Barry Yourgrau was born in South Africa in 1949. He emigrated to the United States as a child. His reading act, a regular feature of the New York art world, combines literary stand-up comedy and surreal oedipal drama. He lives in New York City.

BARRY YOURGRAU

A Man Jumps Out
of an Airplane

Wearing Dad's Head

PALADIN
GRAFTON BOOKS
A Division of the Collins Publishing Group

LONDON GLASGOW
TORONTO SYDNEY AUCKLAND

Paladin
Grafton Books
A Division of the Collins Publishing Group
8 Grafton Street, London W1X 3LA

A Paladin UK Paperback Original 1988

Copyright © Barry Yourgrau 1984, 1987

ISBN 0-586-08662-5

ACKNOWLEDGEMENTS
Some of these pieces have appeared in a previous collection *The
Sadness of Sex* (Whale Cloth Press, 1979), and in the following
publications: *The Paris Review, Poetry, The New York Times, The
Missouri Review, The Iowa Review, Between C & D, Bomb,*
Washington Review of the Arts, *Hanging Loose, Appearances, kayak,
The World, Telephone, The Poetry Project Newsletter, East Village Eye,
Joe Soap's Canoe, Dumb Magazine,* and *This Magazine.*

The author would like to thank the New York State Council on the Arts
and the New York Foundation of the Arts for Fellowships in Fiction and
the Edward Albee Foundation and the Ragdale Foundation for their
generous hospitality. The author would also like to express his
gratitude to Paul Violi.

Printed and bound in Great Britain by
Collins, Glasgow

Set in Optima

Contents

A Man Jumps Out of an Airplane

Wearing Dad's Head

A MAN JUMPS OUT OF AN AIRPLANE

For my parents,
and for Matt

Milk

On a bet, a man climbs inside a cow. Once there he decides to stay. The cow's interior is warm and soft, although very dark. But the man's eyes get by with the driblets of light that do manage to seep in. Food is no problem: there's milk and more milk. 'Fresher than dairy-fresh,' the man wisecracks to himself, chuckling, as he pulls off his socks. No need for clothes, after all, so why bother keeping them on? He bundles them up and stuffs them down the appropriate cavity, thinking slyly of how they'll end up.

Then he lies back and dozes. The movements of the cow, now that she's quieted down, are lulling. The man's friends are still out there, beside themselves: every once in a while they band their hoarse voices into a collective shriek of protest – protest from the world of sanity and reality. But their cries grow hoarser and feebler, and then disappear altogether into the milky stomach mucus with which the man loads up his ears. Slowly, with the contented grace of a baby, he falls into a deep sleep.

Outside the sun creeps away and the moon climbs up over the pasture. The cow wanders slowly, still cautious in her gait, chewing cud. Finally she sinks with heavy care onto the grass, well away from the rest of the herd. Her large, sensitive eyes brim with concern as she tries to fathom her new fate and responsibility.

Village Life

Country girls, red-cheeked and buxom, stand feet wide apart at a counter. They lean on it, elbows propped, forearms crossed. They chat. Their skirts are gathered above their waists.

An old man plods down the line of them with a bucket. He reaches in between the thighs of each girl and puts the fruit he brings out into the bucket. The girls laugh. The atmosphere is easy. They mock the old man, they make cracks and someone ruffles his few hairs.

The old man's tired, stolid expression never changes. When he has finished with the line, he has three buckets of fruit. The girls shake down their skirts, sighing and chuckling.

The old fellow carries the buckets by yoke out to an open shed. He cleans a couple of clay bowls with the sleeve of his jacket. The fruit tumbles from the buckets into the bowls. The old man hangs a blanket across the mouth of the shed. He blows his nose in a big, dirty handkerchief.

By suppertime, the line already stretches a long way back among the houses. It's Saturday night. The young men of the village are fresh-shaven, their simple dark jackets are brushed and buttoned, their hats set carefully on their damp, odorous heads. They fidget, staring anxiously towards the shed. The one at the front of the line pays for his ticket from the snuffling old man and steps quickly into the darkness behind the blanket. After a while – sometimes a short while, sometimes a long while – the youth comes out. Wiping clumsily at his mouth, he hurries, grinning, towards his waiting friends.

Snow

I go to the train station to meet my girlfriend. I am wearing all kinds of scarves against the weather. It is snowing. The train comes in but my girlfriend isn't on it. A conductor covered with snowballs informs me that my girlfriend has had plastic surgery without telling me, and the operation got fouled up, and now she's too ashamed ever to see me again.

I go home, a multitude of ambivalences battling within me. I keep peering about for anyone swathed in bandages, in case she might have come out here secretly on the bus.

At home, I remember the telephone in the freezer. I take it out. The surface of the receiver is brown and wilted, like old lettuce. But the inside will probably still be good. 'She can use this to graft with,' I think. I turn on the tap in the sink and begin carefully scraping off the outside of the receiver. The phone rings in my hands. I don't answer it, I want to surprise her. The ringing goes on a long time before stopping. I start to feel guilty. What if she really needed me? I lose heart with the surprise and finally wreck the good stuff by accidentally tearing off a piece.

I go into the bathroom and begin tying knots in the scarves, out of despair. There is a knock at the front door. The train conductor comes in, dripping, and says, 'Didn't you recognize me?'

Femme Fatale

I have the last pack of cigarettes in the world; but no matches. I am in the bedroom, which has an enormous window, so I have to keep my body between the cigarettes and the window. Everybody is in the other room with the matches. I try to think of some disguised way of asking for the matches without giving away my secret.

I can't think of any. I go out into the other room, hang around for a while in a state of desperate appetite, then sneak downstairs and open the broom closet, releasing the bull. I rush back upstairs and tell everybody that the bull is loose!

They all go downstairs, except for one blonde. To keep her ignorant of my real interests, I seduce her. She tells me she is so glad someone is finally seducing her, because she has just been fired from her job. After we have necked a bit, I suggest she go to the bathroom and prepare herself. She goes off coquettishly, saying she will tell me later all about why she *really* lost her job.

Immediately I rifle through the handbags that are lying around, find some matches and run into my room. But before I can light up I hear her coming out of the bathroom. I hide the matches and cigarettes. We start to fuck. I am unhappy; as I feel myself coming I moan 'No' No!' because I don't want to come, I want to smoke.

Suddenly there is cigarette smoke streaming from her mouth and her fingernails are on fire. I snap into a terrific ecstasy.

Scenery

My father takes me into a dormitory where there are hundreds of figures sleeping in beds. 'Isn't this wonderful!' he whispers. 'Yeah,' I agree, although privately I think, 'Big deal, what's so terrific about a lot of people sleeping?'

Outside, there is a huge walled garden. We walk among the moonlit flowers. My father still can't get over what we've seen inside. 'Have you ever seen anything like it?' he cries. I make some vague movement with my head. His enthusiasm is really bugging me. 'What about this garden?' I think. 'This is what's sensational: the paths and statues; the moonlight and shadows; the aromas.' We walk along, the gravel crunching underfoot in the silence. Abruptly my father halts. I immediately think it's to rest on account of his back or any one of the hystrionic multitude of ailments which enable him to use a cane and make a scene whenever he wants. But instead he grabs my arm and says, 'It was such a wonderful sight, let's go back and have another look!' I gape at him, unbelieving, horrified. 'You really want to?' I ask. 'Yes!' he says, squeezing my arm, putting on his wonderfully-impulsive-guy, life-with-a-capital-L look: 'Don't you?' I smile weakly. 'Okay,' I tell him, shrugging, 'sure, if you'd like to.' We plod back. I can't believe what we're doing, I want to weep with the absurdity of it. The garden beckons like a medieval fantasy. We leave it and come back into the cold hall. It's like an auditorium. From where we stand the beds go into the distance for fifty yards. My father nudges me, beaming, his eyes misty with tears.

Travelogue

I have a bad scalp condition. I go to the doctor. In her office, she hands me a brochure and starts to talk. At first I am thoroughly confused by her terminology; then I realize, looking at the posters on the walls, that I am in a travel bureau. The doctor is very enthusiastic about the country she is selling me on: it has lice perhaps as big as my thumb, she says, and there is no fresh meat available whatsoever. 'So you think this scalp thing might have something to do with *diet*?' I ask, straining earnestly to follow her line of diagnosis.

She stares at me, blinking in puzzlement. Then she shakes her head a couple of times, as if to clear it, and rolls her shoulders, and begins poking through some brochures. Finally she pulls one out. 'Okay!' she says. 'Here's a country where the weather is usually pretty awful right around the time of your trip, and everything is incredibly expensive.'

I look at her, trying to translate her remarks into plain language, trying to find any kind of diagnosis camouflaged among the lines. I can't. I notice, really for the first time, that she is wearing only a bikini and that she considers me through the panes of enormous circular sunglasses, like some species of disco owl. 'You're a funny kind of doctor,' I tell her, and I get up to leave.

On the way out, I pass by a pool. Bathing beauties lounge on its tiled shores, sipping drinks from pineapples through glittering straws. I step towards them, then I remember the disfiguring condition of my scalp. I catch myself and scuttle woefully out the door.

At home I sit in the fusty dimness of the living room, fingering my head. 'She didn't know a lot about medicine,' I think, 'but I'll bet she knows a lot about other kinds of things.' I doze off.

In my dream we are on a desert island. I have managed to get her to take off her bikini. I wear the bra part on my head, Mouseketeer/babushka style. 'So you really think this will work?' I ask her. She looks up from her ukelele and smiles tenderly. 'Not a chance,' she tells me.

Apocrypha

A man is fishing in an unfamiliar creek. He looks over and sees a baby come bobbing around the bend. The baby is in a kind of wicker basket.

The man drops his rod and splashes in hurriedly up to his waist and scoops the kid up before he drifts off into the distance and God knows what harm. He brings the peculiar, dripping burden up onto the bank.

He sits there, bewilderedly dabbing his handkerchief at the kid's cheeks. The little one seems okay despite his ordeal. He has on a little loincloth. The man touches it. He whistles: it sure seems to be gold. He looks around. Whoever was taking care of the kid is nowhere in sight. The man gets up and goes to the top of the bank and peers over the bushes.

A spear appears in mid-air. It goes right through the man's head. The corpse reels dramatically down the bank and crashes spread-eagled with a mighty splash into the creek. Very slowly it spins and starts to float downstream, the shaft of the spear sticking up like a mast.

The baby starts bawling. The bushes at the top of the bank part and a dark, sullen face wearing a plumed helmet looks down.

At home, the dead man's wife hears the clock chiming. It gives her a start. She closes her Bible with a clap and hurries out to the kitchen to get dinner into the oven. She realizes to her shame how badly she had the story jumbled, and she feels a strange and mounting distress as she glances out at the empty driveway.

Journey

A man makes a little proscenium in a living room. He looks around over his shoulder. Then he climbs through. His new surroundings are miniature and picturesque. Snow is falling. He opens a big, dark, high-domed umbrella. He starts up the cobblestones beside a canal. A green barge toots mournfully as it passes: the snowflakes make a cap on its stern lamp. The man waves after it. He quickens his pace. In the silence he is aware of his breathing – the clouds of his breath – of the sounds of his footfall, the rub of his clothing, the miniscule patter of the falling snow.

He hurries along under his umbrella, beside the canal, until he is a small dark point, until he is indistinguishable in the silent scenery.

Later, someone comes into the room, and, going by the table to get a book, draws shut the toy-sized curtain.

Song

For Tony Towle

A man gets lost in a storm and wanders into a strange bar. He takes his drink to a table in a side room and watches the rain swirling down on the unfamiliar streets. He takes a pencil out of a pocket of his coat, finds a piece of paper in another and tries to draw a map of where he might be. But he can't figure it out: the map doesn't make any sense. He crosses it out. The wind rattles the windowpane roughly. The man leans his cheek on his hand and, idling, doodles a few choruses of a song he comes up with in his head. The results have something quite pleasing about them. Cheered, the man puts the paper away and goes back to the bar in the main room, for a refill. 'Okay, I give up, where am I?' he says to the bartender, pretending good-naturedly to be exasperated. The bartender grins back over his shoulder from the ranks of glistening bottles. 'That's a nice little lyric you got there,' he says. The man draws back and looks at the bartender incredulously. The bartender presses a button, and just like that the rain stops.

Out of Water

It's pouring. A girl is at a bus stop, soaked to the skin. She looks like a student, judging from the batch of books under her arm. I tell her she'll catch pneumonia; she should come up to my place and dry off. She says thanks, she's okay, but I insist with gentlemanly concern. She hesitates; but finally, with a worried look, she yields.

Upstairs, she comes out of the bathroom in my robe drawn tight. She towels her dark, glossy hair. She's much lovelier than I'd realized, and I notice with a pang of tenderness that she still keeps on her funny green socks. It must be a custom in her native land – she's a foreigner, judging from her wonderfully liquid accent I can't place. I make her some tea and then I have to tell her that in spite of my genuinely honorable intentions I've fallen completely in love with her, what am I going to do? Her response is to sit with the cup between her hands, staring into her tea, her brow knotted in concentration. I realize she is actually trying to figure out what I should do – a real little scholar. I let out a laugh. 'Don't worry,' I tell her gently. 'I know what to do.'

I go around to the chair beside her and put my hand on her shoulder and kiss her tenderly on the cheek. I get a startlingly oily and fishy taste. It's so unexpected I can't stop myself from showing a look of shocked surprise. She sees it and blushes and bends deeper over her cup. She points a lovely hand at the wet books on the table. They're academic treatises on salt- and freshwater fish. 'Those are my ancestors I'm studying,' she murmurs.

Hula Horror

It's very late at night – very early in the morning. I'm in a thatched-roof hut. Earthern floor. Kerosene lamp. A girl – a fellow tourist – has gotten drunk and is now dancing just for me, lasciviously as she can manage, in the middle of the place. She sways and bobs, come-hither style. She's stripped off her clothing and is attired solely in a 'native' grass hula skirt, colored pink.

I drink, as I have copiously all evening; the gramophone squalls, the lamp throws a melodramatic light, harsh, utterly black in the shadows. I keep time with my glass, thinking, Man, the brochures don't tell you about *this*, and then a horrible realization pops into my mind, like a window shade flying up. That pink skirt, I realize, my skin turning icy – that pink skirt is hideously *evil*: it's an instrument of black magic, a voodoo booby-trap planted here on us two boozed-up, wooly-brained tourists.

The girl of course is utterly ignorant of this. She's not exactly the brainy type to start with. I rise from my chair slowly, wide-eyed, watching in horror as she runs her fingers teasingly through the waving mess of pink strands. I wave my hands for her to stop. 'Don't!' I tell her. 'Stop it!' My throat is all tightened up. She thinks I'm teasing. She giggles, yummily, wiggles her boobs at me and shimmies backwards, away from me, enticing. I go towards her. 'You don't understand!' I whisper desperately. She squeezes her eyes shut for a second and laughs, all dimples. 'Oh yup I do!' she gurgles.

I jump for her. She dodges me and goes scooting, squealing, out the door. I grab as she heads into the night and get a handful of pink grass. It writhes in my hands. Screaming soundlessly, I struggle with it on the floor. Frantically I flap behind me with one hand for something heavy. I get something – an individual-portion casserole of our 'native' dinner – and with it I pound and pound on the twitching strands, driving them into the earth, spraying Spanish rice all over the room.

I sprawl backwards, gasping. The air is full of drumbeats, pulsations. I crawl to the door. In the distance, surrounded by an unearthly, bizarre luminosity, the girl is doing her dance of the seven veils encircled by a ring of fat white candles in the undergrowth. She is sputtering with idiotic excitement, gleefully shouting for me, still absolutely unaware of the nightmare taking place, because she shakes her hips but she doesn't have to: the skirt is clearly moving of its own accord. I watch as it begins to climb up her ribs. She squeals ticklishly and slaps at it.

I can't bear to see what's coming. I scramble up and frantically throw some things into a suitcase. I heave it out the window and clamber after it. Perhaps she will divert attention long enough to cover my escape. I rush into the darkness. I can hear her screaming now. I try to go faster. The moon pops from behind a cloud, suddenly, as if a garish spotlight had been switched on, flooding the way as I plunge down through the ever-pinkening brush.

The Sadness of Sex

A young man stands in the curtains of his bedroom window. Through binoculars he watches the funeral home across the street, where a crowd is arriving for a service. Sad young girls with bare legs emerge from limousines and file across the veranda in a somber promenade. Their sadness invades him, tears fill up the eyepieces of the binoculars and disturb the lenses. Diffractions of giant legs, bare and smooth-skinned, voluptuous, rise to the young man's eyes. Compassion and monstrous excitement struggle in him. One of the mourners stumbles on the steps, showing her thighs. The young man is overwhelmed, he loses his balance and topples backwards on to the bed, dragging the curtains with him.

The binoculars clatter to the floor. They metamorphose into a pair of gilt, high-heeled sandals, with morgue numbers scratched in the rhinestones.

Cuckoo Clock

A middle-aged man and his wife are going at it in the deep quilts of their old brass bed. The big, red-cheeked guy rams it in from behind, driving his wife's blotchy, fleshy shoulders deep into the bedclothes. From down there, under her tangle of braids, come muffled grunts and shouts. Suddenly the twosome sprawl forward. The guy squeezes and clutches ferociously in his ecstatic throes. Through the window the sun splashes on the snow, on the Alps across the valley.

Afterwards, there is coffee made with cocoa and milk, and little steaming almond buns.

Then, still naked, the big guy pads over to his work table. He has on his green felt hat, he smokes his funny, carved pipe. He tinkers with a cuckoo clock in a shaft of sunlight. 'Cuckoo! Cuckoo!'

Out in the kitchen, his wife hangs up the dish towel and gets out the wicker basket. She also is naked. She climbs sideways through the window and steps heavily into the basket of a small hot-air balloon. She casts loose, and the balloon lifts slowly upward. When it comes level with the chimney, she ties off the lines, expertly. She hums a tune to herself as she leans out to take in the laundry, which hangs from pegs just below the clouds.

Demoiselle

I'm in bed with a girl whose head is on crooked. But I know in my heart that if I really do a thorough job on her, really ecstasize her in a way she's obviously never been before, she'll straighten out. I fling myself into the task with messianic relish. I foreplay with the controlled exquisiteness of a French aesthete; I lock horns with the steady languor of a Zen master, timeless and temperate; then suddenly I kick the whole thing into overdrive – a lumberjack in a brand new Cadillac. Off we roar down the coast highway! The rose of our delight crashes over us, drenches us in a hot shower of petals. We roll apart in a daze, and immediately I grope for the cigarettes to celebrate. Her head is perfectly aligned now, just as I knew it would be. But unbelievably, her legs are backwards.

Peeved, I throw the cigarettes away and grab her again. There'll be no mistake this time! At the last minute I wheel her on top of me and make like an oil derrick, we reenact the discovery of oil. I gush, she swoons. I pull out from under her collapsed form, and gasping from exertion, I forage under the sheets. I check her heels, I check her ass, I sit back, panting and vindicated. Everything's pointing in the same direction. Including, I realize, her breasts. Her goddamned breasts are sticking out of the middle of her back! I sink to the pillows, glowering.

It goes like this all afternoon. When her breasts are right, her hands are wrong. When her hands are right, the cheeks of her ass snuggle up under her belly. Finally the parts of her body are in a hopeless tangle and I give up. I sprawl on the floor, utterly wrung out, stung to the very quick of my self-esteem.

She sits at the bureau, humming to herself as she combs out the long red banner of her hair with a grotesquely misplaced hand. She dabs a little extra brightness on her lips: a practiced fingertip brushes once, twice, just above the top knob of her spine, where her lips happen to be. I watch as she dresses, hasty and competent despite the jumble of anatomy – she has an appointment to keep. She comes over to me when she's done and contorts herself to press a hand to my cheek. 'Thanks . . .' she smiles, and from what I can see of her face, she thinks to show by her smile how truly exquisite are her feelings. The smile section is limpid with satisfaction. 'It was just utterly swell . . .' She might as well have said: 'Better luck next time.' I watch dismally as she strolls out, pausing at the door to throw back a tangled kiss, the unregenerate cubism of her body making a mockery of the grand tradition of my powers.

Helium

I open the box and take out the heavy, folded balloon and fix it up to the cannister of helium. The balloon swells spasmodically. Then suddenly it finds its form and goes taut and hurriedly I shut off the gas. It's in the shape of my father. It's a terrific job and worth all the money. There it hovers, against the ceiling, like an obese bumblebee. I get on the bed and tie a line to one foot and pull it after me out the door.

Behind our house is a small park, with a round hill. There's a blue sky, a few clouds and a breeze. I release the balloon and it hurries out, bumping into the wind, until it's at the end of my line. Delighted, I fiddle with the string and my old man dances idiotically under the clouds.

At this point I become aware of shouting. I look, my mother is hurrying up the hill towards me, gesturing angrily. 'What are you doing with your father!!' she cries. 'Get him down!' I start to laugh gleefully at her confusion, but then I'm brought up short by the intensity of her passion. 'Relax, mom, it's a balloon,' I explain to her as she reaches me. 'You must be crazy,' she hisses. She grabs the line out of my hand and starts pulling. 'Mom, it's just a balloon!' I protest, but then I look and it really is my old man up there above the tree-tops. My stomach turns over. I can hear him cursing. 'Hang on, hang on!' my mother cries, fighting his weight and the wind. Suddenly a gust shoves him into the very top of a tree. 'Oh my god!' my mother cries.

I shrink back from her, horrified at what is happening. I can hear the snapping and tearing in the branches as my father roars and struggles, and my mother's shrieks, 'Don't break the line, don't break the line!' I put my fingers in my ears and turn and flee down the hill. At the bottom I look back and my mother is standing silhouetted at the top, wailing and imploring the sky with outstretched arms as my father sails away, a clamorous, wind-blown blob, up into the blue.

The Joke

By way of a joke, a man puts on a disguise. He goes to visit his mother. His mother is also in a jovial mood; she also is in disguise. Unprepared, both of them get a shock at the front door. Neither of them says anything about it through the afternoon visit, which is strained and cautious and overly courteous. Privately each of them thinks the other is well on the way to cracking up, given the get-up, the paint, the tufts of colored hair. Their hearts are heavy and sick when their customary TV show ends. It's with great unease that they look over at each other, that they finally rise to bid goodbye. As the mother watches her son go down the garden path, a tear bubbles along the humpy contour of her papier mâché nose; it is absorbed by a huge nostril. The man waves from the gate; behind his funhouse glasses, his eyes are misty. He walks all the way home, head bowed under its bobbing rubber antennae.

Nothing like this dismal, mysterious episode occurs again; but subtly it haunts their relationship for years to come.

The Shipwreck

For Steven Campbell

After the ship has gone down, there are five of us in the lifeboat. The captain plays a melancholy air on the concertina. The two fat bankers' wives put their heads together and snuffle into their furs. The night is a moist caravan of stars, and the young pharmacist and I stare out past the gunwales, our hearts tugging at our throats.

The captain ends his song and spreads his hands. He asks us to understand ... 'C'est une affaire d'Amour,' he says, the romance of ships and seas. It was beyond him to change her mind, he just wanted us to know that. He doesn't blame her. . . .

A shoal of drowned men drifts by, the little flowerpots of their souls resting on their milky, tattoed chests. The captain blesses them in the language of sailors.

Then he rises and takes up a position in the bow of the boat. Fidgeting with his hat and primping the tassels of his white uniform, he gazes restlessly out to sea.

We follow his gaze to a spot in the waves. The waves break open there and an enormous conch shell bobs to the surface. There is a mother-of-pearl chair in it, draped with velvety seaweed.

The strange craft comes alongside us, propelled by glittering fins. We all turn fearfully to the captain. Without a word to us he clambers down into the shell and seats himself in the chair. He opens a parasol. He looks nervous. The shell moves off.

The women cry out and cross themselves on their bosoms. The pharmacist utters an oath. 'Adieu! Adieu!'the captain calls softly. He waves to us with the dainty fingers of his hand. He blinks as the first foam splashes over him.

Soon there is no more of him, only the suggestion of music and the shadowy movement of lanterns under the sea.

The Wonders

I am in a great house. I go along the corridor. I open a door. A naked girl reclines against the pillows of a bed, her knees drawn up and open. A monkey squats before her. His paws are clasped together and raised, his grimacing face is lifted, towards heaven. It is the age-old attitude of supplication. The room is silent. A candle burns by the bedside, before the heavy curtains. The girl turns her head languorously to look at me in the doorway. On her face there is an expression of elegiac softness, a half-smile: languid, patient, tender.

I close the door quietly. I go down the corridor. 'This place is full of wonders,' I tell myself. I pause at the window, to look down at an apple tree in the yard below. Under its boughs, a bestiary has gathered to watch a girl bathing herself from a porcelain bowl.

Primavera

I go for a walk at night in a school yard in the country. It's early spring. I come around the corner of one of the old wooden buildings, and this is what I see: a hurricane lamp hangs glowing from a tree. In its light a naked man is bent over a naked young girl whose head is in a metal washtub. At first I think, blushing, that they're doing some sex thing bobbing for apples, and I turn to go away; but then I see the guy is in fact holding down the girl's head in the tub: she squirms around, like she's choking.

I hurry towards them yelling. The guy turns around. He smiles as I come up. He's middle-aged and healthy-looking. He holds one hand on the girl's neck and gestures with the other. 'It's a fertility rite,' he explains pleasantly. 'Are you kidding?' I tell him. The girl's hair is spread out in the water, and she squirms and grunts and paws softly at the grass. I reach out for his wrist to make him let go, and he gives a cry and tries to ward me off, and we get involved in an awkward, shifting, tugging struggle, made all the more bizarre there under the lamp by his nakedness. Finally we lose our balance together and sprawl violently over the girl and the tub, knocking everything all over the place.

I manage to pull free out of the tangle and get to my knees. The tub is upended on its side in front of an expanding, glistening pool; the girl droops in the grass, hacking, her skinny chest heaving. I stare at her, dumbfounded: with each watery cough of hers, the air fills with tiny fruits and flowers. They sift around her on to the grass, pale and stunted, a garden of puny litter.

'See what you've done?' the guy says. He sits next to me, rubbing his shoulder. He looks miserable. 'Will you look at that measly stuff! Man,' he groans, 'don't you know *anything* about the seasons?'

Natural Law

A man goes fishing on a windy day. Nothing's biting, and the man starts home in the evening with an empty creel. He stops off at a roadhouse for a drink. He brings his glass over to a table and he notices a fish tank. He goes up to it: there are a couple of gorgeous, stupid-looking trout inside. The man looks at them and then looks over his shoulder. The bar is dim, and empty but for a couple of locals busy with a bowl of peanuts at the other end of the place.

It only takes a second for the man to slip a hand into the tank, grab one fish then the other by the tail, lift them out, bash their heads against the wall and drop them into the creel. He goes back to his drink. He tosses it off and heads out to his car. No one tries to stop him.

Back on the road, a feeling of un-ease, of moroseness, steals over the man. Finally it gets so strong he pulls over. He sits for a long time smoking a cigarette and looking at the creel. He feels wretched: in spite of everything he is genuinely a fisherman at heart.

He pushes the car door open and gets out dolefully under the stars. He looks up at them: there must be millions. He kicks a pebble back down towards the curve in the road and trudges in its wake, lost in melancholy contemplation.

Back around the bend and down the road, a car without headlights bowls along. An out-of-season moose is strapped figurehead-style to the hood: the great, bobbing sweep of the antlers hangs forward like a razor-sharp, hugely pronged snow plow. A pair of drunken poachers are living it up at the dashboard. They pelt each other with peanuts and hoot with laughter. The driver is almost choking with merriment, ducking nuts as he goes bursting into the dark curve.

Warts

A frog makes a noise under a man's window. The man turns over and opens his eyes halfway long enough to grope by the bed for a shoe, which he heaves out of the window. Then he goes back to sleep.

The shoe hits the frog right on the side of its little head and knocks it flying in the midst of its nightly constitutional.

In retaliation it hops along the lawn to the hedge, gets up to the bedroom window by a series of vaulting maneuvers, hops stealthily onto the man's bed and empties its bladder all over the man's foot. Chuckling, it hops out the window and back to the lily pond.

In the morning, the man shambles out to the bathroom. He's all lathered up in the shower before he registers the condition of his foot: it's a mass of warts.

Out in the lily pond, the frog hears the screams. It croaks contentedly, grinning. It paddles over the pond's edge, to take everything in. Gloating, it gets up on the bank and puffs itself full of air and bellows noisily.

At this point a fat boy springs heavily out from behind a tree. Gleefully he pulls both triggers of his father's shotgun. There is a deafening blast. The boy comes plodding through the clouds of smoke to the bank. He peers at the great ragged cavity where the frog used to be. 'Huh?' he says. 'Where'd it go?' He sneers, baffled, into the smoke. Then he shrugs and turns and trudges back for more ammo towards the house, where the howls of anguish still ring down.

Djin

A man buys a wonderful old brass lamp at a rummage sale. He brings it home and plugs it in. There is a terrific explosion. When the man regains his senses he is sprawled against the foot of a bookcase, covered with plaster debris and bits of porcelain. He gropes to his feet and staggers over to the wreckage of the sofa and gapes in horror at the scorching ferocity of what happened. He turns away dumbly and looks at himself in what's left of the living room mirror. He has a black eye and his hair, singed in places, is standing on end.

He stumbles out of the living room, into the bedroom. The phone, he realizes, is ringing. It's right there on the night-table. The man sits heavily and picks up the receiver and a cloud of rancid powder squirts in his face. He drops the receiver, blinded, and tumbles off the bed, hacking and gasping uncontrollably, convulsed.

Outside the apartment, a pair of tiny men in fezes and balloon pants are standing smoking a cigarette. One of them has a big spiked rope coiled over his shoulder. He looks at his watch and sighs. 'So it's still the boiling water, then the closetful of toads, and then it's us,' he says.

Fried Clams

A young girl is lecturing her crewcut boyfriend. She is leaning up against the wall of a fried clam drive-in: one leg bent and drawn up, foot against the wall. The wind snatches at her polka-dot skirt: short and white, with big red dots. The girl is blond, she is eating an ice cream cone. The boy half-listens to her preachy harangue, the subject and style by now quite familiar. It is late morning. The air is wild and fresh and newly warm. The sun leaps around out on the waves of the bay. The boyfriend watches the girl under the pretence of listening. He is realizing how pink her lips are. He smells the warm scent of fried clams in the air, he looks at her little ears, at her little teeth nibbling the ice cream. The breeze surges around her skirt.

'You gorgeous little asshole!' he blurts suddenly. 'I love you!'

The girl doesn't know what to say.

Texas

Some guys are driving through Texas. They're groggy and dazed from all the hours, the awesome monotony. On all sides, they see nothing: scrub plain, as if the earth were flat. There is a smooth line drawn in the dust under the sky. It's the horizon. They drive towards it. The engine drones. Sometimes, a small, single shape appears in the distance. They watch it as it grows, mysteriously. It reproduces. It enlarges, upwards, in creeping increments. Suddenly, it acquires detail: it becomes buildings: a city. For a few strange minutes, they're in it. The fact of scale dazzles them. They crane their necks, watching through the rear window as first the details go. They watch the shapes begin to sink, by gradual increments, all the way into the distance – until there's only the horizon, smooth, dusty, and they're back in the center of a flat world.

This is Texas. Their eyes glaze. They look at each other. They stare blankly and rub their cheeks. They have nothing to say. They see miles of scrub desert in the windows. They stare off ahead, stupefied, waiting for the next speck to appear, to start to reproduce and rise.

Way down near Galveston, a scrawny, crewcut kid in Levis and pointed boots gets tired. The sun's high. His hands are all torn up from turning the big crank handle. He decides to sneak off and go swimming. He pulls off his clothes and jumps into the Gulf. He floats on his back, spouting water. His blisters sting. He thinks: 'To hell with those guys in the car!'

In the Meadow

I climb over the fence into the meadow. There is a crowd of bulls standing about. Women in long white dresses and sun hats and carrying parasols wander among them, chatting. I approach nervously. A woman comes over to greet me and offers me a plate of sherbet. Then she takes my arm and has me stroll with her. I glance at the bulls and see that their eyes are reddened and taut, explosive. The big rings tremble in their noses. 'But isn't this terribly dangerous?' I whisper, hurriedly spooning up the last lemony mouthful. 'Of course it is!' my hostess answers gaily. And turning around, she raises her parasol over her shoulder and whacks one of the huge animals right across the flanks. 'For Christ's sake!' I gasp. The bull lurches away, muscles jostling in its sides, and then turns and lowers its head at us, snorting and pawing the ground. It gives out a bellow. 'Get out of here!' I yell. The other bulls take up the first one's roar. The hostess is delighted. 'Run, girls, run!' she laughs. I tear off towards the fence, as the bulls break. I look over my shoulder and I see the women mincing off in all directions, clutching their sun hats to their heads and shrieking in delight as the great black animals lumber and toss after them.

The Surprise

My date for the evening calls me to tell me she has a big surprise waiting for me when I pick her up. This really electrifies me. She is a pretty wild customer, she must have something extra-special cooked up. I leave my sportscoat and sweater in the closet and get out my zebra-striped dovetail coat, it's totally outrageous, but after that phone call I know I have the nerve to pull it off. I look in the mirror and there I am, a little kinky but definitely loaded with sexy pizzaz. I am going to bowl her over.

I dance up the stairs to her place, an exotic bunch of paper flowers in my fist, I punch the buzzer on the downbeat of the little tune I'm carrying. There's no answer, it's all part of the surprise of course, I whinny like a horse and push open the door.

'Surprise!' a voice squeaks. I look around, finally I see her, she's on the sofa. I drop the flowers, my mouth falls open. She's barely twelve inches tall! 'How do you like it?' she asks. She turns herself one way then the other. 'It took me all day,' she says. 'I'm not quite dry yet, so why don't you make yourself a drink before we go.'

I have my drink, then another, I'm too much in shock to say anything. When she says she's ready I finally get my voice back and try to talk her into having dinner where we are. But she insists on going out as planned. 'Or do you think this is too much for you to handle?' she inquires coyly. 'Of course not!' I retort. 'Why should it be?'

In the restaurant she sits on the table on an overturned cup. I have picked out the darkest, most isolated booth in the place, but even so people won't stop staring – they don't touch their food, they just lean out of their seats and crane their necks and stare. The *maitre d'* finally has to get up on a chair and plead with everyone to ignore us.

I am so embarrassed I can hardly see straight. My date loves it. She has me mash up her ravioli and feed it to her with a matchstick. She asks me if I still think I can handle it. 'You bet I can,' I tell her fiercely. I can see now exactly what her little game is. 'Alright then,' she smirks, 'give me some wine!'

I shove the glass in front of her before I realize the effect a few sips are going to have. Immediately she gets cockeyed. She gives me a lascivious wink, licking her lips. She slides off the cup and starts doing a striptease. Horrified, I hiss at her to cut it out. She leers at me. 'I thought you could take it!' she squeaks. In a panic I grab a napkin and hold it up around her. She hauls off her skirt, she's stark naked. She pitches headlong onto my plate and starts rolling around in the spaghetti.

A waiter appears at my shoulder to clear off the dishes. He stares at the heaving napkin. I grin up at him with all my teeth and shrug my shoulders. He looks at me strangely and says he will come back later.

By now my date has a piece of spaghetti worked in between her legs, she is oohing and aahing, squealing at me, What do I think now? What do I think now? People are buzzing and rising from their chairs. The waiter is on his way back with the *maitre d'*. Frantically I throw down some money. I cram my date up in the napkin and bolt to my feet and shove her wriggling and squealing under my coat. I get ten feet towards the exit when the force of an explosion knocks me flying.

I come to in a heap under a table. My date is sprawled on her back in the middle of the floor. She is shockingly full-sized, smeared with tomato sauce and spaghetti, her ass is churning away furiously, her hands clutch at her thighs. 'Come on, you little prick!' she roars. 'Come on! Come on! Let's see you handle a big, fat, man-sized pussy!'

From Childhood

There are a lot of formally, old-fashionedly dressed men up in a tree. They read financial newspapers and wear bowler hats and starched collars. None of them has on his trousers. They urinate. Streams drip down through the branches, like quiet rainfall.

In the parlor my mother is setting out the tea things. They gleam. She looks out the window at the somber, cloudy afternoon, the stolid green of the trees, the crowded boughs by the hedge. 'Don't say anything to your father,' she murmurs gravely. She tidies back stray hairs behind her ears as she hurries to the sideboard for napkins. I see that at the back of her skirt, the hem is dark and soaking wet.

Zoology

Out in the garden there are naked women crawling around on all fours. Little men ride them – middle-aged, oily creeps from the Levant, in cheap dark blue suits, shiny from use, and straw hats. Their revelry, their contemptuous nonchalance, disgusts me. I want to drive them off, but my companion pulls me back, back into the house.

It's a whorehouse. 'Why do you submit yourself to all this?' I question her angrily, splashing Scotch into a tumbler. 'I've turned to it since you dropped me,' she replies bitterly. I look at her. 'I'm not a *giraffe*!' I insist.

I understand what I mean to signify by this bizarre denial. So does she – but she disagrees with me! Furiously I grab an encyclopedia off a shelf and find the Giraffe entry: several giraffes are shown in nature, in a savanna. Naturally they don't look anything like me.

After this we keep apart in moody silence. I am sullen, insulted. I swallow my Scotch, clenching my jaw. Out in the garden the bastards have taken off their belts and started using them as whips.

Creek

At night vigilantes surround the shack where my girlfriend and I are sleeping. I slide out of bed and go out on to the crude porch in my nightshirt, to confront them. In the oily, here-and-there light of the torches, I realize they're not vigilantes, they're women in Grecian outfits. 'For God's sake!' I whisper at them, glancing back anxiously as I step down into their midst.

We hurry along a dirt lane under the trees. There's a big heady moon up. We turn off by the creek. It looks like spilled silver in the moonlight; it gives off a pale shimmer as we litter the bushes with our garments. With one of them at a time, I dive into the ice-cold waters. I come up shivering and gasping. My heart is thumping, aching, as I look back up the hill, at the shack and its dark window.

Fog

In the fog I go into the wrong room. Luckily there're no embarrassments before I realize my mistake and leave. 'Whoever designed this hotel,' I think, 'should have his head examined.'

At last I get to the proper door: I can make out that the key tag number fits the door number. After a while of poking I get the key to go into the lock. I turn it and go inside.

The door clicks behind me. There is a girl in my bed. She puts down her newspaper and stares at me. I stare at her. 'What's going on?' she says. 'This is my room,' I tell her. 'You've made a mistake.' 'I have *not*,' she says. 'I'm afraid you have,' I insist. I hold up the key and waggle it. 'This matches the door number and it opens the door.' There's silence. The girl looks displeased and thoughtful. 'Alright, you can stay, for tonight,' she says finally. 'But don't try anything.' 'Thanks so much,' I tell her sarcastically. 'Let's not forget whose room this is, shall we?' I add.

I go over to the bureau. I see she's taken it over with her things. Sourly I glance at her over my shoulder but she's got the newspaper up and cigarette smoke rises from behind it. I open the French windows and step out onto the miniature terrace. More 'smoke': it's impossible to see a thing. Anything visible is glistening with damp. I turn back inside. I feel grim and bushed. I go to the closet and push aside her things and take off my coat and start unbuttoning my shirt. 'What are you doing?' she says. I turn around. The newspaper is down. 'I'm getting ready for bed,' I tell her. 'Is that so?' she says, her eyes narrowing. 'And just where do you intend to sleep?' 'In my bed,' I tell her. 'Listen: I'm very tired, this is my room, my bed, I'll be damned if I'll sleep on the floor.' She chews on this one for a while. Finally she says, 'You try anything and you'll be sorry.' Then she shifts all the way over to the very edge of the mattress. Up goes the paper.

I get my pyjamas and go into the bathroom, shaking my head. When I come out, there's no change in the situation. I pause, then I stride up to the bed and lift the bedclothes on my side and get in, courteously but firmly. I settle myself with my hands under my head. The wall of newspaper rises beside me. I lie there in the shadows beyond the sphere of her lamp, and I welcome sleep as a relief from the oddball weirdness of the situation. But something holds me back from sleep, something that nags at me about the whole business. Then I realize what it is.

'So how *did* you get in?' I ask, talking into the darkness. For a long while there isn't any answer. Then behind the newspaper her voice says, 'I don't know. I made a mistake.' Then after a bit: 'What do you expect, with this horrible fog.' 'Yeah, terrible, isn't it?' I agree drowsily, but either she doesn't want anything to get started or I fall asleep because I don't remember her reply.

Aquarium

A couple of girls are locked up in a big aquarium. I try to unlock them but can't find the place where to do it. I stand face pressed up to the dark glass wall. They don't seem to mind their captivity. I decide they're drunk, in a lazy kind of way – they laugh great loose cascades of bubbles and shove at each other the way girls like to do sometimes. I fall for them. The fishes bump into their lazy, swirling bodies, in the hazy glow of the water, in the waving water grass. The fish flit away shyly and come paddling up to the glass. They undulate there, staring stupidly at me with their big, blinking fish eyes.

Nursery Tale

I get onto the rocking horse. I cling low on its neck. It rocks out into the hallway. I look down the length of the hall. The horse turns, positioning itself. Then it tilts backwards on its curved runners, it rears and goes charging down the hall. 'We don't have enough speed,' I think, as through the open door the wall of the bathroom looms. I gasp, and we spring through the wall.

We sail in the night above the houses. Down below are the chimney pots and yellow-glowing curtained windows. We circle. A baby tumbles past. I look about. It's raining babies. Gently, in their diapers, sucking their thumbs, they tumble softly by, fast asleep.

I cling tighter to the horse's neck as now we bank and start to climb. The rushing wind brings tears to my eyes. The houses grow tiny. The stars get bigger and sparkling, the shimmering moon looms ahead. At its edges I can see the folds where the night is pinned to it. As we draw on, a sudden dread makes my stomach quiver. 'We're not supposed to go through there,' I think. 'No, we mustn't try to go through.' The gathered material rushes up. We crash against it. The horse struggles, it forces at the cloth, butting with its head, straining furiously. 'We mustn't, we mustn't!' I cry. In the clamor and turmoil my grip comes loose. The horse goes shooting away from me, head over heels down a dark furrow. Screaming, I slide down the velvet, picking up speed. 'Too fast, too fast!' I scream as I go rocketing frightfully – and then suddenly slow and drift down towards the soft roofs among the sleepy rain of babies. Just before I fall asleep, I look for the horse. I see it, wheeling relentlessly, out of control, heroic, along the turbulent rim of the stars.

Far Region

A man collects enough wood to start a fire. But the fire won't light. Perhaps the wood is wet or rotten, the man thinks. He checks it over thoroughly, turning it in his hands. It seems perfectly okay. Perplexed, anxious, the man painstakingly re-stacks the twigs, sticks and logs into a textbook arrangement. He strikes a match and plunges it carefully into the midst of the wood. Nothing happens. The man stares unbelievingly at the curled-up black match fossil. He has five matches left.

A couple of frantic, cursing minutes later, he has none. He feels his fright bulking gigantically in him. He knows it's his own worst enemy, and he forces himself to try to ignore it. He tells himself he has every chance of being found, of making it. But his eyes are unnaturally white and large as he paces the clearing, hands under his armpits, collar turned up. It still seems incredible what's happening. How could he have been such a fool to have come gallivanting off like this, down an unmarked, barely readable trail!

It's evening now for real. He can see his dense breath, he realizes suddenly, in the hazy chill. Up above, the first stars have a harsh, desolating glitter. The man trudges in a circle, hugging himself.

A hundred yards away, a boy in an odd vegetable and fur garment watches the man from a tree. He is expressionless, unblinking, even when, later, he can hear the man groaning. He pulls up his hood. On its rim the frost gathers, crystal by crystal, hour by hour. Shortly before dawn, he sees it's time finally to go down.

On the Lake

My father and I are out in a boat. Suddenly he gives a shout. The water has been electrified.

We lie frozen in the bottom of the boat, drifting, waiting for the terrifying flashes, the ultimate, sizzling detonation.

Then my father stirs. He peers about and then sits back up. 'I was mistaken,' he says. 'It's only the fog.'

We drift, through furling and unfurling grey regions. A pale boat appears, and moves silently across our bow, as if moving past a shadowy doorway. From a great winch at its stern, a mythical fish, monstrous and golden, hangs to the water. A golden wake shimmers after it.

The yellow flickering plays over our silent, staring faces.

Bones

I can't sleep. My pillow feels strange. I open it up, it's filled with bones. They're white and look as though they come from small animals.

I find myself out in the night, on a street, carrying the white sack of bones. The moon casts dark pools of shadow by the hedges. Near one of them a girl sits. She wears a white gown and her eyes are dark and very large for her delicate face. I have the feeling there is some irrevocable sadness in her life. I sit down beside her on the grass and keep my eyes lowered with considerate, somber compassion. She shows me her hand. Two of the fingers are missing. We put the bag between us and slowly and helplessly we sift through its delicate, clinking trove.

Garden

A girl from another country arrives to stay with us. She's very sweet and also obviously very lonely. I can hear her crying to herself at night. I get out of bed and stand, listening to her, but I don't know what to do.

One day when everyone is out I sneak into her room. My heart is pounding. I go over to the closet and look with trembling hands through her clothes. I go over to her immaculate bed. At its foot sits the blue wooden trunk, painted with flowers, that all of us admired on the day she arrived. After a moment of second thoughts, I lift the lid. Inside are rows of pots: softly colored little flowers grow in them. Their hues are of a delicacy I've never seen before; their scent is exquisite and unfamiliar. I close the lid, agitated strangely.

That night I lie awake, listening. I hear her. I get out of bed and go to my door and stand there. Then I go out into the dark hall, up to her door. I listen. Softly I try the handle.

She is kneeling in front of the blue box. It's open. She is barefoot, in a white nightdress. She turns her head when I call her name. Tears run down her face in the moonlight. I think she's looks extraordinarily beautiful. 'Are you alright?' I whisper. She looks at me, and she nods. 'I'm just watering my flowers,' she tells me softly.

Domestic Farce

A man comes home and finds his wife in bed with a squirrel. He stands in the bedroom doorway, gaping at them. The wife stares back in fright over the covers, which are drawn up over her nose. The squirrel's little head peeps out similarly beside her. The culprits look so idiotic together that the man can't help himself, he bursts out laughing. He sees the nuts strewn all over his wife's clothes on the floor and the sight makes him positively howl so he has to clutch on to the door frame to support himself. The wife and the squirrel exchange wide-eyed glances; but then they catch the bug themselves, and slowly they start to chuckle – the wife in fearful, whimpering surges, the squirrel in its high, hysterical tweeting. Soon all restraints are by the boards; the room rocks with the jangle and din of mirth going full blast.

Then abruptly the husband stops laughing. His face turns ashen. He disappears from the doorway. The wife sits up; she calls out his name. There's no answer. She darts a look of terrible concern at the squirrel and she clambers out of bed and rushes naked out the door. The squirrel twitches in the bedclothes. It hears voices, shouts, and it hops up onto the pillow, down on to the floor, grabs up an armful of nuts, leaps onto the window sill, pauses dead still in attentive silence, and then hops onto the fire escape. At this exact instant the blade of an axe crashes down onto the window ledge. The squirrel bolts onto a nearby tree limb, spraying nuts everywhere. 'You and your goddamned pets!' the man screams in the bedroom, above the caterwaul of sobbing. The squirrel races from tree to tree until it is far away down the block. It fetches up finally in some top branches to catch its breath. Its little heart pitter-patters. The wind carries up to it the scraps of agitated voices; the sunlight makes a glinting speck of the axe head in the distant window. The squirrel sits among the leaves, switching its tail back and forth. It thinks, 'Where the hell does he get off calling me a "pet"!'

Katzenjammer

I am the weekend guest at a house with three rambunctious brats. They race around the living room after breakfast, screaming. 'Pint-sized hooligans,' I mutter, making for the door. I head off down the steep bank in front of the house, towards the bay. Gaining the rocks of the narrow beach, I pause to catch my breath. I look back up at the house, at the tangle of overgrown bushes above which it sits.

Suddenly one of the kids pops out of the bushes. He comes flying towards me, hanging on to the bottom of a vine. His body is riddled with spears. He crashes down headfirst in front of me with a great clatter and starts writhing and gasping horribly. I stand over him, aghast. Suddenly he bounces up and wriggles his fingers in my face. He tears back towards the house, laughing his head off. 'Lousy little trickster!' I scream. I heave a rock after him wildly.

I stalk off down the beach in a rage. 'This was supposed to be a *relaxing* weekend,' I seethe. 'I'll be lucky to get out of here without a nervous breakdown!' I stumble along in this fashion, swearing to myself that if I ever had the misfortune to have kids, I shall immediately strangle them. 'Right there in the maternity ward!' I cry, stopping in my tracks. 'Right in front of the goddamn nurse!' My hands feverishly twist and grapple in the air in pantomime – until I realize I'm getting totally out of control. 'Take it easy, take it easy,' I tell myself, startled by my own violence. I look around sheepishly. I realize I've been walking for a long while without having paid the least attention to the scenery, which is supposed to be famous for its beauty – in fact was a big reason I was so looking forward to coming here. But those pestilential kids have ruined everything!

I seem to be near some sort of marina. A dock goes down into the water, a few small craft bob at tether. The place appears deserted as I wander up. Then I notice there is someone on one of the boats. I step closer, and my eyes grow huge in my head. An absolutely unbelievable girl is stretched out on her stomach on the floor of an outboard, sunbathing. The top of her bikini is untied; the oil glistens on the sun-kissed curve of her back, on the rise and fall of her flanks. A regular dream boat. She lifts her bare feet lazily behind her and scratches the heel of one with a brightly painted toe of the other: I take it all in, transfixed. Then she raises her honey-colored head and looks at me through large sunglasses. 'Hullo,' she says. I gape at her idiotically. 'Oh hi,' I reply.

Hard as it may be to believe, this isn't the end of our conversation. In fact, it's the beginning. In fact it's the beginning of something altogether astonishing! 'Say,' she says, pushing a honey-colored tumble out of her line of sight, 'I was just about to go out in the bay and get some sun, but it's so boring, you know – *all alone*. Wanna come along?'

'Why not?' I inquire, my entire glandular system pouring out onto the rocks around me.

So I manage to climb into the boat and she ties her bikini top together and yank-starts the engine and we go puttering out a ways and then she cuts the motor, and we drift. She turns on the transistor. At first I am reluctant to join her at her scale of undress, but finally I give in to her teasing and take off my shirt, exposing a mass of white flesh I laughingly pass off as my 'lifetime supply of whale-blubber, ha-ha.' With her help I lather it up with oils. Then she points a finger at my trousers. 'Don't be a *prude*,' she insists.

What the hell! I get down to my skivvies and stretch out on a towel beside her. And for the first time in days I begin to feel alive and well. '*This* is what a weekend is supposed to be,' I think: 'sun hot on your back, radio crooning, a lovely stranger at your side as the current takes you where it would.' Shading my eyes, chin on my arm, I look out at the sparkling waters with their distant, darting sails, at the shore with its charming cottages nesting in the woods. Then my eye happens to fall on one particular cottage, and once more a pall descends over my spirits. I brood, gnawing on my bottom lip. 'I wonder what cute tricks those little savages are hatching now,' I meditate darkly.

'There's something preying on your mind,' the girl says, through the brown crook of an arm. 'Oh, it's nothing, nothing,' I assure her.

Then I roll up onto an elbow and gaze into her sunglasses. 'It's just – have you ever – have you ever – ' and I can't stop myself, I blurt out the whole wretched saga, all the torments that have been visited on me – the short-sheeted bed, the soap in the toothpaste, the 3 A.M. firecrackers, the faked monstrosities. 'It's going to drive me off the deep end!' I find myself braying. *'Off the deep end!'*

I realize that I'm shaking all over. The girl puts her hand out to me. 'How awful for you,' she says. 'But you know, I have a saying: Whenever things have got you down in the dumps, the one sure-fire pick-me-up that always works is a good, old-fashioned *lay*. So I was going to bring it up later anyway, but wouldn't you like to do something really dirty with me? It'll make you forget all about that other, stupid stuff. I guarantee!'

The silence that follows these remarks is like the aftermath of an immense detonation.

'Pardon me?' I whisper.

An hour later, as I lie panting back on my towel, I realize how right the girl is, about what she guaranteed. Passion has carried away all my worries in a seething tide of coconut oil and sweat and assorted bodily fluids: a carnal sauna for the anguished spirit. Now I lie here utterly emptied, lightheaded, bathed in relief, in a thoughtless sense of content. All I can do is shake my head and whisper midst the balmy sky and cool, stirring waters, 'Jesus, lady, you are one special kind of *angel*. . . .'

This is greeted by a giggle. I turn my head towards her, smiling. 'Hey, I really mean that,' I insist tenderly. This provokes more giggles. I keep on smiling, but quizzically: something odd is going on. 'Hey, what's so funny?' I ask, unable to keep a slight strain of uneasiness out of my voice. She doesn't answer, she's laughing unabashedly now. Because of the sunglasses I can't tell anything about the look in her eyes. I sit up: suddenly there is a horrifying familiarity to her mirth. My stomach turns over. 'What's so funny!' I shout, grabbing her arm, in a panic. She wrenches free and clambers to her feet, yucking as if she were going to split. She reaches up to her sunglasses and yanks them off. Her face comes away with them. I let out a strangled gasp. *'I'm going to tell mom and dad what you did!'* the kid shrieks, delirious with delight. He tears off shreds of breast and buttock and plunges over the side and goes paddle-wheeling towards shore.

After an obscure interval of several seconds I find myself hanging halfway out of the boat, screeching across the waves: 'Come back! Come back you little – ' The last phrase is quite untransliteratatable, being gnashed to foaming bits in my teeth. My voice box ruptures at this point anyway.

I heave around wildly in the bottom of the boat, flopping between the gunwales, broken noises issuing from my throat. Then I manage to recall that I am in a vehicle. I throw myself at the motor, visions of my quarry being hacked into chunks under my propellor leaping through my head. I tear at the starter cord. The motor blows up in my face with a terrific explosion. I grovel about on hands and knees in the boat bottom, hacking, gasping sulphur. *'Stink bomb – '* I wheeze.

That's how the police launch finds me when it pulls alongside some time later – moaning and babbling and eating handfuls of fouled hair. Two marine corporals carry me on board. The captain comes into the cabin and eyes me disgustedly. Then all three of them shower me with toilet paper and burst out screaming with laughter.

De Maupassant

A man wakes up and yawns and gets out of bed. He feels for his slippers with his feet. His right slipper won't fit. The man looks down and sees the reason: his right foot has grown to monstrous proportions. It must have happened in his sleep. He sits on the side of the bed with his mouth hanging open.

Nothing helps to modify this gigantic appendage's unbelievable dimensions. The man takes half a dozen icy showers, and then sits on the pot frantically kneading his hands while his foot wallows in a tub of ice water. The huge toes stick up above the surface like forms of sea life. Shivering, the man begins to realize that this is the way it's going to be, he'll just have to get used to living on these new terms. But how, with such a grotesque-looking foot! The vistas of shame, of self-loathing, make his head swim.

He hauls the foot back into the bedroom and starts dressing around it. He has a special date for this afternoon — of all afternoons! With great care he at last confronts the wrapping of the foot, trying to camouflage it as best he can as something socially acceptable. Socks won't work; he ends up using a T-shirt and then a scarf. The results look wretchedly absurd and alarming. In disgust the man hobbles to the phone to call up the girl and cancel. There's no dial tone. The phone is out of order. The man hurls the receiver at the wall. He looks at his watch. She'll just be leaving now. He lets out a moan of anguish and sinks onto the bed and covers his face in his hands. The foot protrudes from the heavily scissored bottom of its trouser leg like something ugly from the zoo lashed in place there.

Half an hour later the man plods awkwardly through the doors of the bar. Luckily, it's raining, and the bar is dark. He wears his great-skirted overcoat. His heart rises into his mouth as he sees her at a table. But lucky again, her back is towards him. He forces a brave, almost livid grin and goes up behind her and then launches himself rapidly into the seat opposite her, so she doesn't have time to see all of him. She gasps. His grin freezes. She wears a black, impenetrable veil over the major portion of her face. Neither of them speaks. The man stares. The veil is so large. So wide. He realizes she is sobbing; tears hang from her chin. 'I tried to call you . . . I tried to call you . . .' she is blurting softly. A horrible fear builds in the man, like a flame catching. 'Let me . . . please . . .' he murmurs. He reaches across the table, to lift aside the veil. But with a dreadful sob she grabs his wrist and holds it away, tossing her huge head clumsily from side to side.

Ars Poetica

A man comes in. He has a glass throat. You can see his larynx in there: a microphone disk, a little speaker horn. A mailman comes in with his big bag. He opens the small transparent hatch in the man's throat and pushes in a couple of blue air letters. The man begins to recite – a wonderful poem about being jealous of the clouds; then another poem, not quite as good, about a forbidden voyage.

'So this is how poetry is made,' I think. 'What are some other ways?'

A man in a baggy checkered suit climbs down a ladder from the ceiling. He carries a bucket. In the bucket, beautifully colored fish are swimming. They have been painted. The water rumbles with their brightness. The man crouches and rolls his eyes about and manipulates his hands mysteriously over the bucket. He murmurs in a strange tongue. Nothing at all happens, but it's really quite marvelous just the same.

Horse Opera

A man is awakened from a nap on a muggy afternoon. Someone is trying to be an opera singer. The man swears groggily and sticks his head out the window.

There is a police horse across the street. The policeman is standing beside it, red-faced and confused, his hat in the gutter. The horse sways its flanks and tail, and paws the ground with a hoof and tosses its head – all this in time to the aria it is bellowing out-of-tune with its wide-open horse's mouth.

The man blinks at this extraordinary sight. He pulls his head in from the window and rubs his fists in his eyes and goes over and empties the water glass over his head. Cautiously, he sticks his head out again. The horse is still at it. The cop is nowhere to be seen. The man hears sirens now, in the distance. The horse seems to hear them too, because it stops for a moment and cocks its head. Then it starts up again at an absolutely frantic pitch of expressive fervor. It rears back on its haunches and crosses its front hooves over its heart and squeezes its eyes shut; its great epiglottis throbs in the depths of its throat.

The onrushing sirens quickly drown this heartfelt song. But they don't stop the singer. The horse continues to croon its heart out even after the patrol cars skid up and the angry blue figures swarm out and throw ropes all over it and haul it up a ramp. It is still singing, as the big metal doors swing shut and the orange light flashes, and the big black van goes rumbling away.

Three Ring Circus

I come home after a hard day, and go into the bathroom and find the tub filled with rutabagas. I stare at them. I yell for my girlfriend. There's no answer. I push the door open to the bedroom and get a jolt. The bedroom has been completely excavated, to the horizon, and planted with rice. A straw-hatted figure is bent at work in a distant paddy. The tiny figure straightens up and waves to me. It's my girlfriend. 'Hi hon!' she yells faintly. 'Come join in!' I try to grin at this. 'After a beer!' I yell back. 'What?' she cries. I repeat myself, but she still can't hear. Finally I just wave and nod, letting her know everything's fine, I'll be back.

I head bleakly into the kitchen. I get another shock. There's a giraffe standing at the stove, wearing an apron. The giraffe stirs something in a saucepan. 'Hiya,' it says throatily. It smiles. 'Hello,' I say. I can't think what to say next. There's an awkward pause, which I end by pointing at the fridge and then stepping towards it. 'I'm not in your way, I hope,' says the giraffe, squeezing itself against the stove as I reach into the fridge door behind it. 'No problem,' I tell it. I realize the giraffe is wearing a Rayon body stocking. The stocking has a 'giraffe skin' pattern.

I go out into the living room and drain off half the beer at one shot and try to get a grip on myself. I turn on the TV. It makes a hideous squeal, as if in terrific pain; then a face appears. I do a huge double-take, like a burlesque idiot. It's my own brother, on national television. '*What*!' I cry, grinning explosively. I look around for someone to share in my rampant family pride, but there's no one. On camera my brother clears his throat and smirks. Then he proceeds to unload the most vile and preposterous lies about me, without so much as batting an eye.

Origins

I go downstairs to meet my father for lunch. An elderly Oriental gentleman steps out from behind the mailboxes. 'I'm your real father,' he says.

We go back upstairs. He uses an elegant cane, a slim black implement with a silver pommel. I can't help admire it. When we're seated in my main room, sipping tea, he launches into the story of his life, and thereby the so-called unveiling of my true origins. I listen sourly, one eyebrow cocked. Finally it's too much, I say: 'But look, to be perfectly blunt about it, how do you reconcile the obvious 'physiognomic' discrepancy between us?' He looks at me intently, and then he shrugs. He grins, sadly, and gets to his feet. 'Well, I guess you've seen through my story,' he says. 'Thank you for the tea, anyway.'

I see him out. I come back into the room and stand there abstractedly at the table, hands in my pockets, trying to make head or tail of what has just transpired. The clock chimes the hour. The door of the big closet opens and my father creeps halfway out. He looks about with great agitation. 'The cane!' he whispers fiercely. 'Did he leave the cane?' I stare at him, dumbfounded. 'For God's sake,' he cries, 'are you deaf?'

He comes out a step, peering. Then he gives a gasp and lunges over to the couch and pulls out something that was pressed into the angle of the cushions: the glossy black shaft of the cane. Averting his head from it, he scurries back to the closet and flings the cane into the back and starts piling coats and suitcases and kicking shoes and tennis balls on top of it. 'Help me!' he yells.

When finally we have buried the cane to his liking, we come back to the table and he flops into a chair. He mops at the floods of sweat on his brow. 'An old suitor of your mother,' he says, panting. Then he leans forward and raises a finger at me with stern urgency. 'Now listen, my boy,' he says. 'You're old enough to understand certain things I'm going to tell you.' I look back into those bulging, green and grey eyes of his, and despite myself I feel my knees getting weak. 'That thing in there – you've got to keep it hidden. Whatever happens, *never let your mother see it*!' He seizes hold of one of my wrists. 'Do you understand me?' he cries.

Honky-Tonk

A girl falls down and breaks her neck. The angel sent to accompany her spirit to the afterlife falls in love with her. Instead of processing her, he breaks his heavenly vows and gives her back her life. Then he loses his head completely and runs off with her.

The two of them set up housekeeping in a trailer court on the edge of town. To make ends meet the angel does carpentry work around the place. At lunchtime the girl is waiting for him back in the trailer, decked out in mail-order intimate fluff. The angel barely has time to get off the corset that hides his wings before the two of them are going at it madly between the sheets. The TV glares steadily over the little sink.

At first the angel's deep-seated delicacy is appalled by the world he finds himself in. But in a while his pristine exquisiteness coarsens; the booze and the lust and the slapdash diet makes him bloated, and sometimes he curses without giving it a second thought. The girl gets bored hanging out all the time in the trailer, so the two of them start going out to honky-tonks all evening, and then most of the night. The angel is allergic to the smoke. One of his eyes swells up peculiarly; blotches break out on his skin. Perhaps it's because of these broken-down looks that one night the girl goes out to the bathroom, and keeps going, out the back door. Her hurrying heels crackle on the gravel. There's a pickup truck waiting under the moon with its motor running; there's a tall figure in a ten-gallon hat at the wheel.

The angel stays on alone in the trailer court with his heartache. But mostly he's sinking down in the bars. His fumbled quarters find the saddest songs on the jukebox; his tears and whiskey spill over the selection buttons as he cries along. Or he raises his beautiful angel's voice and gurgles along up into the smoke.

One forgotten afternoon he hocks his angel's wings for more drinking money. Then he's nothing better than one more poor lush with a fancy past.

And these last words are the first words of the very first song he comes to write one midnight of his desolation. He writes more like them, then better than them, and he sings them and one day a passing someone hears them and is struck as if by a revelation. And then another whole story begins, and music is the angel's salvation.

Soup Bone

A man jumps out of an airplane. Sobbing, he empties a shoe box of love letters into the whooshing air. The letters shoot up and stick against the puffy bottoms of some clouds. The man looks, and groans unhappily, but then gets caught back up in the tumult of falling. He gulps and clutches at his head but his hat is long since gone. A cloud rushes up under his feet and the man cringes and crashes into it. The cloud flings him up in the air, as if it were foam rubber. He sprawls back down onto it in a heap. It's a tiny cloud and the man clings to it, desperately, like a shipwreck survivor hanging on to the side of a barrel.

He looks around. Out of nowhere, something hits right next to him and bounces away into the sky: it's a big soup bone, the kind dogs love. The man looks up and sees the looming, on-rushing image of a dalmation hurtling towards him. The dog barks and flails as if skidding on vertical ice. Its tongue trails up over its nose, its ears stream straight up. The man gives a shout and frantically flaps his feet to try to maneuver out of the way. The dog crashes right on top of him. The cloud heaves violently. The man almost loses his grip. The dog scrambles and slides down the man's leg and hangs on to an ankle. 'Let go, let go,' the man shouts at it. He kicks furiously with the leg but the dog hangs on for dear life, whining, eyes shut tight. 'You dumb mutt, let go!' the man screams. He feels his aching fingers slipping. He gives a terrific leg shake and then frantically lets go with one hand to deliver a wild, desperate punch. He misses. The cloud capsizes and pops loose. Screaming and whining and barking, the man and the dog tumble headlong into the wide blue sky.

Strawberries

I'm in bed with a girl whose face, in the darkness, is covered with strange-looking bumps. When we start nuzzling, my nostrils fill with something sweet, something heavenly. Tentatively I put my tongue on to one of the bumps. I nibble. My palate swoons. Feverishly I start munching.

'Stop it!' she cries. She shoves me away, hard. She thrashes to a sitting position. 'I knew it,' she says, 'you're only interested in me for my damn strawberries!' 'Of course not,' I protest, trying to look sincerely shocked. 'How can you say that! It's merely I've never experienced anything like this – and they are, well, frankly, you know, delicious, my favorite fruit, that's all. Honestly.' 'It's what they all say,' she snorts. 'Look, enough nibbling. How's about the real thing, huh?' 'Of course!' I say. 'Just one more teensy snack for energy – ' 'No!' she roars, twisting her head away and smacking her fist into the quilt. 'Sex or nothing!' 'Okay, okay,' I tell her. 'No need to get all worked up.'

So I climb aboard and start up. But it's hard to keep your mind on its proper business, what with your nose pressed against her jaw, where it is teased with the most delicious fruity essences. 'Look, I'm really sorry,' I finally have to say, climbing off and stretching limply by her side. 'I can't understand it, for some reason – ' She bursts into quiet, terrible sobs. 'Oh God, I wish I were dead,' she moans, burying her cheeks in the pillows. I lean over her, feeling heartsore and stricken and ashamed. Obviously this all touches some awful central problem of her life, some rotting prop under her self-image, and I've simply gone gorging my way into it. She's clearly extraordinarily sensitive, and I've shown no consideration whatsoever, just typical, thoughtless egoism. 'Please, listen to me, it's my fault,' I whisper. 'I'm a real jerk, an A-1 prick. You're gorgeous and sexy as anything, you know you are, to hell with the strawberries, they mean nothing to me, nothing! Not a thing!'

But even as I caress and stroke her, even as I plead with her to be assured, even as I excoriate myself for my selfishness, my heedlessness, my brutality, the aromas work away at my fuddled brain. Helplessly, my mouth starts to creep down; helplessly I feel it surround and nip and start to chew; helpless and choking I swallow, in an agony of deliciousness and remorse, as she weeps and twists around under me, inconsolable.

Little Fire

It's snowing in the living room. The tiny flakes dance about, as if precipitated from all directions. They make for a strange, enchanting dislocation – an indoor landscape. 'Boy, isn't this something?' I exclaim to my father, who silently occupies his armchair away from the fire. The casement window is open; through the fluttering curtains I can see a section of whitening landscape, like a picture: the charcoal-colored river, the long, snow-capped wharves on the opposite shore, the grey, sprinkling sky.

Inside, the little fire sizzles and crackles in its grate. I rake another chestnut free from the glow and pry the husk open in my mittens and blow on the steaming nutmeat, to cool it for my mouth. I hear my mother's boots on the carpet behind me. I look back at her. 'How is he?' she asks, rhetorically, pulling back the hood of her parka. She bends over my father and adjusts the scarf about his crystalline shoulders and twists his drooping carrot nose back upright in his perpetually smiling face. Then she kneels laboriously to wipe up the puddle around his chair, where he'd melted over the past hour. I watch her in silence, my mouth full of the luxurious nut. She gets slowly back to her feet, in stages. She lets out a long, weary sigh. Standing beside my father's rotund, happy form, she stares out glumly through the window. 'Two more years,' she muses. 'Then the spell will be over and we can shut that horrible little window.'

Moon and Ladder

It's night. The moon is out. A man in a top hat sneaks along a street carrying a bouquet of flowers and a ladder. The ladder is painted white. The shadows in the street are black as ink. At the silhouette of a house, the man stops. With exaggerated, stylized movements, he looks up the street then down the street, his face framed by the rungs of the ladder. The street is empty. The man props the ladder against the side of the house, under an open window with a flowerpot. The side of the house sways a bit. The man starts up the ladder, all elbows and flowers, in his top hat and boutonniere and balloon trousers.

On the roof of the house next door, the painted silhouette of a cat glides out creaking from behind a chimney. Its mouth opens and closes and emits a 'miaow, miaow' sound. Its long black tail twitches, stiff and metronomic, in front of the huge moon.

From a Book of Hours

Beside a stream a man is reading. He sits against a tree, one knee drawn up as support for his book. Next to him a long slender pole is propped; a line dangles into the water.

The open pages of the book show an illustrated, gilded scene: a tiny figure by a stream, fields giving on to a town beyond. In the fields, men and women bend over curved bundles of wheat. Their scythes make dark punctuations of the harvest.

The man smiles, as if pleased with what he sees. Then he yawns and looks over at the pole. He shifts his gaze a bit and considers the prospect of the town in the distance: the familiar spires and gables. He surveys the fields, before returning to the book.

A shadowiness comes over the surrounding landscape, as if a cloud were passing in front of the sun. It is the man's hand, about to turn the page.

Two Bears

A man rents two bears. One of the bears wears a little blue fez; on his vest is his name: 'Bruno.' The other bear wears a red fez. His vest says 'Hugo.' The man takes the bears home with him.

In his living room, the man pulls off his coat and frees the tails of his shirt and gets a beer from the ice box. He aks the bears what they'll have to drink, but they shake their heads. He sinks back in the armchair and lets out a long sigh and flexes his stockinged feet. After a while he leans forward with his elbows on his knees and he looks at the bears. He asks if either one of them is up for sex with him. The bears stop playing with the hoop they brought along. They glance at each other darkly under creased brows. The man pulls out his wallet. 'I'll make it worth your while,' he says. The bears look at the money. The bear named Hugo finally shakes his head. The other bear, Bruno, glances at Hugo. He thinks to himself, and he shrugs. He takes the money and pushes it carefully under his blue fez. He follows the man into the bedroom. He shuts the door.

The bear named Hugo stands at the fireplace. He taps the hoop up and down. Then he lets it fall. He pads over to the television. He looks at the grey, blank screen, at the row of knobs. He wanders over to the armchair. He lowers himself into it and lounges back, gingerly. He lifts the beer can and sniffs it, uncertainly, under his black olive nose. From the bedroom, he hears sounds. He hears the other bear give a sudden, snarling growl. He hears the man making hoarse, fierce noises.

The bedroom door opens. The bear scrambles out of the chair. The man comes out. He finishes adjusting the fit of his pants. He strolls by the bear, into the kitchen, snapping his fingers. The bear named Bruno shuffles out. He comes shuffling stiffly over to the fireplace. The other bear watches him. When

Bruno finally raises his eyes, they are ashamed and vulnerable, ready to take offense. The two bears look at each other. There is a long pause of silence. Then suddenly the bear named Hugo starts sputtering. Bruno watches him. He pushes him in the chest. Hugo turns with the blow and hangs on to the mantlepiece with one paw and clutches his low belly with the other. He shivers and sputters with stifled laughter, his vest and red fez jiggling, his eyes squeezed shut, his hams quivering. A big, embarrassed grin spreads over Bruno's snout. He glances over his shoulder. He swats Hugo on the arm. Hugo quakes uncontrollably. Bruno looks down at the floor, grinning. Then he takes off his blue fez. He holds it cupwise in his paws and gazes at it.

At last Hugo turns back from the mantle. He wipes his tearing eyes, shaking his head, still chuckling. He sees the fez in Bruno's paws. He looks at it. He falls silent. The two bears stand head to head, in silence, gazing at the money in the fez.

From the kitchen come the sounds of ice, liquid, whistling.

Golden Years

On the bus, I meet a guy who says his hobby is jails. I go with him to his house to take a look at a cell he has constructed. In the backyard I get a shock: there is a primitive sort of stockade there; inside are my mother and father, looking wretched and frightened. 'What the hell's going on?' I demand. 'Do you know them?' asks the guy. 'Of course I know them!' I tell him.

I lead them down the street, away from the house. They're very shaky, and they lean on me, walking slow. The marks of the manacles are still on their wrists. 'He seemed like such a nice young man when we met him,' says my mother. 'Oh for Christ's sake!' I burst out at her, furious at her feebleness, at my own apprehension of the vast evil of the world. 'Can't you be more careful? Don't you understand people prey on people like you? How could you have been so naïve!'

This excoriation produces a chastened silence. We move along, heads bowed for our various reasons. After a while my mother looks up and glances at my father and says, 'But you know, the food was very good.' 'Yes,' my father agrees hurriedly, 'the food was excellent, surprisingly!' But then they see the look on my face, and there's nothing further said the rest of the way.

Talk

A man develops a highly sophisticated way of communicating. It's a language of arcane and inspired symbols, dedicated to the art of being witty. It has exquisitely abstruse features. No one can understand the man, but that doesn't perturb him. He goes for long walks, and then sits in a scenic area of the park and tells himself cunning, subtle, utterly brilliant little jokes at which he chuckles and wipes his eyes and shakes his head, knocked out by his own genius.

One day a tubby black and white dog follows the man into the park. It watches the man settle himself onto his bench and begin murmuring his witticisms. The dog laughs and tells the man he doesn't have a bad sense of humor at all. The man sits frozen to the bench. Slowly he turns and looks at the dog. Disbelief gives way to horror. 'Nobody in the whole world can understand me,' he thinks, 'except for this dog? How clever does that make me and my language?' The dog sits wagging its tail, looking on pleasantly. Then it grins. 'You little bastard,' the man hisses.

That night the man stays up until the crack of dawn, tinkering feverishly with his linguistic complex. The next afternoon, haggard, he makes his way to the park. The dog comes trotting in after him. He takes his seat on the bench. His hands are shaking. He sits on them. He looks down along his shoulder at the dog, which is seated nearby on the grass, its head cocked and uplifted in a parody of solicitous attentiveness. The man glares at it. Then he shuts his eyes and launches pell-mell into the spectacularly funny and convoluted fruits of his night's labors. He finishes, gasping. There's dead silence. The dog looks up at him blankly. Finally it says, 'That's funny?' The man's head reels. He grips the bench with white knuckles. His whole career swims frenziedly before him. 'You pompous little mutt, let's see you do better!' he snarls. 'Okay,' says the dog, and it hops onto its haunches and tosses off a series of Noel Coward-style drolleries on contemporary themes, all linguistically polished up like a batch of rare gems in a velvet box.

The look of horror turns sickly on the man's face. 'Stop it, stop it!' he blurts out finally. 'Those aren't funny,' he adds, in a stiff, miserable voice. But it's obvious they're all killers, every one of them. For a long time the man sits staring wretchedly at the dog. The dog wags its tail quietly, looking off discreetly. Finally without a word the man rises and wobbles off slowly towards the exit of the park, his head sunk down between his shoulders. The dog gets up and follows at a distance for a ways. But then it stops; it leaves the path and goes over to a tree and raises its leg; then, smiling to itself, it trots off in another direction.

Tired Magician

Late at night a magician pulls into a roadside diner for a pre-bed bite. He is tired and a bit on edge from money worries. He orders coffee and pie. He's the only customer in the place, but the service is slow. He gets his coffee but not his pie. Finally from his seat he aims a finger at the pie cooler and via levitation slides the door open and edges the plate out. Due to weariness, however, his concentration is off, and the plate falters and then crashes to the floor.

The little gnarled counter guy spins around at the far end of the seats. A second old face appears behind him out of a doorway. The magician feels very sheepish and stares down at his coffee.

He gets his pie. The counter guy kneels down and picks up the many scattered pieces of broken plate. When he goes for a mop, the magician leans over the counter and wags his finger back and forth through the air, thereby cleaning the floor spic and span of its mess. He does this out of injured professional vanity. The old guy reappears with the mop. He drops it and looks narrowly at the floor and then at the magician. The magician gives a casual, apologetic grin and shrugs. The old guy takes a step backwards. He lifts his hand a funny way and there is a blue-lighted detonation that knocks the magician flying out of his seat.

The second old guy comes running out of the doorway. 'What the hell!'' he says. 'He was acting strange,' the counter guy grunts. 'I didn't like it, not tonight. Gimme a hand.' The two of them drag the magician behind the counter. He has a dark, scorched bruise between his eyes. They cover him with aprons and then lock the door to the back. Then they pull off their masks so their little green antennae spring up free behind their ears, and they hurry out behind the diner, to set the flares for the landing.

Call of Nature

I walk in the woods. I see a man pressed against a tree. His pants are at his ankles. My first thought is that he is answering the call of nature. But then I realize he is rotating his hips heatedly against the pit of a low-forked branch. Suddenly his hands grip wildly at the bark and he slumps forward. 'Oh, baby,' I hear him groaning. 'Oh, baby, *baby*. . .'

Shocked, I hurry away from this scene. On the other side of a hill I stop and try to collect my thoughts. I remember reading somewhere about practices such as these, but coming upon them in the flesh, on an afternoon stroll, is something else again. I look around at the greenery. The glimmering agitations of the leaves begin to take on a whole new personality. I shake myself and start walking. 'It's not possible, it must be the full moon,' I think.

But it isn't. Two weeks later I'm hiking in different country and I come around a bend and stop in my tracks. A man lurches backwards away from the path, into the undergrowth. He looks wild-eyed, his face is flushed red. There is a violent odor of alcohol in the air, an atmosphere of debauch. A bottle of whiskey lies next to a pine seedling, which is bent to the ground in unnatural submissiveness. The man sprawls down onto his seat. He flaps awkwardly, trying to get back up and at the same time cover his fly, which bulges enormously. 'I didn't know it was just a seedling,' he croaks desperately, 'honest, I didn't know it was just a seedling!'

Horror Movie

A man is lying in bed. A young woman comes in and begins briskly attaching him to various machines and performing various physical procedures. At first he's confused, then he realizes he must be in a hospital, the girl is a nurse. But then he realizes she's not in white. She's in black: like a mortician. 'My God, I've died in my sleep,' he thinks. But then he decides there's been a terrible mistake, he can feel his heart hammering, he's not a corpse, he's alive. 'I'm alive!' he cries in an emotion-strangled voice. The girl smiles back at him from a counter piled with instruments and plastic containers. 'Sure you are,' she whispers. 'But you won't be after I'm finished with you.' The man stares at her, stupefied. The girl holds up an enormous hypodermic needle and squirts out a jet of fluid. Then in one frighteningly swift, almost ritualistic motion she whirls around and plunges the needle through the sheet into the man's leg. The spasm of pain jerks the man screaming into the sitting position. His hands flounder in the air. Then a switch goes and the machines tear him to pieces. The girl backs into a corner and sinks down, giggling and drooling.

Two more people die in this gruesome fashion. Then a kind uncle writes a letter. 'My dear favorite niece,' it begins. 'I'm afraid I've recently become an honest-to-god invalid. . . .' And the girl moves out to his isolated cottage in the country, to take care of him.

Full Moon

A couple of bored young girls sit around on a summer evening. Their folks are out. They lounge about on the side porch, reading aloud from a dirty book they found upstairs under the sweaters in their dad's bureau. They're in their undies. Their young legs loll over the side of the swing rocker in a youthful, graceful sprawl.

High above the porch roof, the full moon, which notices everything, notices them and pumps itself dizzy sending down syrupy rays, which fall thick and golden along the curve of a young thigh, the turn of a bare ankle. The girls scratch themselves and eventually grow tired of giggling at the book. They get up and open the screen door and go into the kitchen and start making an apple-spice cake.

Down the street, under the moon and the shade trees, a deranged sex-murderer – a certified monstrosity – comes wandering on the loose. He pants and gasps, dragging his maimed foot behind him, its toes lost to the prison-hospital dogs. His skulking back is all matted hair and blood, from the guards' whips; his enormous arms are scabbed with crude, self-inflicted tattoos. He moves from tree to tree with an aimless, tormented urgency, clenching and unclenching his horrifying hands.

At the tree across from the girls' house, the madman stops. He stares awestruck at the lighted kitchen window, where the girls, as if on display, are languorously licking the cake icing from the beaters. He moans and clutches a low bough, and elm seeds flutter down around him in a moon-gilded shimmer. The vein in his neck bulges. His huge bloodshot eyes roll up towards their unnaturally low brows. His mouth falls open and from between stump teeth a slim tendril of spit winds silvery and Art-Nouveau to the ground.

The screen door opens and slams. The girls go padding over to the swing rocker with the warm cake. The aromas float through the moonlight, across the street to the madman under his tree. His nostrils flare grotesquely. His eyes show only white. He stammers something and then his mouth snaps shut and the blood roars in his tiny brain and an eerie, high-pitched whine rises from his throat. Trembling extraordinarily, he jerks his huge claw hands up in front of him, and springs out into the street.

Up above, the full moon, which notices everything, notices the impending catastrophe and groans. 'Not this *again*,' it thinks. It decides to intervene, if for no other reason than to forestall one more gross insult to its reputation. In one second it withdraws all its energies from the swing rocker and stokes itself and pivots and blasts the charging lunatic with enough golden moonlight voltage to blow up a squad of oxen. But alas, it doesn't work.

Big Red Nose

Police surround a house. A dog runs out and they open fire. The dog keeps running, pink tongue flapping, black and white tail bobbing, until it's out of sight down the street. The cops reload, shrouded in gunsmoke.

The front door bursts open and a clown rushes out: big red nose, bag pants, a rubber-bulb noisemaker squawking insanely in his hand. A hailstorm of gunfire catapults the clown straight up in the air and down onto his back, vaudeville-style.

Suddenly shots ring from the house. The whole scene erupts in gunplay. An upstairs window explodes and a life-sized dummy, crudely handmade, comes sailing out. Bullets tear it to bits before it hits the ground.

Flames shoot up from the roof. A fire engine shrieks and clangs. A bullhorn bellows. A laundry truck comes roaring down the street, guns blazing from every window. The cops fire and scatter. The truck leaps the curb and crashes into the side of the house, smashing a gaping hole in the wall. The occupants stumble out and are nailed by a spotlight in the sudden darkness. They gasp and stagger about, hands in the air. Up above the fray, a yellow ladder sticks out of the chimney, slanted at the moon. A lone figure, wounded, drags himself up the rungs.

Sport

I'm fishing. A girl goes by in a red canoe, paddling carefully. When she has cleared me, I take my line out of the water and recast, powerfully. The fly streams through sunlight and shade. The girl's head jerks back, her arms fling out and the paddle goes flying and she tumbles into the water.

Immediately I know I've got a fight on my hands. She thrashes ferociously, taking line with her. Then she dives under some boulders and hides. A handful at a time I start taking back the line, creeping along the bank stealthily, keeping the tip of the rod as far out over the stream as I can to avoid snagging. But then I step loudly on a twig and that does it: she comes roaring back out into the midstream, towards the canoe, and I have all I can do to keep the line going out and my hand clear so it doesn't get torn off. When she breeches for air just before the canoe, I set myself and slam her. We go at it tooth and nail with my rod tip bent into the water and her mighty eruptions into sunlight – flashing yellow tank-top, emerald hiking shorts – and spectacular, spraying crashings.

At last I feel her tiring. The momentum swings in my direction. I work her in closer and closer to the bank, staggering to keep my balance on trembling legs against a final desperation run. Then I find the harness with one hand and I splash down into the rocks, and with what's left of my strength, I land her.

She lies sprawled on the bank, drenched and gasping. When I've got some breath back myself, I look her over. She's long-legged and young, the good-looking outdoorsy type. The fly is caught in her lower lip. I grip her by the arm and warn her, 'Get ready,' and then I twist out the hook. She yelps. I push her hand away and dab the little red wound with peroxide. As I'm putting the bottle away, she sits up. 'That was quite a fight,' I tell her admiringly. 'You from around here?' She glances up at me from probing and tasting her injured lip. 'None of your damn business,' she mutters. I purse my lips at this. I close up the tackle box with a deliberate gesture. 'Hey look,' I tell her. 'It's a sport, see? Fair is fair: I caught you. But I happen to be a nice guy and so I'm going to return you to the water.' 'You are?' she says, and her eyes get big, making me realize how young she is, all the more reason to put her back. 'Yes,' I tell her. 'But first you do have to give me one of these.' I lean over and take a kiss. She gives a modest little laugh. Then we wade into the water and find her paddle for her and get her back into her red canoe, and she even comes up with a wave as she goes off somewhat shakily on her way again.

My Father

I find a document that shows my father was born hundreds of years ago. I bring it downstairs to my mother. When she finishes reading it she looks off to the side, chewing over a thought. 'Well no wonder . . .' she murmurs to herself. A flicker of a smile plays over her lips. 'No wonder *what*?' I demand, if possible more stupefied by this comment than I already am. 'Oh, nothing,' she says. 'Well,' she says, handing the parchment back. 'It's quite something, isn't it?' 'Yes,' I tell her, 'it is.'

I go up to my room and sit by the window and wait for the sight of my father coming home from work. Certain things about him now fit glaringly into place: his preference for shoes with buckles; his fondness for, and extraordinary knowledge of, sea-chanties; his eccentric habit of going up to bed by the light of a candle; his continual mutterings of amazement at ordinary things like hot running water or bananas or umbrellas – even smallpox vaccinations. With a sudden start of insight I realize that all those smelly dusty wigs up in the attic aren't my mother's at all, they're his.

I hear the report of his walking staff on the sidewalk. I look down: he comes marching along, his briefcase in one hand, his staff hefted smartly in the other. My heart beats wildly. His whole manner now possesses something suddenly heroic. He has breasted the passage of the centuries. Involuntarily I start to rise to my feet. How will I approach him in his new stature, how will I behave? My mother appears on top of the porch steps below me. She says something to him, wagging her finger. He stops. She rushes down the steps and jumps into his arms and he laughs, and with one powerful arm around her and his feet planted wide he swings her about so her skirts fly up. My heart feels fit to burst at this sight and I exclaim out loud, 'What a splendid figure of a man my father is!'

Renovation

They are working on the road. Big-wheeled yellow machines strip back the paving, and underneath, in rows, lie delicate old women in housecoats. All of them have at least one of the features of my mother.

Then some workmen come up into the room where I'm sitting. They walk around me over to the wall and start prying at it with crowbars. 'Got to keep at it once you've got the subconscious open,' the foreman explains.

A great deal of mortar and bricks clatters to the floor. Dust billows. The men pull objects out of the wall and throw them back out of the way – tricycles, cribs, skates, furniture: all of it familiar to me from a long time ago. Peering over their shoulders I can see a scene faintly through the dust. A group of figures sit at a table: my family at a meal. It is all very pale and wobbly. The workmen reach their hands in, poke crowbars right through my father's face, through my brother's shoulder, through the back of a chair, through a bowl of potato salad. The people in the scene go on obliviously, mouthing animated silences.

'Well, that's going to be it for today,' the foreman announces finally. He points to his wrist. 'Quitting time – got to go home and start the weekend!' He grins and tips his hardhat and leads his crew out to the street. Their boots crunch in the rubble.

I stand at the torn opening, looking at it. It's still much too faint really; it goes in and out of its forms and I can't hear anything. The dust hurts my eyes and makes me cough. I turn away and go out of the room, shutting the door behind me so the dust won't get into the rest of the house.

I go outside and look around. The exposed roadway is covered with tarpauline; from the edges, the multiple old women's feet stick out. Barricades have been set up to keep people away.

I walk back inside slowly with my hands in my pockets. 'Well, there's not really much I can do,' I think to myself. 'I'll just have to wait 'til they come back Monday.'

Sheep

There are sheep outside my window on the supermarket roof. They're plump, thickly wooled. They plod about in a way that is delicate and airborne. I step carefully across to the roof. The sheep are very friendly. I hold out my hands for them to lick, as I look at the sky. The sky is full of sheep: they funnel up from the horizon like little grey and white clouds. Here, on the supermarket roof, they mill around me going 'baaa-aa' complacently.

I climb back through the window. In the dining room my girlfriend is reading the paper. 'They all seem to be streaming up from the southwest,' I tell her, pouring myself a cup of tea. She turns the page. 'That's good sheep country,' she says.

Angels

An old, miserable guy goes down to the banks of the river. He raises his arms to the heavens. He beseeches the angels. He calls on them to make things better for him. They show up, but their mood is ugly. They tell him he has a scrawny neck, that they're tired of guys like him. When he complains, they knock him down. They beat him with their thick fists. They roll him into the river. They walk off stolidly through the mists, not saying anything, breathing hard. Under their robes their shoulders are big and violent, under the great horns of their wings.

Bomb

A man happens to look behind his couch and see a bomb. His heart freezes. He stares at the stiff black hands of the alarm clock strapped to the grease-cloth package. His ears fill with the sound of ticking. At last he is able to rouse himself from terror-hypnotized immobility. He tiptoes towards the door.

In the first scenario, he gets out in time. He runs for the police who put on strange iron and rubber suits and creep in behind the couch and daintily ensconce the bomb in a special wicker basket, where it roars like a volcanic toy, furious but harmless.

In the other scenario, the bomb goes off just as the man reaches the doorway. The roof of the house bursts open. The man is thrown into the sky. He lands upside-down in a tree. After a while, he shakes himself. He manages to grip and slide and finally tumble to the ground. He gets up and holds on to the tree trunk unsteadily. As far as he can tell, he's alright. He looks around. He's on a hill; he doesn't recognize at all what he can see of the green, silent countryside. Dazed still, tottering slightly, he starts off down through the trees, looking for a road. And that's how his great adventure begins.

Evening

A girl sits in her room by the window, which is open to the evening. She is robed demurely in white. She smiles, sadly. On the small dustless table beside her is a thin cake of soap in a dish. Every few minutes she breaks off a piece of the soap and places it delicately in her mouth and chews. Her lips are frothed with soapy foam. It glitters like infinitesimal jewelry in the last rays of the sun.

Across the street, the youth who loves the girl hopelessly paces the terrace of the cafe. He smokes wretchedly, in distraction. Time and again he stops and looks up at the window at his sweetheart, and his heart breaks. The spit in his mouth turns sour and poisonous, and he covers his lips with his handkerchief and turns away.

Out back among the overgrown weeds and flowers of the garden, the father of the house finishes his business in the privy. As he wipes himself, he whistles. Then he stands over the seat and inspects what he's done. He comes out into the humid, mellow air and stands around leisurely, whistling. He snaps a couple of roses off a bush and smells them and sticks them, boutonniere fashion, into the outhouse door. Then he strolls over to another bush and shakes off a handful of blackberries and stands around eating them from his unwashed hands.

From the guest-bedroom window, his wife watches him. 'Old idiot,' she mutters. She sighs. Then she puts on a luxurious smile, and she rolls back into the middle of the disordered bed. Across the room the youth's best friend crouches over the bidet, splashing himself. The wife chuckles, watching him, her eyes shining. 'And now we're going to get it all dirty again,' she says.

In the Ice Age

A man skates on a frozen pond. The ice is dark and clear; the man glides along. Below him, the faces of a multitude stare up. The man is skating over them. He is skating over his ancestors. He can see the details of their features as he looks down, whirling along.

A creek winds off; he takes it. The skating here is marvelous, thrilling, a kind of Eden. The man follows the sheer black thread as it winds between the banks. On either side bare woods spread in perpetual winter. He draws his scarf closer. The milky bodies slip by beneath him. Mile after mile he moves along, without effort, in a trance of motion; not a sound rises from anywhere in this marvelous landscape.

Hermione

A man finds a photo of a lovely girl. He puts it in a frame and stands it on the table in his living room. When he entertains, he nods toward the photo: 'My new *friend,*' he announces softly, smiling enigmatically, shyly. One day he places a rose in a bud vase beside the photo. Later, a lovely mother-of-pearl hairbrush. As the days go by, the trove increases piece by piece: a lace antimacassar, a scroll of antique colored paper tied with a blue ribbon, a fluted tumbler of frosted glass, a pair of red ballet slippers whose ties trail over the side of the table.

The man appears to be very happy with his creation. His friends soon realize the exact nature of the girl in the photo. But they are discreet, affectionate. 'Hermione,' they repeat delicately, when the man finally reveals the identity of his loved one. 'What a wonderful name!'

One day the diary of Hermione appears, in marbled covers, on the table. Each day an entry is added, such as: 'Today I had my hair washed. Mama was very kind, though I was cross and out of sorts because the washing is so tiresome. I have so much hair! But afterwards it was very nice indeed, sitting in the shade in the garden and eating sour apples while Mama brushed my hair and sang all sorts of little songs I love.' And so forth.

When the man dies, quite young, his friends preserve the living room exactly as he left it. Through their connections they arrange to have the diary published, with a preface by a brilliant young art professor who never knew the man personally but is beguiled by him and his creation. 'A delicate, primitive romantic,' he writes. 'An enraptured, gentle dreamer.'

Greenland

It's deep in the night. My cousin is intoxicated, from drugs and alcohol. It makes him very spirited in his decadent, mannered way. He leads me through the rooms of his great house, knocking back the doors with a flip of his long white hand, shouting mocking and melodramatic greetings at the inhabitants. Extraordinary sights confront me: an artificial elephant constructed from pearl and ivory and tin, a group of painted men and women in a stupor around a golden brazier, a sunken pool crowded with long-tailed birds. My cousin breezes on ahead, throwing back his oddly shaped head to let out an abandoned, drawling laugh. Somewhere, in one of the rooms, I lose his track. His laugh comes to me faintly through the wainscoting, over here, over there, somewhere in the reaches of the house. I give up finding him. The night is dying. The room is inhabited by a softly faun-like creature. She lights a long white pipe for us from a candle in a bowl. Later, as we drowse, she lifts the hem of her stained velvet skirt and shows me, by candlelight, the map of ancient Greenland inscribed on the soft inside of her thigh.

Snot

I am sitting across from a girl on the subway. She's beautiful. I watch her pick her nose. She licks what comes out on her fingertip. At the next stop she gets off and I follow her. 'You know,' I say, drawing beside her on the stairs, 'you're very lovely, but eating what you pick from your nose does a disservice to it.'

We go to my apartment to make love. Afterwards, she lolls against me. She rubs between her toes and tastes what she finds. I take her wrist sharply. 'Honestly!' I tell her. 'Where did you get these appalling habits?' She shrugs. She laughs, impishly. 'Make some tea,' she says.

I sit at the table, sipping tea, when she returns from going to the bathroom. As she picks up her mug, my gaze drifts down to her thighs under my robe. I splutter in my cup, pointing: trickles of urine make their way down. I roll my eyes and shake my head and hold up my hands helplessly.

She giggles. She takes her tea over to the bed and curls up. 'Tell me again how pretty I am,' she says, grinning at my consternation. She rolls a finger between her legs and sucks on it idly at the side of her lovely mouth, chuckling, as she waits for my answer.

Mask

A man goes to a party where everyone is wearing masks. His eye falls on a little redhead in a tight-waisted outfit. He keeps track of her and finally starts talking with her in an archway, under a flickering taper. She seems a saucy and mischievous type – and, the man bets, passionate too. He gets the feeling he's going over with her. He asks her to dance.

The party is in a rented ancient palazzo. The dances are stylized and centuries old. Some people seem to know them but the man and the girl don't. They get into the spirit, but sometimes they miss the sequences so badly it makes them laugh. However the sight of all the masks and pomp stirs up a strange, lascivious atmosphere for the man. 'It's like Venice or something,' he says in the girl's ear. She grins.

After a while they go out on to the balcony. They're both sweaty; the scent from the formal gardens beyond hangs ripe and intoxicating in the air. The man feels druggedly erotic. He looks at the masked, kittenish creature at his side. 'Let's go for a walk,' he says.

The two of them go down wide stone stairs which look painted in the moonlight. They walk along past topiary, and hear noises and see it's people necking heavily in the shadows. They look at each other and go on, almost hurrying, further into the grass. Finally they sink down by a low, sculpted tree, just beyond the edge of the moonlight. The man pulls the girl to him and they kiss and she bites him.

He shoves her away and feels his mouth. There's a dark speck on his fingertip. The girl grins at him and lounges back luxuriously. The man seizes one of her wrists and kneads it hard in his hand. He calls her something obscene and then he moves onto her and pushes her mask up into her hair.

Later, people have gotten naked and are having a sort of orgy in the stone pool at the foot of the garden. Masked women rise head and shoulders out of the water. They try to climb out, glistening, and then they slip and shriek and splash back in. The man and the girl watch from under the tree. They have on each other's mask. The girl's barely covers the span of the man's eyes. The man's looks like an industrial helmet on the girl. They hold hands. There is a tiny scarred bump on the man's lower lip. The girl picks a blade of grass and carries its little bubble of dew back into the shadows and dabs it carefully where the damage was done.

Blood

A girl comes up to me with blood pouring out of her nose. We staunch the flow and clean up her chin and neck. She says her female metabolism has gotten all screwy recently because of an affair she's been thinking of having. I tell her I don't really know all that much about female things: all I know is what I've heard here and there. I help her off with her blouse, which is badly stained. 'Who were you thinking of having an affair with?' I ask her. 'This guy . . .' she says, shrugging, and she looks at the floor. I look at her shoulders, which are rounded and pink, and at the roundnesses of her bra, which are also pink. She sees me looking and she flushes and hugs herself modestly and her nose begins to flood again. 'Oh no,' she says. The blood is bright, the color of cherries, and it has a delicate, almost floral smell to it. I get a towel, then another, then a third. By the time things are more or less wiped up and clean again, the girl and I are surrounded by a crimson litter of towels. My own shirt is soaked. I shake my head as I go over to the sink. 'Whoever it is, I suggest you have this affair very soon,' I tell her.

The Cousin

I'm down in the driveway, helping my old man clear some
brush. My mother calls from the front steps: 'Stephanie's here!'
The old man and I look at each other. 'Oh Jesus,' I say. We go
on up. She's sitting in the kitchen, drinking tea – Stephanie, my
cousin, who killed herself two years ago. Her hair is just as long
and dark and untidy as ever, but it's the disturbing whiteness of
her face I notice. The old man of course grabs her, gives her a
huge hug, launches pell-mell into a discussion of things. I peck
her on the cheek quickly and take a chair and sit watching the
conversation, feeling her clamminess clinging to my lips.

A little later we walk out into the woods. She insists on
showing me her wrists, not once but twice, even though I tell
her it frightens me. 'So what is it like – where you are,' I ask her
finally in a hesitant voice. We're sitting on a log. 'What's it like?'
she says, and she gives me a furtive look and her upper lip
quivers. 'I don't know . . .' she says, and she shrugs and bites
her lip, trying to suppress the giggles, thinking about what it's
like. Her eyes have a wild, loony darkness in them; she just sits
there, shaking with giggles, trembling with spooky, secret knowledge. She keeps it up for so long it gets really awkward, as I sit
beside her, trying to grin along. I realize how absolutely little I
know about her, how strange she always was. Once when she
was staying with us I said something very rude and spiteful to
her (about how much tea she drank), which pained me with
guilt afterwards, especially after we got the news. I was going to
bring it up when we came out here. But it doesn't seem
appropriate now, considering the way she is. The pallor of her
skin is horrifying.

We return to the house. The old man and I go back down to
the driveway, to finish what we can before dinner. 'How long is

she going to stay' I ask him, dropping some branches on to the pile of what he's cut. 'As long as she wants,' he says. His voice and face are grim, occupied. 'Well, after dinner I'm going,' I tell him. 'I'll stay somewhere else, I can't stay in the same house with her. She gives me the creeps.' 'She's your cousin,' he says, 'and she's had a very unhappy life. You'll stay.' 'I'm going!' I tell him. 'She scares the living piss out of me. How can you stand it?' He looks up at me, lifting one eyebrow, one of his withering, hanging-judge looks, so that I flinch. Then he reaches down for a sapling. 'Your problem is, you're not tough,' he says, quietly, scornfully, not looking up.

The Greek

I am brushing my teeth at the washbasin when I notice a spear in the bathtub. I go over to it and lift it out, it's a heavy spear with an ornate bronze tip. The tip is razor-sharp. The thing's a deadly weapon, a fearful weapon that must take an enormous man to wield it. I wonder to whom it belongs, but I won't show it to my father until I've kept it for a while to admire for my own.

I sneak back to my room with it, my toothbrush still in my mouth. I open the door and there is a huge, muscular guy sitting on my bed examining his feet. He has beautiful feet – all of him is beautiful in fact, like a Greek statue. Golden hair ripples down over his shoulders. All he has on is a kind of fancy loincloth.

He looks up, regards me vacantly for a moment, then goes back to his feet. Right away of course I know the spear is his. A bit awestruck, I step over the huge eight-shaped shield lying on the floor and place the spear carefully against the wall. Other pieces of armor are strewn over the floor: an Argive helmet with a red brush plume, a breastplate ornamented with sinister images, a set of golden shin protectors, a stubby sword, a big tangle of straps. I would love to handle every one of these things, but I don't dare. I place my toothbrush on the table and wipe my lips so I won't drip on anything.

The Greek guy finishes with his feet and lounges back, looking sullen and preoccupied. Suddenly he heaves himself lithely to his feet and goes to the window. He stares out moodily. I come up behind him and see out there the swimming pool and my father floating on his back in his blue bathing shorts. His big belly sticks up in the air; his body is strangely congested with dark, fat muscles.

The Greek guy swears arcanely and spits on my rug. He starts pacing about, slamming his fist against his thigh. The room is small, I have to dodge to keep out of his way. I am startled that he seems to be mad at my father. He goes back to the window and rolls his bottom lip in his teeth. He growls under his breath, fiercer and fiercer. Abruptly, he turns around. His face is like a thundercloud, his icy blue eyes are smoking. He reaches for his armor.

'Oh my God!' I think. 'He's actually going to fight my old man!' With a sickened stomach I watch him tying on his breastplate and fitting on his shin protectors. I keep glancing out at the pool, at my poor old man floating out there. Why has he got those sinister muscles? But whatever he's done, I'm sure he couldn't have meant any harm. I want to explain this to the Greek, I want to at least warn my father – but I am too terrified to do either. The atmosphere of violence completely numbs me.

The Greek finishes adjusting his helmet. He picks up his shield. He shouts something towards the ceiling and brandishes the shield in the air. He grabs me and plants olive-smelling kisses on both my cheeks. Then he strides out the door.

I drag myself to the window. The back door slams, the Greek goes trotting across the lawn rhythmically, like a perfect animal of prey, his huge shield almost covering him. Without breaking stride he rears back and heaves the spear. 'Dad! Dad!' I squawk, spraying toothpaste all over the window. The spear goes hurtling into the pool with a great splash. My father jerks up, he bolts out of the water with a power that is horrifying to see. The Greek comes through the pool gate and delivers a terrific blow with his sword. My father blocks it with his forearm, he swings the deck chair. It clangs against the shield.

I can't bear to watch. I sink to the floor, pressing my eyes shut, hiding myself in my arms. A phrase blares through my head, over and over, like a hideous loudspeaker: 'Bleeding *like a pig*! Bleeding *like a pig*! . . .'

Dummy

A man is bothered by dreams in which he appears as a ventriloquist. 'We all know what that's a symbol for,' he thinks. He confides his concern to an old friend of his at the neighborhood bar. The friend listens intently, his gaze fixed on the floor between their stools. After hearing the man out, he raises his head and looks at the man. Then he smiles and assures him there's nothing at all to worry about, the man is taking everything much too melodramatically. He makes a fist with his hand and taps the man on the cheek with it. He winks. Then he excuses himself and goes off unsteadily towards the john. He's gone for a long time. Puzzled, then hurt, the man finally gets up himself and goes out to the men's room. He sticks his head in the door and his heart stops: his friend hangs by his belt from the toilet-stall door frame. His tongue sticks out huge and purple, like an eggplant.

From that day on the man is haunted by the image of his dead friend in his dreams. Typically, that poor slob is standing in tears before a dark, looming judge. He strains helplessly to plead his case not to go to hell. But his gruesome tongue prevents him. Horrifed, the man has to do the talking for him.

Lattice

I go fishing in winter. I lose my footing on a snowy bank and fall in. The cold dumbfounds me, and I remain below. It's a small stream, but very deep. The green, dark slabs of the sides go down into caves — narrow and slippery tomb entrances where the motions of the water have washed everything to smooth stone: the great slabbed walls of the boulders, the little scattered pebbles.

I paddle in place, still in my fly-tufted fisherman's cap and deep-woods parka, the pockets of which undulate about me like a lazy skirt of fins. My boots plunge and rise ponderously below me, up and down, ineffectual. All is silence here, a corridor of darkened shale and the long pulsations of the moss-colored, somber current.

At night, I watch above me the glow of the rescuers' fires on the banks, under the snow-heavy branches. Figures move trudging along the verge of the water; suddenly they spear the current with the glaring streams of flashlights. For a moment the fiery lights criss-cross around me, like an underwater lattice. But then they break apart, and veer off elsewhere.

At dawn, everything is greyness and silence. Then the ice forms overhead, and I slip down among the boulders and they never find me.

Box

I live in a box. On its corrugated horizon I have painted a girdle of trees, some plump hills, the arc of a meadow. There is a little lake, with a rowboat and a party lunching on the bank – and a pretty swimmer, far from shore, who smiles though a luxury liner, laden with flags, oddly steams in her direction. Clouds puff above the lake, casting no reflection, and a kite floats in the blue like a bow tie.

At night, the rest of the world hovers under its darkness. But I gaze up at the menagerie of my heavens: stars in the shape of tennis shoes and brooches shine there, and the smoky scarf of a galaxy blows among them. There is a little cork, with astronauts peering out: a monkey hangs from the tip of a melon-slice moon and offers the voyagers a smaller moon – a shimmering banana.

Now I smoke and dream, my hands under my head on the pillow. My gramophone tinkles softly, pouring its wine into the night.

I muse, and my soul sways up before me. 'Dreamer,' it complains. 'Look how you waste your days shut up in here like somebody's parakeet. Mr Good-for-nothing! I'm so tired of you. One day you'll just be swallowed up, like an ornament, like a moonbeam. Your head is full of moon-junk! . . .'

Thus my soul sways and grumbles. 'Oh, to think that I belong to you. . . .'

And tenderly I reply. 'Little worried potato, little radish! Don't you see, it's really a carriage we're on. Look: how we go rolling over the dusty road, and how the arms of the trees and hedges jostle us! The moon wants to come down with us. The streams want to wrap themselves in our wheels. And back there, that's our dusty wake – it's full of fireflies and jewels.'

Woodsmen

Men are working in the woods. I take a seat on the pine needles and watch the movements through the trees. I hear the sounds of their talking. I lie back in the coolness and shadows, covering my eyes with my arm, and let myself be lulled into a doze by the distant voices, the blurred echoes. In my dream, they're working beside me. They chat with me pleasantly as they carve from wood the roots, the boughs, the blossoms, the detailed leaves: the forest. 'And soon we'll do you,' they promise.

WEARING DAD'S HEAD

Again, for my parents,
and for Matt

'The thoughts that we can clearly grasp are very little thoughts
... all greater thoughts are undefined and vast to our poor
childish brains.'

Jerome K. Jerome, *Idle*
Thoughts of An Idle Fellow

'. . . On those evenings my child's heart was rocked like a little
ship upon enchanted waves. . . .'

Isaac Babel, 'Gedali'

Childhood Memory

My father comes into my room. 'Look,' he says. He carefully opens his hands; a luminous, gold-colored butterfly sits in the bowl of his palms, like a light he has carried into the dark room. I prop myself up on a hand in the pillows, gazing in awe. The butterfly remains still for a while; then it twitches its wings. We watch it flutter in a curving, luminescent course to the window, and then under the sash and out into the night.

We go downstairs and noiselessly out the back door onto the dark lawn. My father points up at a tree: a halo flickers around its crown. In its topmost leaves a golden colony hovers. 'They'll be there all night,' says my father, his voice a whisper. I stand beside him in my pajamas, spellbound and feeling a strange, tranquil enchantment, as if the night had turned into my bedroom. 'Where do they come from?' I ask my father. 'From the moon,' he says softly. We look at the moon. 'At least,' he says, 'that's what I've always been told.'

Picnic

I drive with my parents for a picnic. We stop by a cliff. My father tells me to bring out the picnic basket. The wind lifts the lapel of his jacket. He looks at my mother wildly. He gives a hoarse, trembling moan. He clutches fumbling at her hand. My mother cries out and gapes at him as if stricken. Hand in hand the two of them clamber hurriedly out of the car and lumber towards the cliff and, screaming and shrieking, jump off. There is the brief, diminishing sound of their screams; then abruptly, nothing.

I stand by the car, staring at the edge of the cliff. The wind flutters in my ears. After a while, I fearfully approach the cliff edge, and crouching timidly on my knees, I peer over it. My parents lie near each other on the rocks, like rag doll replicas of themselves. Their clasp has come undone. The waves splash over their shoes, up over their legs and hips. I crawl backwards several feet, and then rise.

Back at the car there is a note pinned to the picnic basket. I look at it, but it means nothing to me, as I'm not old enough to read cursive script. I poke somberly through the contents of the picnic basket, most of which is beyond my taste. I open a bottle of pickled onions and sniff it with displeasure and put it aside. I find three slices of cake. I eat one and part of a second, and half of a pear, which I chew sitting in the open back seat of the car. Then for a while I just sit without moving, with the car blanket over my knees as I gaze at the cliff, listening to the sound of the waves coming in and the rustle of the wind. At length, slowly, the light begins to fade around me. I climb down stiffly out of the car. I stand beside it. After a long pause of hesitation, I turn, and start off back down the dirt road by which we'd come — slowly at first, then with gradually rising haste, until my tottering steps are scrambling along through the evening's gathering shadows.

By the Creek

I come into the kitchen. My mother screams. Finally she lowers her arm from in front of her face. 'What are you doing, are you out of your *mind*!' she demands. I grin at her, in my bermudas and bare feet. 'It's okay,' I tell her in a chambered voice through my father's heavy, muffling lips. 'He's taking a nap, he won't care.' 'What do you mean he won't *care*,' she says. 'It's his *head*. For god's sake put it back right now before he wakes up.' 'No,' I tell her, pouting, disappointed that her only response is this remonstration. 'I'll put it back in a while.' 'Not in a while, *now*,' she says. She moves her hands as if to take the head from me, but then her hands stammer and withdraw, repulsed by horror. 'My *god*,' she says, grimacing, wide-eyed. She presses her hands to her face. 'Go away! Go away from here!' 'Mom,' I protest, nonplussed. But she shrinks away from me. 'Get out of here,' she cries.

I stalk out of the kitchen. Hurt and surprised I plod heavily up the stairs. I go into my parents' bedroom. I stand at the foot of the bed. My father lies on his back, mercifully unable to snore, one arm slung across his drum-like hairy chest in a pose particular to his sleep. I look at him. Then I back away, stealthily, one step at a time, out the door. On silent, bare feet I steal frenetically down the hall, down the front stairs and out the front door. On the street I break into a run but the head sways violently and I slow to a scurrying walk, until I'm in the woods. Then I take my time on the path, brooding, my hands in my bermuda pockets. I come to the creek and stand balancing on dusty feet on a hot, prominent rock. The midafternoon sun lays heavy, glossy patches on the water and fills the trees with a still, hot, silent glare. A bumble bee drones past, then comes back and hovers inquiringly. I get off the rock and stoop down, bracing the head with one hand, and pick up a pebble. I get back on the rock and fling the pebble at the creek. It makes a ring in the water. Another ring suddenly blooms beside it. I look around at the path. A friend of mine comes out of the trees. 'Hi,' I say to him. 'Hi,' he says, in a muffled, confined voice. He stops a few feet from me. 'You look funny,' he says. 'So do you,' I tell him. I make room for him on the rock. 'Where's your dad?' I ask him. 'In the hammock,' he says. 'Where's yours?' 'We don't have a hammock,' I tell him. 'He's in bed.'

Half an hour later there are half a dozen of us standing great-headed at the side of the creek.

School Days

A schoolgirl is squatting at the side of the road, her skirt hiked up and her knickers down at her ankles. I watch her pee. Then she hurriedly pulls everything back into place and scrambles off, her satchel bobbing against her back.

I go over and look at what she's done. There is a little puddle in the mud. All sorts of tiny ivory creatures – a charm-bracelet menagerie – are swimming about in it. I get some pebbles and start flipping them into the delicate, crowded water, to observe the turmoil that ensues.

I hear footsteps and I turn around. A big, plain, severe-looking woman comes trudging up. She uses a walking stick and wears the school's green blazer. She makes me hand over the last of my pebbles, and boxes my ears for me, for teasing animals.

Animals

My father turns into a gorilla. At nights I sneak in to visit him in the monkey house where they've got him locked up. I bring him what he wants: perfectly ripe bananas. 'You're really sure,' I whisper again, 'that it isn't a gorilla suit? I mean, it looks very much like a gorilla suit.' 'Of course it's not a gorilla suit,' my father snorts irritably, flinging a banana peel behind him and ripping another helping off the bunch. 'You think for the sake of a joke – you think as some kind of gag I'd let them lock me up in here?' His huge flaring nostrils quiver menacingly. 'I suppose not,' I mumble.

After he's eaten his temporary fill, my father waddles over to the little window at the back on his stumpy, bowed legs. A faraway moon hangs between the window bars. The moonlight falls cold and white on the narrow crown of my father's great dark skull, on the massive expanse of his thick-tufted shoulders. He lets forth a booming, mournful growl and raises his fists and slowly pounds them on the smooth plating of his chest. I draw back, awestruck by this exhibition of percussive thudding, this behemoth distress.

After a while my father leaves off and comes shuffling over to the front of the cage. He hangs his woolly head. A soft, sad light flickers in the dark hollows of his eyes. 'You know what I miss sometimes,' he sighs. 'I miss those little green shoots I used to nibble, up there on the heights of the rain forest. . . .' I look at him. 'But dad,' I tell him, 'what can you mean? – you've never been anywhere near a rain forest in your life!' 'So what?' he snaps. 'You haven't ever heard of Species Memory? I'm a gorilla, aren't I? Don't be such a damn fool!'

One night I persuade my mother to come along on a visit. I have my arm around her as we approach the cage. In the dimness her eyes are large and shiny and full of trepidation. 'Hello, dear,' she says in her halting voice. 'How are you, my darling!' My father stares at her. He drops the chunk of wood he was gnawing and backs away a step. He lifts a great, horny hand, pointing. He bares his dazzling white teeth. He starts hopping up and down. 'Dad – ' I protest. My mother shrinks back; then she screams. 'Dad, for god's sake!' I shout, horrified at the sight of my father furiously rubbing away at his enormous groin. I hurry my mother out the clanging door. 'I don't understand, I can't imagine what got into him,' I gasp, as we stand trembling outside in the shadows under the eaves.

My mother refuses to return again. 'I happen to be a gorilla,' my father insists incorrigibly. 'What does she expect, a bunch of little flowers?'

Soon afterwards, my mother turns into a llama. At nights, after I drop off my father's request, for an assortment of nuts, I creep on under the stars to the corral where my mother resides. She trots up to the fence. 'It's really all for the best, I think,' she says, nosing at the sheaf of mountain grasses I've brought for her. 'Everyone here is very gentle, and I have to tell you, I find this coat of white fur immensely compatible. Feel it, just feel how luxurious it is.' 'What, just reach in, through the fence?' I ask her. She smiles at my hesitation. 'Come now, I won't bite you,' she chides me. Warily I reach in. I stroke the soft, plush fur on her neck. 'It's very soft, it's lovely,' I tell her, bringing my hand back. My mother regards me for a long, tender moment with her large, brown, tranquil eyes. Then gracefully she dips her head to eat. 'Sweet, sweet the mountain leaf . . .' she extemporizes, browsing through the greenery.

Family Car

We drive in the family car. 'Have another hard-boiled egg,' my father says to me. He takes a bite of his sandwich, steering idly with one hand. 'The pickles are wonderful in this,' he calls over his shoulder to my mother in the back seat. 'I used up the entire bottle,' says my mother. 'I *love* gherkins,' I inform the two of them, cracking the egg on the dashboard. 'I *detest* bread and butter pickles, I can't see how anyone could actually *stand* them.' We come over a hill. 'Look at all the mud down there in those fields,' I murmur, staring out of the window.

The car plows into the mud, shuddering and drifting sideways, out of control, wheels racing and racing. An arrow explodes through the window, gashing my father's brow as it slams quivering into the dashboard. Blood pours down his nose. 'Comanches!' he cries. 'They've broken the treaty!' He throws open the car door and clambers out. Snow blows heavily. My father wears a parka with a huge, tufted hood. Tears and blood stream down his face as he clears the windshield with the red-bristled brush. 'Millions have been killed,' he weeps. 'Millions and millions!' A thick batch of photographs spills out of his pocket into the snow. I stare down at them. Each photo is an individual snapshot of each one of the slaughtered innocents.

The wheels thrum on the road as the car cruises along. 'The *second* biggest state west of the Mississippi,' my father repeats, pondering. 'That's a hard one. Texas must be the biggest. California?' 'I think you've got it *exactly* backwards,' I chuckle triumphantly. 'And what about Atlanta?' asks my mother. 'Atlanta's not a state, mom,' I call back patiently. 'And it's not exactly *west* of the Mississippi,' I add. 'It's not somewhere over there by Nevada?' my mother says, perplexed. '*Nevada?*' I protest. 'You've been in this country fourteen years and you still don't know where Atlanta is?' my father exclaims, looking up at my mother hopelessly in the rearview mirror as we lean into a curve.

The curve twists unexpectedly, and the car roars off the road and plunges out over a chasm. My father's door flings open in midair and he is sucked out, screaming without a sound. He cartwheels over and over down a slope, hideous to see, and crashes finally upside-down onto a cactus. Staring through the window I hurtle silently past him. He lies impaled on his back, drooping unnaturally, his arms hanging down past his head. The car plunges into the water of a lagoon and sinks down into an outcropping of coral. I try to force the door open, but it won't give. I batter it with my fists. In a chaos of bubbles I tumble about in the front seat, locked in a life-and-death, hand-to-hand struggle with a marauding alligator. My mother swats at it with a broom. 'Not in my kitchen you don't,' she cries. 'Not in my kitchen you don't!'

The car drones along steadily, its big engine humming. I look back at the rear seat. 'Mom's asleep,' I whisper to my father, with a gesture of my head. 'Good,' he replies softly, glancing up at the mirror. 'She deserves it, after that magnificent lunch she packed.' 'I'm not asleep, I'm simply dozing,' my mother informs us from under the handkerchief spread over her face. My father glances up again at the mirror and smiles privately. 'You do whatever you want back there,' he says. 'Your Highness,' he adds. He looks at me and we exchange a grin. I resettle myself in the wide, warm seat. 'Another ninety-seven miles,' I announce softly, as a mile post skims by. My father checks his watch. 'Another two hours still,' he says. He sighs, and shifts himself about in his seat. He glances at me contentedly. 'You know if I were you, I might make use of this time to think up one of those funny stories of yours,' he suggests.

Tongue

Some friends of mine have removed my tongue and hidden it. I look all over the house but I can't find it. The thought begins to seep in that it's possible for the rest of my life I may very well not be able to talk at all. Images of an empty mouth and a truly vacant smile flash like horrific neons through my mind. I suddenly become intensely shy and embarrassed about my awful disability. A practical joke, I realize, may have ruined everything for me. An incredible shame takes possession of me now at the thought of being the kind of person destroyed inadvertently by some people's heedless idea of fun. I want to hide myself away from the world, to shrink from life.

This desire is so strong and irresistible to me that I realize I am in fact shrinking; in fact I have shrunk already, to the size of a young child. 'This is terrible,' I think, gaping down at my little feet and then at the looming furniture, through eyes that feel uncomfortably large in my head, like figments of a sentimental drawing. Big silent tears start to drop down my cheeks.

Suddenly a huge door flies open. A party of giants – my friends – bursts uproariously into the room. The sight of me stops them all cold. One of them almost drops something like a loaf of peeled salami – my tongue. They rush up to me, exclaiming in shock and alarm. They try to cram the great tongue back into my head, but of course it's far too big now and won't go at all. Finally they see it's useless and they leave off manhandling me. The women burst into tears and huddle together wailing in horror. The tongue lies on the carpet like a piece of sodden firewood. The men pace around me, red in the face, pounding their thighs with huge fists. 'You pathetic fool,' they shout at me, 'what have you done, what have you done!'

In a Room (Butterfly)

I trap a butterfly with a glass. Later, I can't find it. My cousin, who has come for the day, watches me search. At last I notice she seems very pleased with herself. She has her hands behind her back. I lunge for her, but she scrambles away.

I chase her into a room. It is dim in there, shadowy, hot. She orders me to lock the door. 'Now give it back,' I tell her. She shakes her head, not speaking. She looks at me. She pulls her dress up over her head, and off, keeping one hand closed the whole time. She lies down on the cot, naked, and watches me over her shoulder. I stare at her, feeling frightened and intoxicated. I hear the two of us breathing. She extends her hand on the pillow, and opens it: the butterfly sits in her palm. Its wings are like ruby lace. She reaches back and sets it on to her shoulder. Her hair is tumbled over her face. I watch in agitated silence as the butterfly wanders down slowly over her still, brown, naked back.

Cleavage

A strange disease afflicts my father. By daily stages he is transformed inexorably into a full-figured blond woman – a bombshell. 'Now I think we had better prepare ourselves for certain difficulties cropping up in your relationship with your dad,' suggest my mother, patting at her slightly sweaty forehead in the drone of the lawnmower, as we sit with iced tea on the patio out back. 'What sort of difficulties?' I reply, swallowing. I stare fixedly past her shoulder at the golden-haired figure of my old man shoving the old mower across the daffodils and weeds. Voluptuous swellings magnificently press out the pockets of his checkered flannel shirt; golden limbs flow from the baggy flapping of his much-patched chino cut-offs. My mother purses her lips and regards me. 'I think you understand perfectly well what I mean,' she says.

In the evening, at the dinner table, my father glances at me and scowls as he takes the peas from my mother. 'Listen my boy,' he mutters in his shockingly normal voice, spooning peas, 'would you kindly once and for all stop gaping at your father's décolletage!' I turn a deep, profound red. 'I'm sorry,' I mumble, staring at my napkin in my lap. After a few moments I sway clumsily to my feet. 'I don't feel so good,' I blurt out. 'I think I better go lie down.'

My mother comes upstairs to find me. I lie huddled on the bed covers, groaning. 'You look awful,' my mother declares. 'You're running a fever, obviously. Get into that bed right this minute.' 'It's nothing, I'm okay,' I mumble, shuddering. 'I just shouldn't have eaten all the mint in the iced tea this afternoon, that's all. I'll be fine.' 'You'll be taking aspirin and drinking gallons of fluids, that's what you'll *be*,' says my mother, hefting one of my feet and yanking off the shoe. 'You're a very, very sick young man,' she declares grimly.

I toss and turn all night. In the morning I wake up with a splitting headache and a bladder fit to burst with fluids. I maneuver unsteadily out to the bathroom. In front of the bathroom mirror, I freeze motionless. 'Oh my *god* – ' I gasp. Trembling, I raise a hand to the blond tresses cascading onto my pajama collar. The hair is silky in my fingers. I move my eyes, and stare down in horror and awe at the twin globe forms in state on my chest. I edge a hand, now shaking, into my pajamas, to feel. I gasp and suddenly slump, grabbing out at the washbasin for support. 'Mom!' I call miserably. 'Dad!'

Eventually, my fever passes. I come back downstairs and take my place once more at our unnatural dinner table. My mother sits in the middle, trying determinedly to maintain her dignity in the face of truly harrowing circumstances. My father and I sit stiffly at the far ends. Every so often, roving, furtive glances flare between us. The awkwardness is palpable. The silence is measured out in the clank of a fork scraping up rice, the sawing of a knife through a fibrous pork chop – the grinding of mastication, the gulping swallow of iced tea. All of a sudden my mother puts down her fork. She turns. She looks at my father. She turns the other way. She looks at me. She turns again, and looks straight ahead. She seems to tremble. Slowly, she tilts back her head, and opens her mouth astonishingly, and roars with laughter. She laughs so hard the cultured pearls of her necklace jump about on her collar bone. Tears stream down her cheeks. The lamplight flashes on her gaping teeth, flecked with morsels of food. My father and I stare at her sidelong. We glance at each other. For a short while we grin unsurely down at our plates. Then gradually we just sit staring off beyond the table, blond and nonplussed and stunning in our cardigans, as my mother quakes howling into her handkerchief between us.

Oak

I'm eating lunch. Through the green shutters of the window I watch a sheep trot by on the road. A flock of them comes ambling along placidly behind. A pretty shepherdess appears, hurrying. I smile. She wears a starched white bonnet and she hefts the long crooked tool of her trade with a big blue bow tied around it. 'How charming,' I murmur to my mother, who sits in her rocking chair, puffing on her corncob pipe as she whittles a clothes peg with her penknife. I spoon up another portion of yellow chowder. Then I put the spoon back. I hear querulous bleating; shouting. I push back my chair and lean out the window. 'Hey!' I exclaim. I throw off my napkin and hurry out the door into the sunlight of the yard. The flock stands about in a large group. The renegade of the bunch is loose in the primroses. Bleating, it tries desperately to chew off as much as it can while wiggling about to avoid the punishments of the shepherdess. She curses at it, whacking it with great blows of her decorated crook, as if it were a rug she was beating. 'Hey – hey there!' I shout, hurrying around the baa-ing flock. 'Stop abusing that animal like that!' The shepherdess glares around under her bonnet. 'Why don't you just get lost,' she snorts, apple-cheeked and nasty, as I come up. 'I certainly shall not,' I reply, dumbfounded. 'How dare you address me in that manner on my family's property!' 'Why don't you stick your family's property up your arse,' she retorts, sneering. She turns away and raises her crook again. '*Why don't I stick my family's property up my a –* ' I repeat, my eyes widening at every word. Furiously I grab at her crook. She snatches it out of my reach. Her blue eyes flash. She hefts the crook, measuring me with it.' 'What in hell – ' I protest, falling back and raising my hands in protection. The shepherdess moves towards me, grinning menacingly. She makes as if to deliver a blow. I flinch. She swings. I duck frantically. The crook sweeps over my head, its bow fluttering and whirring. 'You bucolic hooligan!' I sputter, scrambling backwards. Chuckling ferociously the shepherdess steps up to swing again. I curse her and turn and rush through the dodging sheep back into the house.

'What's up?' says my mother, narrowing her old eyes as I run over to the fireplace. 'What's it? A ding-dong? A dust-up?' 'Some maniac of a shepherdess has gone berserk out there with her crook!' I pant, rummaging through the clutter of implements by the hob. 'First she was beating up a sheep and then she tried it on me! But I'll fix her!' 'Not with that goof-ass twig broom, yer ain't gonna,' my mother snorts. She points with her pipe. 'Git the pestle from the butter churner. It's oak.' I go over to the butter churner. Hurriedly I scrape off the yellow tufts from the long pestle shaft, from the wooden barrel of the head. 'It's solid,' I agree, feeling its weight. I turn towards the door. 'Now yer mind now,' my mother warns me, limping over to the window for a view of the proceedings. 'I know how them Bo Peeps go at it. She'll fake yer high to the left, then try to come under low right and wham yer jewels up in yer watch pocket.'

I stalk back out into the yard. Sheep stray everywhere, confused and bleating. A number are now in the primrose beds. The shepherdess stamps among them, whacking and cursing. 'I told you to stop that!' I shout, halting a few yards off. The shepherdess wheels about. Immediately she sizes up the change in the situation. Her pink brow lowers. She steps out towards me, scowling cautiously, crook at the ready. 'Now we'll see how you like a dose of your own medicine, you little pastoral sociopath,' I mutter. We circle, sheep baa-ing out of the way. I can hear her fierce snorting of breath. Suddenly she lunges at me. I fall for the feint, but I remember my mother's words at the last moment and wildly I parry the low right blow that follows. I step in and deliver an awkward, lurching stroke that catches the shepherdess off balance with a loud clunk on the side of the bonnet. The crook flies into the air. The shepherdess topples into the grass. I stare down at her. I drop the pestle. 'I've killed her!' I blurt. I sink to my knees and peer horrified at the big buttery smudge where the blow landed. Buttery blond curls stick out in a sweaty thatch on her forehead. Her blue eyes stare unseeing at the blue sky. I bend over her, reaching gingerly under the skewed bonnet to feel her temple. I stare at the pinkness of her lips, frozen in a scowl. Suddenly there's an explosion in my eye. With a yelp I keel over backwards. The shepherdess springs on top of me and grabs me by the throat. She throttles me and punches me and pounds my head again and again into the grass. Her pearly teeth are bared, the cords stand out on her red-flushed neck. 'Help . . . help . . .' I sputter feebly, swatting at her, helpless. Suddenly a bucket blurs overhead. Milk splashes onto me – the shepherdess goes flying. 'I *said*, What in blazes is going on here!' my father cries, standing over me, the oak bucket still swaying from its handle in his fist. 'Can't I tend my cows of a morning without all hell breaking loose in my absence?' I sit in the grass, swollen-eyed and drenched, leaning on a hand and shaking my head for lack of speech as I gasp for air. The shepherdess lies sprawled motionless on her crumpled bonnet. A sheep nuzzles her bared ankle. 'Not his fault,' declares my mother, appearing among the sheep at my father's side. 'She started it,' she explains, pointing with her pipe. 'Yer know how shit-biscuit them Bo-Peeps kin git sometimes. . . .' 'Would it ever be possible for you once to speak in English instead of that repulsive backwoods gutter-lingo you affect!' my father demands of my mother in exasperation. He turns from her, shaking his head, and joylessly regards the shepherdess. 'Well, she won't be starting anything else for the rest of the day, at least that much is certain,' he says. 'I'd better drag her over into the shade. And now for god's sake get these sheep out of here,' he cries, 'before they chew up my lawn and whatever's left of my flowerbeds!'

Towards sundown two of her menfolk come for the shepherdess. They have yellow, curly beards and pink cheeks, and wear round fleecy hats and fleecy white vests. Sullenly they load the shepherdess and her crook onto the back of a pony cart. I stand in the yard, holding a chunk of raw beef against my eye while with the other I watch the cart bump and creak slowly down the lane, followed by the flock of sheep. 'Well good riddance, they're a nasty lot,' observes my father, his tankard of home-brewed ale in hand. I sigh, a long, complicated one. 'I suppose so . . .' I murmur. 'I must admit though, if you could overlook her personality, she certainly was a very pretty girl. . . .' My father splutters into his beer. He lowers his tankard and stares at me. Then he mutters something and stamps off, shaking his head. I remain where I am, watching the cart one-eyed until it is a point lost where the woods converge on the lane. I turn wistfully towards the house. My father tours through his flower-beds, shaking his head at the ruins of his primroses. I can hear him muttering into his tankard, as the smoke of my mother's Dutch oven drifts out into the evening air, and the first star gleams in the evening sky over the meadows and dales.

The Viking

My mother sits at her dressing table, braiding her hair. 'I see you,' she calls out pleasantly, looking past her shoulder in her hand mirror. 'I see you!' She hums to herself as she puts the mirror down and reaches for a tortoiseshell pin. I inch along, buttock to heel, clanking, trying to work myself in between the bookcase and the bed. 'I can still see the tips of some *very* funny-looking horns,' my mother sings out, mirror again in hand. 'It's either a great big bison back there, or it's a Viking.' I try to hunch down further, but my hat is just too big. I pull it off. My elbow cracks against the edge of a shelf. I grind my teeth and clutch at my broadsword to keep from howling. 'Now what was *that* violent noise?' my mother wonders mildly. She takes up the mirror, inspects herself, and puts the mirror down. 'There, all done,' she says. She turns to the room, fiddling with her watch strap. 'And all alone, all alone and defenseless, dear me,' she announces, and she gives a hyperbolic sigh. Squeezed in behind the bed, I squat on my knees, gripping my sword and my ax, sweating in my synthetic bearskins, waiting for nightfall, and the raid.

Lullaby

I go swimming at night. I leave my clothes under a bush and feel my way to the edge of the creek. I slip in. The night water is oily, soft, warm. I start out into the current. An owl hoots in an overhanging branch as I pass beneath, its horns and high shoulders silhouetted against the orange moon. Frogs honk among the lily pads. The current carries me along, bobbing quietly. The deep-rimmed, yellow-lit dials of an alligator's eyes watch from the cat-o'-nine-tails as I drift past. Up on the bank a heron sleeps on one spindly leg. I make my way through the water lapping at my ears, through the night that's all around. Fishes flutter against my legs and along my ribs. A turtle and her young surface nearby and paddle along with me, their shells gleaming and slick in the moonlight.

The creek turns a bend. A great bared tree root arches out into the water. Pausing, I look back towards where I've come from. A canoe is making its way quietly down the creek in my wake. The canoeist barely uses the paddle; just one languid stroke, and the paddle is put away. The sound of a voice softly singing reaches my ears. I edge back into the watery shadows under the tree root. The turtles crowd in around me. We watch as the birch vessel comes gliding up. My mother kneels in the middle of it, her long, fine hair let down about her shoulders. She runs her hands through her loosened hair, bathing it in the moonlight while she sings low, and drifts. Her song is the simplest of refrains, the little round that guards the night. Over and over she chants the names of her family – my own name, my father's – commending them softly, under her care, to the water and the woods and the world.

Rite

At night some men are beating an animal down in the garden. I watch from my window; it all takes place in silence, slowly, a tableau in the midst of the flowerbeds. At last the animal manages to break free. It bolts clumsily through the flowers into the woods, a cowed, erratic, lamely darting white shape.

Later I come downstairs to make some tea. The back door is open, and I can see some of the men gathered there, grim, talking low in the darkness, drinking.

I can't sleep. The shadows flit and tremble on the wall. Later I leave my bed and go down again. They're still there, in the rubble of bottles, talking about it, some of them weeping as they point out in the darkness to where it took place.

The Raid

During the night some redskins attack. My father comes into my room. His hair stands up in tangled handfuls. There is dirt on his face. He tells me they've carried off my mother. He sits on my bed, breathing heavily and grimly. He looks exhausted. He reaches out a heavy hand onto my shoulder and squeezes me powerfully and stares off into space. 'Come,' he says finally, 'get dressed.' I pull my pants on over my pajamas and put shoes on my bare feet and hurry out behind him. The collar of his shirt stands up, making ludicrous shapes under his ears.

Later, they find her. The porch is lit with hurricane lamps. I watch from behind the screen door. My father sits by the porch railing; the people from across the street stand around him. There is a box on the wicker table. My father reaches into it and brings out pale lengths of a plastic necklace, the beads dirty white like giant, dusty pearls. They're chipped and pocked. My father runs them caressingly through his fingers, over and over again. Tears stream down his cheeks. 'Oh those barbarous swine,' he groans. 'Look what they've done to her! Look what they've done!'

The Lifebuoy

Lightning flashes. The waves slam against the pilings. I lean into the heavy wind and spray, hanging on to the tossing linkage of the safety barrier chain. My father's head and shoulders appear and disappear among the crests of the waves. His arms flap about to summon the lifebuoy I have hold of. The noise of the wind and the water and the boom of thunder squash away his cries. 'Hel . . . ! H . . . p!' is what I hear. I set myself to toss. I see my father's bulging, desperate eyes. Lightning flares lividly. And then suddenly I'm backing away from the chain. The lifebuoy dashes against the walkway. It goes wheeling off crazily in the wind. I retreat slowly, crouching, mesmerized by what I'm doing and what I see. The storm feels muffled and numb, yet concentrated and huge. My father struggles in confusion and frenzy in the midst of it. There's a look of dawning horror on his face, then a wave obliterates him from view. For a moment I see his spasmodic, grappling arm reappear, but then I break into a terrified run, away from the pier, chased by pelting sheets of rain.

I arrive home soaking wet and shivering. 'My god, I was so worried,' says my mother, hurrying me into the kitchen. 'What a storm! Where's your father?' 'He's coming,' I mumble, my teeth chattering. I pull off my soaking clothes and huddle shivering in a blanket by the kitchen fire. An hour passes. My mother turns around from the kitchen window, which the rain still lashes. 'Where can he be? He's much too late,' she says. 'He was on his way, you say?' I nod my head vigorously, not looking at her. 'Alright, we might as well go ahead with our supper,' she says grimly.

We draw the table up near the fire. We eat our stew in silence. The fire blazes in the hob, and the light licks and dances over the table, over my father's waiting bowl and spoon. I feel the onset of a luxurious, drowsy warmth and contentment. I look up at my mother. I grin at her intimately. I look back at the table. I feel her eyes on me. 'I see,' she says. 'So that's what's going on.' I hear her sniff. A tear drops heavily onto the table. I keep very quiet. She uses her apron. 'After your clothes are dry,' she says quietly, getting to her feet, 'I want you out of this house for good.'

Frontier Days

I hide in the leaves. My father comes around the side of the house. He wears only underpants and slippers. Half his face is white with shaving cream. His eyes blaze. In one hand he hefts the length of a broad, thick belt. I hold my breath, shifting on my haunches to follow through the big leaves of the rhododendron his stalking approach. He passes abreast. I burst out of the bushes, screaming and brandishing my tomahawk. I have on full Sioux war regalia. My father bellows and starts violently backwards. The rake end of the leaf rake catches in his heels and he sprawls all at once to the ground. The belt goes flying into the grass. I swoop down on it and snatch it up, dart back a step and whack my father on his bald spot with the rubber blade of the tomahawk, and go racing off into the back woods, yelping and waving the belt aloft in triumph. Shouts of pain and outraged fury clamor after me.

The trees mount in a long slope behind our house. I scramble up a good ways, then turn and scurry briefly along a bumpy ridge, and at last plunge slithering down a bank into my secret hideaway. It's a sort of wide overgrown pit, unknown to the greater world. In the middle of it a scrawny, solitary tree raises itself. I stand before this, panting happily, the broken feathers of my headdress dangling over my ears and shoulders. The tree's branches are stuffed and garlanded with plunder: my father's old hairbrush, a silk tie, his tweed flat cap, his old corduroy nightgown, his initialled eyeglass case, his second best hickory walking stick, one of his favorite pipes and a box of pipe cleaners, the top half of a pair of his flannel pajamas, and two rolled-up, weather-beaten issues of his professional magazine, their original mailing wrappers still in shrivelled evidence. I hang the belt up beside these, and add from my fringed pouch the two other splendid trophies, both foamy with soap. I step back and gloat sweatily.

Through the surrounding woodland, fragments of a continuing apoplexy make their way. Keen ears aren't needed to pick them up. Still gloating, I cross over to a mound of brush at one side of the pit. I crouch down and reach inside, all the way up to my shoulder, straining. Finally I bring out an empty coffee can. I maneuver off with it until the string running from its bottom back into the bush and then out into the woods is sufficiently taut. Then I take a deep breath and compose myself on my knees in the leaves. A prodigious sulk disfigures my war paint. Actual tears well in my eyes. 'Mom, mom!' I call piteously into the can. I push aside feathers and hold the can with both hands up to my ear. 'Hello?' a tinny voice comes back. 'Hello?' 'Mom,' I whimper. 'It's dad! He's furious at me again, and all because I had a little accident with his shaving mug and his nail scissors. It was just a terrible, unfortunate little accident, I try to tell him, but he won't understand!' 'Oh, no, not all this, again,' says my mother's tinny voice. 'He's so irritable these days, it's simply impossible.' 'I keep telling him it was an accident,' I whine. 'Please, mom, you have to help me! *Please* . . .' 'Yes, alright, don't you worry, I'll see what I can do,' she says. 'Thanks, mom!' I whine. I shove the can back hurriedly into its hiding place. Gleefully I clamber up the side of the pit and start up the branches of a maple tree. From a distance below comes the noise of repeated woody violence and then the slamming of a door. I steady myself on my moccasins in the crotch of a high bough. Through the leaves I survey below the now-empty back lawn, the thrashed remnants of the leaf rake on the back door steps, and beyond the further side of the house, the long curve of the driveway. A figure emerges on to it from the lower woods. It's my mother, called forth from her garden. She has on her great-brimmed straw sun hat, her voluminous beekeeper's veil, her brilliant white gardening shift, her yellow gardening gloves and boots. She marches determinedly up the driveway, a basket full of her green beans and daisies on one arm, a flowing white handkerchief held aloft in her opposing hand to advertise her office and her mission. High in my tree, I grin like a savage. I throw back my head, I raise my hand in front of my mouth and send out a long, pulsating ululation over the woods and the house, exulting, as the wind plays in my feathers.

Buttercups

I crawl through a hedge, and stop dead. A butterfly the size of a dog is feeding at a stand of buttercups. It lifts and lowers the massive, yellow and black lace of its wings, as it spears the buttercups with the thin, curving blade of its proboscis. Its enormous shadow spreads lazy and tumultuous into the grass. Breathlessly I lift my air rifle to my shoulder. I squint along it. My heart pounds aloud. There's a sudden thump. The butterfly jolts stupendously. Its huge, florid wings swing open, one crazily half-flapping. It starts to roar about frantically, struggling up into the air and then diving swooping back towards the grass. I cower, horror-struck. I shoot again, wildly. The thump dies into the clamor of wings, the heavy, grassy silence. The butterfly comes wheeling towards me, hobbling at an insane angle. I shout and pull the trigger again and again. The great shadow storms across the grass. I hurl myself frenziedly to the ground, as the wings sweep overhead and plunge into the hedge behind me. I scramble to my feet. I bolt towards the buttercups and huddle there, staring back at the golden wreckage broken and torn in the hedge. I stare, moaning softly, as the scent of buttercups floats up into the humid air.

Age of Reason

Trouble with a leg forces me to bed. Every evening the doctor comes and pries a hole in my plaster cast and extracts a tiny, wriggling, lizard-creature. Sometimes it gets free of his tweezers and he runs around the room after it, upsetting chairs and lamps. He comes back at last with the struggling specimen and holds it up to the light to let me inspect it. His long, dingy hair hangs over his collar and sweat gathers under his spectacles. In the lamplight, amazed and a bit mortified, I peer at the little parasitic fellow, all wriggling tail and feet and desperately flicking tongue. Its skin is clear and jellied, like a fetus, so that the light shines through it. Finally the doctor claps it up in his battered black bag, and smacks his lips as he reaches for the drink I have poured for him on the night-table. My case, he assures me, is a medical astonishment, and he has taken it to heart. He grows passionate, discoursing on it. His waistcoat is stained with a mixture of formaldehyde and ink. He is writing me up for the medical journals, and his particular inspiration is this: to write his article in the form of a poem. Once again he recites the opening lines. The force of his declaration carries him away. He rises to his feet, he flings out his arms, as the little room fills with the rolling, magnificent periods of his verse.

Lightning

Outside the house, thunder rumbles. Rain begins to fall. I go into my bedroom to shut the window. I see something in the backyard. I gape, flabbergasted. My mother sits in a chair in the middle of the lawn, knitting. 'Mom!' I shout at her. 'Mom!' My voice is lost in a crack of thunder. Rain pelts down. I swear and hurry downstairs and go out into the rain, shouting. My mother lifts her head and smiles at me as I come up. 'Hello, darling,' she says. 'I'm just out here having a bit of a thrill. This silly knitting of mine can grow into such a bore.' 'Are you out of your mind?' I demand, squinting at her under a raised forearm. Water streams down the sides of her cheeks from her plastered hairdo. Her blouse is already soaked. 'For Christ's sake, come inside, right now,' I protest. 'It's dangerous to be out here like this!' 'Oh I'll be alright,' she says. She holds up her knitting needles and clacks them together. 'See? Not metal – plastic.' She grins, rain bouncing off the front of her head. There's a vicious, cracking peal of noise close by, and then a great, jolting basso blast. The ground trembles. My mother sits cowering. Slowly she raises her head and stares up at me, frightened and grinning triumphantly. I lose my temper. 'Listen, stop this absurd nonsense and come inside!' I demand. I reach out and take hold of a drenched arm. 'Let go of me,' she protests. I try to pull her to her feet. 'Let me go!' she cries, wrenching about and whacking at me with her knitting needles. I let go of her. 'Mom, for Christ's sake – ' I exclaim. 'You've got no right to interfere in someone else's fun,' she cries, resettling herself angrily in her chair and fiercely resuming her knitting. 'If it scares you so damn much, just go on back inside.' I stand over her, staring at her ferociously through the soaking drive of the rain. There's a stunning, blinding flash. I slam backwards into the grass. I lift myself around heavily.

143

'Mom – ' I stammer in a thick voice. My mother sits, cringing and immobile in her chair. She glows, incandescent. As I gape at her, the intensity of her light gradually fades. A thin trail of smoke curls up from her head. She turns about slowly towards me. She gazes at me, and blinks. 'Whew . . .' she declares, with a stunned grin. 'That was a *jolt*.' She grins at me, blinking. She looks down at her lap. 'Damn,' she says. 'Look at these stupid knitting needles, they've melted!'

Bonfire

The light of a fire trembles in the night sky. I go across the lawn from the house and down through the trees out into the meadow. Some figures are wandering there; they're all in flames. A great load of brush has been piled high and ignited. A woman in a gauzy dress approaches me. She's barefoot. She smiles and says something to me, but it's impossible for me to make out the words in the whoosh and crackle of the bonfire, and in the woman's own flames, which are like a shifting booth of light around her. I show I can't comprehend, and she stands, smiling at me and nodding her head. Then she turns her flaming back to me and watches the bonfire as it lunges furiously, higher and higher, into the sky. Flickering figures drift about in the surrounding blackness, like satellites.

Later, I sit in the moonlit coolness of the formal garden. There's still a glow over the treetops, and the smell of smoke among the flowers. I watch the old gardener as he goes along bent-backed through the shadowy flowerbeds, to and fro, grumbling to himself as he tips his ancient watering can.

Adults

My father titters. He has turned himself into a girl. A throng of blond curls sits on his balding head. A powder-pink sweater stretches to the point of ripped seams over the bra bumps of his burly chest. A pleated skirt surrounds his voluminous girth, and white ankle socks shine under his stocky, hairy, powerful calves. He swishes about clumsily in the parlor, preening and giggling, and then heads off waddling down the back hall, a hand bent-wristed on his hip, out into the garden and the moonlight. I stare out at him from the kitchen window. Lifting little fingers, he holds his hands far out to either side, and bends his big nose and sniffs a hydrangea. He pitter-patters in place, beside himself with delight at what he smells.

Shaken, I go upstairs and break the news to my mother. She puts down her sewing. She crosses to the sewing-room window. 'Yes, I see what you mean,' she says, peering down under the brim of a hand against the pane. She sighs. She turns back into the room, shaking her head. Mysteriously, a smile plays at the corner of her lips. She goes out, into her and my father's bedroom. When she reappears she has on a cloak, black tie and tails, and a top hat. She carries a cane. She squints jauntily through a monocle. The thin line of a moustache is pencilled along her upper lip. 'Dearie,' she announces to me, 'I think it's better if you go to bed now. This sort of an evening is for adults.' She pats me on the cheek, seeing how shocked and speechless I am. She winks, and steps off in a swirl of her cloak.

From my bedroom window I stare down open-mouthed at the garden. The slight, top-hatted figure of my mother strides out towards the bloated pixie who is my father. My father wiggles shyly at the sight of my mother's advance, and retreats one coy step, and then another, and then scampers off heavily into the rhododendron bushes. His sweater comes flying out powder-pink into the moonlight. My mother snatches it in midair and brandishes her cane in a display of lusty enthusiasm. Then she crouches, and stalks towards the rhododendrons, calling ahead teasingly. Suddenly she stops. She straightens and looks around. A flying kid glove bangs against the screen of my window. 'Go to sleep!' my mother's voice orders from below. I turn off the lamp. After a while I lie down on my pillow as bidden, but I can't sleep. I stare in confusion at the ceiling, hearing laughter from the garden, and the strangest of noises.

Oasis

I take a job guarding a harem. I cut a small slit in the stripes of the great conjugal tent behind my sentry post. Through this aperture I have a particular view of the privacy in which the sultan conducts his delectations. The great raised bed is right under my nose. Sometimes, as I squint down through, the face of the exalted companion of the evening is almost brow to brow with my own. I stare into dark, almond eyes swooning upside-down below a shadowy veil – a veil damp with the sweat of ardor, fluttering to the warbles of love. I smell the scent of perfume through the ever-present aromas of dates and tobacco. My head swims. Suddenly the veil veers aside, driven there under a storm of cries. I crane on tiptoe, straining with a livid eye to follow the last, whimpering denouement of the exalted evening. Finally I turn away, and come fumbling back to attention, my fez slightly cockeyed, my hand shaking as I bring the engraved scimitar upright against my shoulder. A thin drop of sweat runs prickling down my cheek and onto my neck.

At other times, my view through the slit is of another perspective, a perspective profoundly unauthorized. The full majesty of the sultan's nakedness is displayed from the rear. I stare at the exalted hairy rump, as it jostles and shudders to do the work of pleasure. I gaze awestruck at the stupendous exalted balls, each one as big as a man's fist, as they clang against the exalted thighs like clappers of a majestic bell, striking out the moaning cries that rise from the shadowiness beyond. I pull myself away, overwhelmed, scarcely able to draw a breath as I peer around in wild apprehension down one then the other tasseled length of the awning. The flames of the tapers throw trembling shadows of ropes into the sand.

By days, my off hours, I lie stretched out on a carpet in my humble quarters, wreathed in the fumes of cheap tobacco, restless with sights and visions.

Once, emerging from his tent, the sultan stops right beside me. He rocks back on his heels and drinks in the night air. Then he notices me. All at once, he grins, right at me. His fez is tilted at a rakish angle. 'And what do you think of our oasis?' he cries, sweeping an exalted arm at the panorama before us. Under the stars and the sickle moon, the palms hold up the curved wings of their fronds. Plodding camel bells jingle among the dark tents, where oil lamps flicker, and dark eyes gleam. The ubiquitous sweet scent of dates is borne on the desert breeze. 'It's – It's – wonderful!' I stammer. The sultan looks at me. Then he throws back his head and roars with laughter. 'Yes, yes,' he nods ferociously. 'That's it, you're absolutely right. It's wonderful! It's *wonderful*!' he cries to himself, and he tramps off across the sand, chuckling as he goes, moving with that peculiar, wide-legged stride he always displays at this exalted hour, on his way back to the tent of state.

Story

My father and I quarrel and he cuffs me and I lose my balance and tumble down the carpeted stairs and bang my head into the foot of the banister.

I lie in bed with my head festooned in bandages. Every evening my father comes into my room with another present for me. A science book, which perhaps I'll read; an instructive game, which I'll certainly never play. Then he wheels me out onto the screen porch and turns on the lamp and reads me a story aloud, which normally he never does. The stories are hoary favorites of his from his own childhood, and they bore me terribly. But I love the sound of his voice as he reads, hammy and low and at times awkwardly urgent. Then he puts the book aside. He reaches down and from under the lamp table he brings out our paper hats. He has fashioned these with his own hands from the Sunday paper. He spreads mine wide and carefully seats it on my swaddled head. He fits on his own. Then he turns off the lamp, and in our hats we sit together waiting for the moon, a pale giant, to rise above the woods across the street. He tells me about these woods, as my mother used to when I was still a very little child. 'Yes, it's all true . . .' he murmurs, squeezing my hand in his, his great wavering hat nodding in the dark. 'The woods are full of all sorts of things – lions, tigers, savage crocodiles. . . . And two valiant soldiers,' he adds, squeezing my hand. 'The young one wounded, the other, who loves him, to nurse him. . . .'

Pirates

I am taken prisoner by pirates. They put me in irons but release me after I agree to join them. Our ship leaves the coast and enters the muddy reaches of a river. Here the wind falters and then the water becomes too shallow for navigation. We take to rowboats and after an afternoon of arduous pulling, put ashore under trees. The pirate captain says we will eat now; after dark we will move on foot to our raid's destination. Two laughing, stinking types – my 'shipmates' – come out of the woods from foraging with a squealing pig in their arms. The one who wears a brass ring in his nose thrusts his cutlass blade against the pig's throat, and laughing all the while, the two of them let the frantic pig wriggle out of their grasp so that when it lands it's done the work itself of cutting its own throat. The pig rushes briefly in idiotic posthumous circles in its own blood. I turn away, horrified. 'Go bring me the ears,' says the captain, grinning at me sadistically as he scratches under his shirt for lice.

The sun sinks. The night is moonless. We move inland. The first mile or so is through dense woods and after much confusion and crashes and cursings, the captain angrily submits and we go under the light of a small torch. Then we reach a main road and the torch is doused and we go across. The woods are sparser here. We come to a smaller road and follow it, keeping just off the edge, breathing heavily, weapons clanking in the silence. They have provided me only with a cudgel, apparently not trusting me with a cutlass or a pistol. Suddenly I crash into the back of the man ahead of me, who has stopped. He elbows me savagely. It's the brute with the nose ring. 'We're here,' the captain announces in a fierce whisper.

The dark shape of a mailbox stands beside the entrance of a driveway into the trees. Part of a house is visible, set back on a high lawn. I regard all of this with disbelief. 'But this is where my parents live!' I gasp. 'What's that?' says the captain, eyeing me over several shoulders. 'Nothing,' I reply, and I sink back out of his sight. I am in shock. I hear mutterings all around me about a fabulous treasure of vacation slides. We start in a body up the driveway. I can see now the car my mother wrote me they've been trying to sell. No lights show in their window. They're asleep of course, they go to bed early. My heart is sickened, feverish. What would pirates want with my old man's vacation slides? They are good slides, it's true, but worth a raid? I cover my mouth, thinking of what's in store for my poor elderly parents. We reach the lawn. The first man goes tramping through my mother's zinnias. Suddenly the cudgel flails in my hands.

I go racing up towards the house. 'Mom! Dad!' I scream. 'Stop him!' the captain's voice shouts. Explosions roar around me. 'Save your ammunition, save your ammunition!' the voice screams. I fling up the welcome mat and find the key and throw open the door and go rushing down the hallway, crying alarm. The lamp is on in my parents' bedroom. I burst in. My father is sitting on the side of the bed in his pajama bottoms, fitting on his spectacles. His grey hair stands up in sleepy wisps. His false tooth is in the glass on the night table. 'What is all that noise and shouting?' he says. 'What are you doing here? I thought you were out west communing with nature. Why are you wearing that funny eyepatch?' 'There's no time for questions, we must run,' I gasp, grabbing him by the arm. 'Come on!' I cry, then looking around, I let go. 'Oh my god, where's mom?'

The bedroom door crashes against the wall. The pirates fill the doorway, all black moustaches and yellow teeth, headkerchieves, drawn cutlasses, smoking guns. 'Ha!' cries the captain. He comes swaggering into the room towards us, in front of his troop. 'What's going on?' says my father, rising to his feet. 'Who are these awful people, are they friends of yours?' 'They're pirates, dad,' I mutter unhappily. The captain reaches us and raises his cutlass into my face. He sets the point slowly against my chin so I have to tilt my head back. 'We're going to hang you by your guts, you mutinous dog,' he announces savagely. 'This is an outrage!' cries my father. 'How dare you? Stop that this instant!' 'Dad, don't,' I tell him, through clenched teeth, squinting down the length of the blade. 'Shut up, greybeard,' the captain sneers. He gives a quick vicious prod so that I jerk. 'What we want from you,' he says, addressing my father but glaring at me, 'is to tell us exactly where the slides are.' My father gasps. He draws an arm up in front of his once burly but now wizened chest in a pathetic gesture of defiance. 'Never!' he cries. 'What do you say?' grins the captain. He presses the cutlass slowly so I have to bend my back. 'Dad . . .' I plead out of the side of my mouth. There is a long, deadly pause. 'Do you think I'll wait all night!' the captain gasps furiously and his jab makes me stagger back into the night table, upsetting the tooth glass. 'Dad, please – ' I whimper. 'Stop!' cries my father. His voice breaks. 'They're in the closet, over by the secretary.' The captain grins lividly. 'Ha!' he says. He pulls the cutlass away with a sharp flick of his wrist. I squeal in pain and clap a hand to my chin. I look at the palm: there is a drop of blood on it. The captain swaggers over towards the closet, gesturing with a thumb over his shoulder for someone to guard us. 'Don't cry, bag-of-bones, we'll take good care of your treasure for you,' he says, and he cackles derisively. He pushes his men out of the way and flings open the closet door.

There is a tremendous choral explosion. The captain rises into the air like a rag doll and sprawls down onto his back. There is no more front to his body whatsoever. My mother and the next-door neighbors, all in nightgowns, step through the smoke firing blunderbusses and muskets. 'Now we'll show them!' cries my father. Flintlock pistols blossom in each of his hands. They belch flame. Our guard screams and topples to the floor, clutching his face. My father throws the pistols aside. A saber and a dagger take their place. 'Cover my back!' he cries. Stupefied, I do what he says and stand behind him. I look around for a weapon, all I can find is the cudgel I brought with me. Furious cries and clangings and explosions sound in the room at my back. Suddenly a pirate bursts in front of me. A brass ring hangs over his frenzied snarl. It's the pig sadist. His berserk one-eye glitters at me. Cursing him, I cower under my cudgel as his cutlass rises high above my head and the spit of his own invectives sprays me. My life flashes before me. The cutlass flashes down with ferocious violence, past me, into the floor where it quivers wildly, sunk on its tip. A hand and forearm are still attached to its handle, gruesomely, all by themselves. The pirate gapes at this spectacle in one-eyed astonishment. Then his astonishment transfers to his chest, where, to a deep gurgling in his throat, the blade of a saber secured in two neuralgic hands sinks full length into his ribs, up to the hilt, then withdraws, covered in blood. He slumps, lifeless and gushing, onto the bed. 'Are you alright?' cries my father, the bloody sword in his hands. 'Yes, I think so,' I gasp, my knees trembling. Then I gasp again, pointing in horror. 'Your shoulder!' I cry. 'What?' says my father. He peers down his nose at the red stain at the top of his arm. 'Ach, it's just a flesh wound,' he says. He looks past me and he grins, pale in the face and looking rather foolish with his tooth missing. 'Well, I think we're all done for the evening,' he says.

. . . Some hours later, when many things have been cleaned up and seen to, the three of us sit by ourselves alone at last in the kitchen. The blackberry cordial my father brings out for special occasions is open on the table. My mother is putting a safety pin into the bandage on his shoulder. I have a Band-Aid on my chin. 'So you see we've known a raid was coming for quite some time,' my father says. 'Everyone in the neighborhood has been very helpful and kind, especially the Lewises from next door. I must say we didn't expect to see you! But when the time came, we were ready for them.' 'I'll say you were,' I agree. 'But you know, there's still one thing in all of this I don't quite understand: why would they want your slides?' 'Oh, that,' says my father. He shifts in his seat and puts on a grin of debonair self-effacement, and I realize he is trying to evoke the debonair movie heroes of his younger days. His tooth is back in place. 'Well, I'll resist the obvious temptation of saying they're all 'gems' . . .' he jokes urbanely, pausing to let this bon mot sink in. 'But in fact,' he continues, 'for some reason people seem to value them very highly.' 'Did you know,' my mother breaks in, 'that next month the library is going to have an exhibit of your father's slides?' 'Just prints of them,' my father corrects her. But he's beaming proudly. 'But at their expense.' He leans back in his chair and slings his unbandaged pale arm over the backrest and regards me with a cool, wry twinkle in his eye, his characterization now in full flood. 'So you see, Mr Adventurerout-west,' he says, the lamplight in his wisps of hair, 'maybe we live in a quiet little town here, and perhaps we are getting on a bit in years – but we still manage to have our share of excitement. Wouldn't you say?'

In the Jungle

He's dead,' says my father. The Indian lies face down in the path. Around him are scattered blood-stained library books. I reach out my hand to examine one, but my father warns me sharply not to touch it. I stand up. No marks show on the Indian's half-naked body, but the corpse is charged nevertheless with a brutal, hideous violence. My father stares about into the jungle. 'Your eyes are brown like his,' he says. 'If they see that, we won't last a minute. Put on your sunglasses.' I take out my sunglasses; but a hole has been cut in each lens, in line with the iris. I show this to my father. He nods grimly. 'They're clever,' he says. 'Very clever. Never mind.' He takes out a handkerchief and ties it over my eyes for a blindfold.

He grips my hand and we move off again on the path, he leading me along behind him. I hear whining and screeching in the foliage overhead and then the strange chirping drone on either side, like anxious blood in my ears. I feel myself sweat. 'What was in those books?' I call out to my father. 'Never mind,' the answer comes back. 'I'm putting on a voice changer now.' There's silence. 'It's better if only one of us knows,' a deep, thickened voice explains.

Habeas Corpus

I go into the bedroom. My girlfriend is sprawled on the bed in a pool of blood with the handle of a kitchen knife sticking out of the middle of her back. I hurriedly retreat out the door. After a while, cautiously, I enter again. My girlfriend sits propped against the pillows, fresh from her bath, nibbling a pear as she reads a book. I sit down on the side of the bed. I stroke her bare leg, hot and pink from the bathwater. I look up at her. I grin sourly, shaking my head. She smiles back bashfully behind her pear. Her shyness is heavy with guilt. I reach out a finger and prod her on the side of the nose. 'Can't you read something besides those horrible murder mysteries?' I tell her.

Udders

I get involved in a game of strip poker. The others have somehow persuaded a cow to join in. The cow stands stupid and uncomfortable in the cigar smoke. My tablemates ply it with booze. It is decked out in a pathetic catalogue of bedroom apparel. Naturally it always plays a losing hand. It can't manage with its garments, and everyone makes full use of the opportunity to handle it, in the name of assistance. I watch in disgust as a beefy bank-manager type fumbles with a lacy garter on the cow's flank. His hands are trembling. 'Will you look at those udders, will you look at those udders,' he keeps mumbling. His face is flushed crimson. The cow shifts a leg, quaking, big-eyed. 'Count me out,' I mutter finally. I throw in my cards, for good. Without further ceremony I push back my chair and go out on to the patio. I take a couple of deep breaths. The salacious laughter rises behind me. I hurry off unsteadily down the steps, drunk, feeling unclean and despicable. 'These package vacations are a nightmare,' I think to myself. In this frame of mind I wander about the lakefront for an hour. Not a soul is about. Lugubriously I make my way back. I stop at the foot of the patio steps. The sound of mooing goes out into the night, above the swarming of abandoned laughter, the yelps and cries. Silhouetted shadows come and go in the French windows' curtains; horns toss about and disappear. Sourly I turn to leave again, when the French windows burst open. The bank manager staggers out into the moonlight. He wheels down the steps, his shirt tails loose, his suspenders flapping at his knees, and lurches straight into me. 'Oh my god, oh my god,' he moans, half in ecstasy, half in horror. I shove him away from me. His face is smeared with milk.

Climatology

The barometer drops. 'We're in for a change of weather alright,' I observe. I go over to the window, to look at the sky. It's still blue and empty. I see a girl coming along the field just beyond the fence. She stoops awkwardly through the rails and hauls after her the burlap bag she's been carrying. She sets it down, opens it and reaches in. She brings out some lumps of white stuff. She tamps them crudely between her hands a couple of times and then starts flinging them into the air. The white lumps expand and float off. They're clouds, I realize. They stay low to the ground because the girl's arm isn't very strong. 'Well, I'll be damned,' I think, watching the clouds snag in the branches of a birch tree and start to jam up.

I hurry downstairs and out the back. The girl is under the tree, poking at the clouds with a stick. They've piled up with alarming suddenness and have grown black and threatening. 'Watch out there, careful,' I shout, as I cross towards her. The girl turns around and looks relieved at the sight of me. 'Oh thank you,' she says, as I come up behind. 'I'm so glad – ' But her sentence is cut off by the flicker of lightning from the black-crowded branches, and the petite clap of thundering. 'Get out of there!' I cry, yanking her back and giving her a shove out of the way. I grab a big piece of branch that's lying in the grass and maneuver under the tree with it, spearing up at the branches and hunching my shoulders as the little thunder roars and tiny hail pelts me. Finally I just throw the stick aside and grab the birch bough overhead with both hands and shake it with all my might. The black cloud tilts and wobbles and suddenly goes whirling off into the blue sky, flashing and roaring.

I step away from the tree, a bit unsteadily. 'Are you alright?' the girl exclaims. 'I'm just so sorry – ' 'Never mind, no problem,'

I tell her. 'Only a little moisture.' 'And your poor tree, it's ruined,' she says. We contemplate the torn, denuded, considerably scorched branches. 'Oh, it's a sturdy tree, I'll prune it and it'll be as good as new,' I reply. I laugh, running my hands over my wet hair. 'Maybe I can give you a hand with the rest of your bag,' I suggest. 'I've always been proud of my throwing arm.' The girl flushes and shakes her head. 'I feel so foolish,' she says.

She fashions the patties. I fling them about in the air virtuosically. 'It's a summer job,' she explains. 'It's my first day, I'm afraid I'm not very good at it.' 'I must say I find it quite remarkable,' I tell her, 'that this is how weather is made.' 'Yes, it's really incredibly simple, isn't it?' she agrees. 'But then, just about everything is, when you really find out about it, don't you think?' 'I suppose so,' I reply, amused by this philosophizing vis-à-vis its philosopher. 'Sure,' she says, pausing to scratch her nose and leaving a trace of cloud on the side of a nostril. 'Last summer, for instance, I had one of those jobs distributing the effects of entropy through this part of the solar system.' I halt in the middle of my pitching motion and turn around and stare at her. She looks back. 'You don't mean last July, when everyone went insane losing things!' I protest. 'That was you?' She laughs, coloring. 'Yes, that was me,' she says. She shrugs. She looks off, an abashed grin on her face. 'I guess, when you come down to it, I am just pretty much of a klutz,' she reflects, a bit ruefully.

Plumbing

I get a job as a plumber. I dress in white overalls and big round boots. I ring a doorbell. A woman answers, in a negligee. 'Oh,' she says. She looks me up and down. 'You're new,' she says. She steps back, holding the door open for me. I step inside modestly with my canvas bag. She closes the door behind her, smiling. 'Brand, *brand* new,' she says. She steps right up against me and claps a hand between my legs. 'I see you brought your tools with you,' she whispers. I take hold of her wrist and lift her hand away. 'Could I trouble you,' I ask, 'for a cup of coffee before I start to work?' She looks at me, chuckling. 'Why?' she drawls. 'Don't you like to do a job while you're still sort of half-asleep?' She chuckles brazenly at the look on my face. 'I do,' she whispers, her lids drooping down. She drifts off towards the kitchen, eyeing me over her shoulder.

Later, we're on the kitchen floor by the sink. Her negligee lies flung off in a gauzy heap; my overalls are piled neatly beside my boots. My bag is open. I work away between her knees with a monkey wrench and long bright hoops of copper tubing. 'I have to be extra-careful here,' I mutter through clenched teeth, straining. 'I don't want to strip any threads on these intersection nuts.' 'I don't care, I don't care!' the woman hisses wildly. 'Just do it, do it!' She grabs hold of my hair with both hands, swinging my head from side to side. 'Easy, easy!' I protest. I strain, red in the face. 'I got it,' I blurt out, 'I had the torque setting all wrong!'

Afterwards, when we've dressed, she offers me lunch. I decline awkwardly. 'Full schedule today,' I mumble, indicating my bag. 'Oh I see . . .' she says coolly. At the door she remembers a lamp in the den that's not working properly. 'It has three settings,' she explains to me. 'It works fine on the first one. It works fine on the second. But the third one,' she says, and she tilts her head coyly, 'on the third one it just sort of goes all dark and spooky and makes this loud kind of buzzing noise!' I stare at her. She stares back with wild, glittering eyes. I swallow. I let out an uneasy little laugh. 'Lady, that's not my line,' I tell her hastily. I feel about for the door handle. 'Lady, let me be blunt,' I advise her, coloring. 'If you have something like that in mind, you require the services of a certified electrician.'

Mosquito

A mosquito bites my mother. She swells shockingly and then floats upwards and lodges against the ceiling. 'What's going on?' I demand, coming into the living room for a magazine. 'Some funny little thing bit me,' my mother replies, 'and this followed.' I groan in despair. 'Mom,' I protest. 'Why are you always doing these things!' 'Don't be a fool,' she says peevishly. 'I told you what happened. D'you think I want to be up here like this?' A response immediately sounds in my head, but I don't say it. I grit my teeth and go out to next door and get the neighbor, who is very kind and has a stepladder and is used to my mother's ways. Then I go to the kitchen phone and call the doctor. He says my mother has a prescription, she knows what to do. I make a sarcastic jibe at this last statement and let out a laugh, trying to get him to join me in it. He doesn't. He says to call him if there's still any swelling in the morning.

I go back to the living room. My mother is down, sitting plumply on the sofa with the neighbor beside her. She has apparently just commenced her in-depth narrative of the episode, and I hastily deliver my information and make my exit, before I get trapped into the audience for a command-performance recital. The neighbor sits beside her, looking rapt.

Back in my room, I try to read. After a while I look out the window and see her slowly walking the neighbor to the front gate. He carries the stepladder. A couple of times she bobs into the air, and she yelps with nervous laughter and flaps her feet, and he gently pulls her back down.

163

Night Work

A man can't sleep. He takes a job driving a cab all night. On his first shift a woman gets in. 'By the river,' she says. They drive downtown, across the sleepy clacking of the bridge. At the far end of the bridge the road simply descends underwater. The man is surprised but strangely unalarmed. The cab sinks down below the lamps and sidewalks, into the waves. 'This is fine here,' says the woman. When she pays, the scales on her body shimmer in the man's eyes.

The next night the man's father gets in. He wears a chamber pot on his head. 'Happy birthday!' he says, and he gives the address of the party. The man explains that he would like to go, but he has to work. He taps his mouth, unable to stifle a yawn. 'But all your friends will be there!' says his father, and he names them. They are all names from elementary school. The man turns around to ask about this, but a passing car honks loudly, startling him. Then his father isn't there.

Two nights later, the passenger is a pale young man with a leopard. The beautiful cat purrs and languidly shakes its chains on the seat. Its master stares ahead in silence, tears dripping down his cheeks. The following night, a young girl turns into a violin on the way to the train station.

The man asks the other cabbies about these peculiar happenings. They just shrug and yawn and resettle themselves sleepily in their seats. Perturbed, the man wonders whether he should quit. But in the mornings he finds himself strangely rested.

So he stays on. Each night he pulls up to the curb with his roof light on; he leans his cheek in his hand. He drowses, under the dark windows and the stars, waiting for his next fare.

Monkey

I stumble across a girl in the jungle. 'Please, help me get these vines off!' she says desperately. 'And as recompense, I'll let you do whatever you want with me,' she adds. I give her a disapproving look for this last remark, as I crouch beside her to inspect the situation. The vines are thin, but immensely sinewy. They grip the girl's legs below her shorts. It's like being grabbed by dozens of clamping digits. Little, scented buds show here and there, like floral jewelry on fingers. I get down onto my knees. At length, by dint of our mutual prying and pulling, the girl is divested of her botanical clutchings. 'Look at what they did to my poor legs,' she says, extending one limb and then the other, each scored with pink tracings. She shakes her head and rubs her legs and sighs. 'Anyway,' she says. She looks up at me with a brave smile. 'Thank you. I'm all yours.' I laugh coolly. 'Hardly,' I tell her. 'It's not really my style to take advantage of young ladies in distress, you know.' 'It isn't?' she says in a tone of surprise. 'Well of course not,' I inform her. I'm irritated. 'What do you think, I just lurk all day in this overgrown weed patch, looking for the chance to get the drop on girls?' 'Well that's not exactly what I meant – ' she says, but the dialogue is interrupted by a sudden, splatting thump on my cork helmet. I lurch a step. 'What the hell – ' I cry. I crane my neck wildly. A monkey clambers high overhead against the sky, screeching in hysterics. A terrific stench fills the air. 'Jesus Christ,' I hiss. I snatch off my helmet and stare at the muck splashed on it. 'I just bought this,' I protest miserably. I squat down and snatch off handfuls of greenery and start vehemently to rub, screwing up my nose against the stink. The girl's laughter rings in my ears. 'Alright already, for Christ's sake,' I call back over my shoulder. 'I'm sorry,' she sputters. 'I'm sorry, it's just so – ' Quaking, she bursts into another gale. I suffer it, gritting my teeth. 'Listen, do shut up,' I mutter. I snatch some more leaves. 'Will you please shut up!' 'Your face!' the girl gasps. 'The look – on your face – when the monkey – ' My temper flashes. I jump to my feet and swing around. 'I said cut it out!' I snarl, and I give her a shove, much harder than I intend, because she goes sprawling backwards into the shrubbery. She stares up at me, shocked. Then slowly, she grins. She lounges back in the leaves, and turns her head to the side, and grins up at me sidelong. . . .

Later, as we lie together, she makes a confession. 'Those vines didn't really grab hold of me,' she says. 'I fixed them on with glue.' I turn from contemplating my helmet drying on a bush, to regard her. 'You did?' I ask, bewildered. 'Of course,' she says. 'I wanted to meet you.' I hear this with astonishment. I assure her I'm flattered – very flattered indeed. She gives me a kiss on the cheek. 'I set things up with the monkey too,' she whispers. 'You *did*?' I protest, my eyes by now practically saucers, as I feel more and more like an audience volunteer in a nightclub act. 'Of course, of course,' she laughs, her mouth at my ear. 'Who do you think planted this jungle?' she says.

Barnyard

A girl is feeding the white ducks. I watch her through the window. I put down my seed catalogue and get up and go outside through the muddy barnyard towards the duck pond, kicking chickens out of the way. 'You're new here, aren't you?' I call out, stopping a short ways from her. 'I haven't seen you around before.' The girl looks back over her shoulder. 'I've been here since I was a kid,' she says. 'You just haven't been looking right.' 'Is that so?' I reply, narrowing my eyes and grinning at her cheekiness. I watch her scattering her crumbs to the waddling ducks. The arm showing from her white cotton blouse is brown and plump. My eyes narrow even further. She throws out the last of the crumbs and gives her apron a shake and takes up her bucket and with a glance starts to walk off past me. I check her, my hand on her arm. 'You're cute, sloe-eyes,' I mutter, and I sink my teeth into the plump brown of her bare neck. Then I screech and hop backwards, clutching at my shin. 'My god, what are those clogs – *iron?*' I sputter, hopping. 'Walnut,' she says, grinning. She puts a hand on her hip and tilts back her head and bursts out laughing as I hop about with increasingly frantic ill-balance, until my shoe sticks in the mud and I sprawl down with a splash onto the seat of my pants. This makes her clutch her chest and start to howl. Then suddenly she stops. She puts down her bucket and bends over at the waist, and concentrates, and let's loose a long, slow, resounding fart. 'What the hell – ' I demand, as chickens scatter, clucking. She stands back and roars with delight. Finally she wipes her eyes. She gives me a look. 'I've got to feed the hens,' she says. She picks up her bucket and sashays off swinging the bucket jauntily through the barnyard. I sit watching her in the mud. I curse myself. At last I maneuver in stages to my feet and make my way stiffly back to the farmhouse. I change my trousers and contemplate my course of action as I stand close and backwards to the kitchen fire, drinking hot cider.

In the evening, after late milking, I cross under the big yellow moon to the barn. I mount determinedly up the straw-covered ladder to the hayloft. The girl is there. She looks around from her milk buckets as I appear over the top. 'I thought you learned your lesson . . .' she says, with a wary grin. I don't speak a word. I stand across from her, grinning boldly back at her. Slowly, wordlessly, one button at a time, I undo my flies. 'Hey – ' says the girl. She feels about behind her for the big-toothed wooden rake. 'Hey, wait a minute – ' Without a word, grinning, I empty my bladder in the lantern light. The stream of piss arches out, strong and cidery, and splashes onto the straw and the planking. The girl stares with widening eyes. Then slowly, her eyes narrow. She raises them by degrees, and looks at me. She chuckles.

Down below the cows shift in their stalls. After a while, they begin to moo fearfully. They hear tumbling on the straw, thudding on the planking, yelps of laughter and the crash of buckets being knocked over. Milk gushes down the ladder. The cows moo in anguish. The hens in the henhouse next door begin to squawk. The pigs grunt in their sty. Straw from the thatched roof showers past the window slowly, as the moon bumps its cheek against the barn eaves, trying to peer in.

Bags

I get involved in a robbery. The cops come looking for me at my mother's house. I'm holed up in my old bedroom, which my mother uses now for her sewing room. 'You must just go downstairs and turn yourself in,' she says, turning back to me from the window. 'Never,' I tell her. 'I'll never turn myself in!' 'What did you get that's so fabulous and wonderful worth this?' she says. 'Take a look,' I tell her, and I heave open the top of the suitcase on the bed. She stares, incredulous. 'Grocery bags?' she says. She looks at me as if I were retarded. 'Mom!' I protest. 'Have you any idea how scarce wood is getting these days, how valuable paper products are? Right there in that suitcase are all sizes you could want, although I think my cut was mostly medium-sized bags. But there must be almost two hundred of them.' My mother looks disgusted. 'If your father were alive, he'd have a fit,' she says. 'I'm going down and letting the police in. I'm sorry, you'll just have to make the best of it.'

'Mom!' I cry. Before I can stop myself I have her by the wrist. She stares at my encircling hand. There's an awkward pause. 'You can't!' I whisper desperately. 'So it's come to this,' she says, contemptuously, drawing herself up to her full five feet one inch. 'Of course not,' I reply, hanging my head, and I let go of her. The cops start up once more with their bullhorn. Fear leaps wildly through me. I grab her wrist again. 'Listen, I'll cut you in,' I tell her. 'On those *bags*?' she laughs, trying to pull away. 'I'll give you a third of them!' I tell her. She stares at me. 'Half!' she says. I am shocked. 'Alright,' I tell her. 'Half.' I relax my grip and she twists away and steps back a few feet, rubbing her wrist. 'I'm going to have a terrific bruise,' she says. 'I'm sorry,' I tell her. 'You know I didn't – ' 'Oh shut up,' she says. 'We have to think how to get out of here!' She steps over to the window and peers out carefully past the edge of the drapes. The cops have a line of men crouched across the way. She lets the drapes go and stands bent in thought. 'How about the roof?' I suggest, but she flaps at me harshly to be quiet. She looks back out of the window. Suddenly she spins around. 'Get the bags and follow me,' she says. 'Where to?' I ask, but her housecoat is already out the door. 'Mom!' I call out after her. I drag the suitcase off the bed and struggle with it frantically through the doorway. The first tear gas cannister crashes through the drapes and goes rolling, fizzing dark smoke, towards the sewing baskets.

Footprints

I find footprints of someone in the garden. The impressions in the dirt are short and broad. I bend closer; I make out the distinct markings of what suspiciously resemble claws. I stare at them. 'These aren't from any normal human,' I think. I rise up slowly, and look out at the path meandering past the great stands of gladiolas. I swallow and look back at the house, which is silent and still. I look over at the granite garden bench. A hoe stands against it. I hurry over and snatch up the hoe and brandish it like a staff. I start along the path, warily, following the prints, my jaw clenched. I pass the gladiolas. The path turns. I stop, and reconnoiter. The footprints continue, past a Grecian-style bust on a pedestal that stands in front of rhododendrons. My heart hammers. In the dirt lie torn, thorny stems, as if flung there in the midst of a frenzy. I stare at them as I go by. The path turns again. I hear water, the playing of a fountain beyond a hedge. I inch along, trailing the footprints as they follow the hedge. At the end of the hedge, I stop. Gripping the hoe, I peer around. A girl is sitting under a tree, beside a small, low fountain. Her back is to me. She is barefoot. She turns her head suddenly and looks at me. She smiles. 'Hi,' she says. I stare at her, at the rose in her chubby hands. Petals have fallen onto her dress. 'I stole this, isn't it pretty?' she says. I don't answer. She smiles again and turns away. I stare at her feet. They're short and broad. She leans sideways on an elbow. She sighs. 'I have a blister, on my heel,' she says, looking back at me. 'Do you think I could put my foot in the fountain?' I don't say a word. She looks at me. 'Come sit with me,' she says softly, sniffing the rose. I grip the hoe so that it trembles. I draw it back slowly, ready to protect myself. 'It's alright,' she says softly, putting out her hand with the rose. 'Please, come and sit with me here. It's nice, you'll see.'

Later, the hoe leans propped against the tree. I lie with my head in the girl's lap. She brushes the rose along my cheek. I feel the thin trickle of a thorn. The fountain plays off to the side. 'And I don't want you ever to think nasty things like that again,' she says, referring to my misunderstanding about her footprints. 'I'll do my best,' I tell her. 'It was all a silly mistake. I know perfectly well girls aren't bears. . . .' I smile quietly to myself. I look at my wet handkerchief rigged coolingly around her stocky heel. I look at her chubby, dirt-rimmed toes. I feel her hair on my face. I turn my mouth to meet hers, and we kiss softly. After a while, she sits back up, and lounges back on a hand. 'The air is so fragrant here,' she sighs. She savors it with sensitive twitches of her nose. 'It must be all these wonderful flowers.' 'Now there you make a mistake,' I inform her, closing my eyes against the sun. 'It's not the flowers at all. It's that little pot of honey hidden over behind the tree.' She lowers her head slowly and stares at me. Then she twists her head away and grins, her cheeks darkened with her blushes.

Traitors

I'm arrested as a spy and a traitor. My mother comes to see me in jail. 'Hello, mon petit,' she says with a rueful smile. 'Alas!' 'Did you smuggle me a gun or a file?' I whisper desperately through the bars. 'Certainly not,' she snorts. 'This is your destiny. You must face it like a man!' I look at her. I hang my head. 'I'm so ashamed, for the family,' I murmur. 'You don't blame me?' 'Blame you! Good heavens, why should I?' she demands. 'Your father was a traitor, your uncles were all traitors. Even my own dear father was a traitor. Now there was a traitor – *there was a traitor*,' she says, smiling off at her memories. 'I never knew all this,' I protest, astonished. 'Oh, I could tell you things . . .' she says dreamily. 'But enough,' she declares. 'Right now is right now. You lift that head up, young man. You throw back those shoulders. We'll show them what a *traitor* looks like! So what if you let them nab you!' 'I was stupid,' I admit, staring down at the floor. 'So, so stupid . . .' 'Can't be helped!' my mother replies. 'What's done is done!' She turns, grimacing. 'What on earth is that wretched banging out there?' she says. I glance over my shoulder at the high, barred, too-familiar window. 'My *scaffold* . . .' I inform her morosely. 'Good!' she declares. She shows a fist, proud-eyed. 'Let them make it big and strong and full of nails to hang *my* traitor of a boy!' she cries. I raise my eyes for a moment and regard her uneasily. I look back at the floor. 'Mom, I wonder if we're really on the same wavelength about all of this,' I murmur. 'There's only one wavelength I know of,' she retorts. 'Chin up, spit in the eye! Come on in there now!' 'Alright, mom, alright,' I protest wearily, running a much-bitten fingernail down the long, cold iron of a jail-cell bar.

The next morning, at dawn, I'm led out in manacles into the chill air and up the wooden steps erected under the jail wall. My knees keep starting to sag. I recognize my mother's large, festive sun hat in the throng of bloodthirsty early-risers. A manicured hand waves enthusiastically to me. I acknowledge it in miserable embarrassment, wiggling my fingers in front of my thighs. 'Give 'em hell!' I hear her cry. 'Mom, come *on* – ' I murmur. The hangman raises the noose. I feel its dreadful weight touch my shoulders. I gasp at the shock. A bouquet of flowers arcs into the air and plops at my feet. 'For Christ's sake, mom!' I sputter. I look up wildly for her valediction. But she is gabbing away under her sun hat to a neighbor, pointing up at me with animated pride, as the trap door suddenly opens.

In the Kitchen

My father is sitting in the kitchen. He is bare-chested and burly, laughing, flushed. His deerstalker hat is tilted back on his head. A fat cigar juts out, curling smoke, from his bared, carnivorously grinning teeth. He rubs oil into the stock of his shotgun. A bottle and a glass sit by his gun tools on the table. My mother stands in the corner of the kitchen, watching in distaste, her fingers pressed fearfully into her ears. My father chuckles at the sight of her, his eyes glinting. He swings the gun up so it points straight in the air, and looks at my mother with big, teasing eyes, and pulls the trigger. There is a terrific boom. Plaster showers down everywhere. My mother shouts and stamps her foot. My father roars delightedly and pulls the other trigger. Tumultuous smoke and plaster dust fill the kitchen. A pot crashes down off a shelf. My mother rushes cursing out the door. My father sits, delighted, throwing back his head with laughter, his cigar in one hand, his drink now in the other. He looks around at me, where I crouch timorously by the sink. 'Ah, women, they love this kind of thing,' he grins, winking.

Later, I help my mother sweep up the debris. The air is still cloudy and strong-smelling from gun and cheroot. There is a great ragged hole in the ceiling over the table. My father's voice reaches us from the garden. It is his singing voice, meandering painfully through a run of sentimental songs. My mother pauses to watch through the window. 'Look at the old fool,' she mutters, 'with his ridiculous hat and his noxious cigar. One day you wait, I'm going to grab that stupid gun of his from him and shove it up his bum and he can pull the trigger all he wants!' She glances over at me. 'Did I say that? Dear, dear me,' she says.

Dinner Table

'Let's eat,' says my father. We go into the dining room. Halfway through the meal the phone rings. My father puts down his napkin and pushes back his chair and goes out to answer the phone himself, since he's expecting a call. I seize the opportunity to right an inequality that's been vexing me since we sat down. I pick up my father's plate and hastily scrape what's left on it onto mine, and bolt everything down. My father had given himself by far the larger, tastier portion to start with. He comes back into the room and sees the two empty plates. He looks at them. I sit quietly, trying to look vacant. He doesn't say anything. He walks behind me. Suddenly he grips me by the back of the collar and heaves me out of the chair, on to the floor.

I lie on the floor, shocked. After a while, I get to my feet, my face burning. I set the chair back upright. I go out of the room into the hallway on trembling legs. I make my way towards the kitchen, and pause in the doorway awkwardly. 'Dad, I'm sorry,' I tell him, in an unsteady, chastened voice. 'I was only joking.' He stirs eggs in a bowl. The flame is on under a frying pan. He glances at me. He closes the lid of the egg carton on the counter and takes it over to the refrigerator. 'The sooner your mother gets back from her trip, the better,' he says.

Magic Carpet

My father arrives on a magic carpet. 'Come on,' he says. Sitting cross-legged together, we lift magically into the air. We glide over the backyard. Our rectangular shadow passes over the sheets my mother is hanging up. She rushes out from them to the back gate. She waves at us and shouts indistinctly. I lean over, excited and scared, and wave cautiously down to her. She signals frantically for me to come back. My father gives a lazy, sardonic laugh and opens and shuts a fat, much-ringed hand in farewell to my mother's diminishing, tiny figure. She dwindles to a speck.

The carpet swoops off, speeding higher, up in the sky. Gulping, I press myself as flat as I can, gripping the tassled edge. Miniature houses and trees blur far below. 'How do you like it?' my father shouts, grinning at me. There is a cruel glint in his eye. I try feebly to match his grin. He wears a great egg-shaped turban with a streaming feather pinned by a jewel, and an opulent silk robe that flutters violently about his neck in the wind. He laughs at how scared and pale I look. 'Have a date!' he cries, indicating the bowl in front of him. I shake my head wretchedly. Amused, he picks out a date and holds it up for inspection between fingertips and puts it in his mouth. 'Can we go slower?' I plead. He looks down at me, his eyes large with mock disbelief. 'Slower?' he says, his mouth full. He swallows. '*Slower*,' he shouts, throwing back his head and booming with laughter. '*Slower*!' he roars, tossing his head from side to side at the word. As if in response the carpet suddenly surges forward, higher, faster. I cling to it desperately, whimpering, terrified, as the gusts of my father's laughter mix with the roaring of the wind.

Safari

My father and I are on safari. He wears a deluxe pith helmet with a decorative red strap and reinforced air holes. His sumptuous safari jacket is festooned with gussets, map pockets, zippered pouches, epaulettes, and a broad belt drawn with flair about his pot belly. I have on a similar outfit, but in its humblest, most discounted version, one that is mere crown and brim above, and bare, meagerly buttoned twill below. 'Yes, you look the spitting image of a dashing young hunter,' my father declares, pressing my shoulders back straight and resetting my helmet by forcing it down painfully over my ears.

All day long the two of us track across the great savannah rising temporarily from our backyard. We're after lion. In the stupefying glare of noon we pause, leaning on our guns to watch a herd of Thomson's gazelle undulate along the heat-wavering horizon of the used-car place a block away. The vicious black dog from next door gives chase through the dust, baying, frantic, ineffectual. Taking up our guns we continue on, through a terrain of high grass. We emerge somewhere along the alley that runs behind our backyard, and follow its course between trash cans to the spindly birch tree across from our back gate, where we come upon a watering hole. We stoop in the brackish shallows, tipping water over our heat-stunned heads with our pith helmets. A pair of blue herons look on from a distance, motionless on a leg. Across the dull-gleaming way a hippo yawns enormously. An elephant gazes around at us, big-eared, over a high dark shoulder, and lazily unfurls its long, dark trunk high in the air, and squirts a stream of water gushing over its ancient back. My father and I retire with our canteens to the sparse shade of the birch tree. We resume my instruction in the use of a gun. 'That's it,' my father nods, red-faced and mopping at his cheeks with his profusely cologned safari handkerchief. 'Keep that butt firm up there. Remember, that caliber of weapon kicks like a horse. It can snap your shoulder in half like a breadstick, my boy – like a breadstick! Alright now,' he says, lounging more deeply against the birch tree in his sweat-blotched, sumptuous khaki. 'Remember: don't *pull* the trigger. *Squeeze.* Slowly! *Squeeze*!' I squeeze. In the dust of the alley there's the precise metallic click of hammer striking empty chamber. 'Excellent,' says my father. He grins. 'We'll make a hunter of you in no time,' he declares, as I let the heavy, stumpy gun down, grinning from ear to throbbing ear under the low brim of my helmet.

At dusk we make our way in through the gate to our campsite on the back lawn under my mother's maple trees. My father builds a fire and dons his ascot. As night falls we eat from a black iron pot hung over the briquettes. Then my father retires behind the mosquito netting of his tent, and I climb into my hammock. I'm keeping a journal of our safari for summer school social studies. I write, bare-headed and tender-eared, swaying quietly. A huge, burnt-orange moon rises low and heavy in the night sky. A buzzard flaps across it. Somewhere in the dark a hyena laughs at the stars, demented, forlorn. Crickets drone in the grass. There's a commotion in the mosquito netting. My father struggles out from his tent. At last he approaches the hammock. 'Idiotic zipper,' he mutters, flinging something into the grass. He holds out his hand as he jerks his ascot back into place. I surrender the notebook. He stands by the hammock, looking over what I've written.

'Yes, yes,' he says, screwing up his eyes in the difficult light. 'Your penmanship could be improved, as always.' He frowns. 'I hardly think,' he says, his frown deepening as he reads on, 'there's any need for so many of these picayune observations about minute differences in our mode of dress. Yours is a training outfit, after all. It's an extremely elegant cut, and it was more than expensive enough, I can assure, I still have the bill. Where's your pen?' I give it to him. I watch him blacken out the offending lines, one after the other. 'And Thomson's gazelle does not have a "p" and does have an "h",' he adds, scratching in the correction. After a final, penetrating scan, he closes the notebook up and hands the materials back. 'Good work, my boy!' he says, patting me on the cheek. I smile wanly. In silence we look out together at the massive, star-shot equatorial night. A breeze stirs, bearing strange savannah odors of dust and animal. A bat flits low. The hyena cackles again, and the vicious dog from next door howls behind a window, and the crazy old lady who owns it and had the argument with my father about our property line spies down on us from her lamplit curtain. 'Magnificent, isn't it?' murmurs my father, his face a woodcut in the light of the hurricane lamp.

There is the clatter of a screen door closing. Footsteps sound beside us in the grass. 'Ahoy there, you hunter chaps,' calls my mother's voice. She appears in the light carrying a paper bag. 'I brought you your beef jerky for tomorrow,' she announces, passing the bag over me to my father. He goes off to the tent with it, peeking intently inside en route. My mother makes a face. 'Disgusting stuff,' she says with a shudder. 'How was the chili?' 'I don't know,' I mumble. I shrug. 'It was okay. I guess.' The mundanity of her question irks me, as does her presence in general at our camp. I stare at the edge of the hammock. 'You didn't put in enough spices again,' my father complains, coming back. 'Darling, you know how you shouldn't be eating things highly spiced,' my mother reminds him. 'It's deadly for your blood pressure.' 'Nonsense,' my father grouses. 'What's the good of chili if it isn't hot and spicy?' My mother listens to him sourly. 'Well, I'm not going to argue,' she says. 'Anyway, I've packed you fellows a good lot of zucchini bread as well.' 'With loads of butter, I hope,' says my father, glancing avidly towards the tent. My mother sighs. 'Yes, with "loads" of butter, god help me,' she says. 'Honestly, I don't know why I do it, I'm just helping you dig your own grave,' she exclaims. 'One day you'll open that mouth of yours, my dear man, and your heart will simply come flying out, like a great big wad of phlegm!' 'Mom, jeez!' I protest. 'Nonsense, nonsense,' mutters my father. 'Butter is extremely healthy.'

My mother shrugs in resignation. Shaking her head, she looks around. Suddenly she starts back. 'Great Scot!' she exclaims. 'What is that gargantuan beast of a thing doing devouring my maple tree?' 'That happens to be a giraffe!' my father informs her. He hurries under the hammock lines to her side. Together all three of us stare at the great shape in the nearby leaves. 'The queen of the plains!' my father goes on, his voice lowered pointedly. 'And she's not feeding, she's performing her nocturnal custom of scratching her neck.' 'Well she better not harm a single leaf up there if she knows what's good for *her*,' says my mother. 'Not after all the money and labor I've lavished on that tree spraying and pruning!' She takes a step, flapping her hands. 'Shoo! Shoo you!' she cries. My father shouts and grabs at her. 'For Christ's sake!' I howl, writhing in my hammock. The giraffe sways off into the night.

'My *god*!' my father explodes. He stamps away, flinging up his arms. 'Here I am, out in this primordial wild,' he bellows, 'trying to show this boy an adventure of a lifetime he'll never forget, at immense expense, and you have to come out here interfering with your ridiculous suburban nonsense about a ridiculous tree!' 'No tree of mine is ridiculous,' my mother replies, trying lamely to muster her hauteur. She looks about, bravely tilting her nose in the air. She gives an artificial laugh. 'There, that thing, that's *ridiculous*,' she says, pointing a scornful finger off into the dark. 'What is that silly-looking zebra animal?' I roll my eyes. 'Mom!' I whine. 'Just because it's got stripes doesn't mean it's a *zebra*!' 'It's a bongo deer, obviously,' snorts my father. 'Everybody knows that!' I add. 'Well, well,' says my mother. 'I can see I'm among frightfully expert hunters. And since they're so hostile, I shall bid them both good night before they take out their guns and shoot me. Mind you have a blanket on when you turn in up there,' she warns. Gruffly I suffer her kiss. She gives one to my father. 'Goodnight, you chaps,' she says. 'Goodnight,' we mutter. 'Don't worry, my boy,' my father murmurs, as my mother's footsteps diminish. 'Tomorrow will be a big day for hunting, you wait and see.'

It's late morning when we come upon the lion spoor near the used-car lot. We crouch down beside it. It's an evil-smelling puddle of dung, pale and flyblown in the dust. 'He's not far now,' says my father grimly. We raise our helmeted heads and gaze off across the rows of family sedans and the shimmering plains beyond: a herd of wildebeest drift across, lumbering and stately, like barges under sail. My heart thumps as I scan the rear of the herd for a sign of laggards, for their consequences — predators. We take our lunch under the broiling sun, saving some of the zucchini bread for later, for energy. By midafternoon we've recrossed the alley. We come back into our yard. All of a sudden my father halts me. He points down the far side of the rear fence. Under a swirling cloud of flies lies sprawled the carcass of a lone wildebeest. Its tongue hangs lewdly into the grass. Its whole chest has been torn away. I stare at the raw cavity of bone and blood. My father grips my shoulder and pulls me down with him to a kneeling crouch. He points at the crabapple tree, by the next-door fence. 'There,' he whispers triumphantly. I stare white-faced into the shadows: I make out the lineaments of a tawny, sinister mass. My breath catches and my stomach dives. 'He's napping, after his lunch,' whispers my father. 'We won't take him right now, asleep like that, we'll wait until he goes to feed again, towards dusk.' He looks about. 'We're downwind securely here,' he says. 'The breeze won't shift quarters this time of year. But we're too exposed like this. We need cover. Go get the lawn chair, it's behind the tent.'

I creep off, as silently as I can. My heart hammers with appalling violence. I creep back hurrying with the lawn chair. Stealthily we open it up and get down in the oblong of shadow behind it. The screen door clatters at the back of our house. My mother comes out with her laundry basket. She sets it down in the grass. She waves to us. We stare back at her, stunned. She goes back inside. Rolling my eyes I turn and direct a look of outraged disbelief at my father. He takes out a handkerchief and mops his brow under his helmet, shaking his head. 'Unbelievable!' he mutters. He is still shaking his head as he rises up on his knees. He peers muttering over the bright yellow thatchwork of the lawn chair. 'Alright, a few hours of waiting,' he says gruffly, coming back down. Suddenly he looks up. He sniffs the air. 'What's that smell?' he whispers, sniffing. 'It smells like cologne! — You're not stupid enough to be wearing cologne in the vicinity of a lion!' he demands. '*Me?*' I reply. 'Do you know what happens if a lion smells that!' he whispers. 'But you're the one who's wearing it, dad!' I protest. 'What nonsense are you talking!' he hisses. 'Your *handkerchief!*' I whisper lividly, jabbing a finger at it. 'What?' he says. He stares down at it. He sniffs it.

'Perhaps you're right,' he mutters, looking puzzled. He shoves the handkerchief deep into an elaborate pocket. 'Doesn't matter,' he shrugs. 'As long as we're downwind. Where's that bag, anyway, we should finish the zucchini bread now.'

In silence we eat, and drink from our canteens. Then we settle down to wait. I fall into a drowsy, anxious reverie. I hear over and over my father's words: that a charging lion covers a hundred yards of ground in approximately four seconds; the first fifty in under two. That when it rushes from that close, a hunter has one shot, and one shot only. That if he thinks of missing, he should think of the wildebeest. . . . I force my gaze away from the carnage by the rear fence. I swallow. My mouth is bone dry. I blink at the sweat in my eyes. I grip my gun, feeling once more how crude and unassuring a weapon it is, with its stubby barrel and heavy trigger and cast-iron sights. I gaze over enviously at my father's spectacular gun lying against his knee: it's a show-piece of telescopic sights, calibrated cross-hairs, custom-articulated stock, hand-tooled butt inlaid with cursive ivory monogram. Its magnificent barrel gleams. I wipe at the sweat again in my eyes. My ears ache under the pinching grip of my helmet. Slowly, the shadow of the lawn chair lengthens. The garish intensity of things fades, and then suddenly the light turns exhausted and soft and fraught with melancholy. I turn towards my father. He slumps open-mouthed, his eyes shut, his helmet tilted towards one shoulder. His jacket is littered with crumbs. As I stare at him, his mouth drops even lower, and a great, snagging snore issues from it. 'Dad!' I whisper, aghast. I shake him. 'Dad!' He starts. His eyes spring open, unrecognizing, alarmed. 'What?' he says in a loud voice. 'Sssh!' I hiss at him. I point vehemently. 'Isn't it time?' I whisper. He looks at me blankly. 'Oh,' he says at last. He sits up, blinking. He rubs his hands over his face and licks his lips. 'I seem to have dozed off for a moment,' he mutters. 'Must have been that zucchini bread of your mother's. She's always putting too much butter on it, it makes a man bloated.' Blinking, he feels for his gun and turns himself laboriously and straightens his helmet and gets upright on his knees. He peers over the top of the lawn chair. 'Get ready!' he whispers.

My stomach ties into a knot. My hands go clammy and

tremulous as I grip my gun. I peer stealthily around the lawn chair. The terrible, sand-colored shape is there under the crabapple. Slowly, it seems to stir. A huge, tufted tail flicks. The whole mass starts to raise itself. The screen door slams behind us. My father and I whirl around. My mother comes marching across the lawn, hefting a broom. 'I can't believe I could actually be so stupid as to bring my wet laundry out and then completely forget all about it after going back in for my clothesline and pegs,' she cries. 'Now it's much too late for anything to dry, but I'm going right into that tent of yours and give it a good sweeping, it must be filthy with all that tramping about in the dust you do all day!' My father and I gape at her, eyes bulging. 'Can't you see – there's a lion – under that tree – !' my father sputters, his larynx barely surviving the intensity in his voice. 'A *what?*' says my mother, coming to a halt and staring at him. She turns slowly towards the tree. My hair stands on end. A lion regards us from under the crabapple. It growls softly. 'Mom – ' I stammer. The lion comes waddling forward and rears up and flops on my mother. Shouting, my mother swats at it with her broom. I jump to my feet and bring my gun up frantically, but there's no target in the welter of broom and flying elbows and tossing mane. '*Mom!*' I screech. My father bellows beside me. He points his gun straight in the air and pulls the trigger.

There's a deafening blast. The broom goes flying into the grass. My mother sprawls onto her back and the lion collapses in an immense, awkward pile. Smoke drifts over the lawn. Frenzied barking erupts from the yard next door and starts an echo through the neighborhood. My father hurries forward. He stands over the lion with his smoking gun. 'My god, look at it, you've ruined it!' he moans at my mother. 'Ruined it!' 'You didn't have to shoot that horrifying gun,' my mother gasps, sitting up clutching her chest. 'You practically gave me heart failure!' I stand behind my father, peering around his elbow in astonishment at the jumble of quilted limbs and spun plastic hair. 'But that's not a *real* lion!' I stammer. 'Of course it isn't *real*, it's a training lion!' my father retorts, shouting to be heard through the caterwaul of barking and scratching and thumping from the other side of the fence. 'It cost a fortune to rent something this authentically ferocious, and your idiot of a mother has just gone and smashed it to bits. Look at it!' he cries. 'The ear's torn off, the snout's dented like a soup bowl, all the batteries and circuits are probably in splinters! Do you have any idea of the expense of replacing one of these things?' He throws his gun down in disgust. 'Well how was I to know it was going to come springing out at me like that,' my mother protests, scarcely audible in the din. 'I was simply on my way to clean your silly – ' An explosive surge in the barking completely drowns out her voice. We all look up at the fence. I gasp. 'Good god!' my father blurts. He and I shrink back a step.

The monstrous head of the dog next door roars down at us from above the redwood planking. Its huge jaws writhe and snap, its tongue slings spit and foam over its flashing incisors, its eyes strain white and berserk in its black, Cerberean skull. 'Now you, you shush up there!' my mother admonishes it. 'Go away! Vamoose, you odious beast!' 'Mom, don't *do* that stuff!' I shout. 'Hoy!' my father cries lamely, edging out a half-step and reaching for my mother's arm. The dog's jaws lunge out violently, snapping. Our whole family flinches back in unison. For an instant the horrible head seems to flounder above us. Suddenly two black shapes like clawed boxing gloves appear clambering and scraping on the fence top. Immense shoulders heave into view. 'My god, it's coming over,' my father sputters in amazement. 'It's gone mad. Run! Run for your life!' He wheels and goes galloping towards the house, his helmet toppling off onto his heels. My mother hesitates, then scurries after him. I start wildly in their wake. Suddenly I see the bright yellow of the lawn chair. Without thinking I veer towards it and fling myself down heavily behind. Feverishly I work my gun up to my shoulder. Roaring, slavering jaws and thundering, flailing limbs loom huge between the notched V of my sights and my helmet brim. I gulp and think 'Squeeze!' and close my eyes. I squeeze. There's a precise, metallic click.

A scream gags in my throat. My eyes fly open on the giant blur of a paw as the lawn chair crashes back over me. The dog plunges past, thundering on baying towards the house. I flounder about tangled in the chair, crying out inarticulately. At last I struggle free and I lurch around on my knees, unhelmeted, squawking in terror for my parents. I scream, and throw myself headlong into the grass. The dog runs past, away from the house, howling, scattering pieces of wet laundry. It rushes skidding to the rear fence near the wildebeest and starts to scramble frantically at the planking, its tail between its legs. 'Noisy rotten bully!' my mother shouts, charging by and flinging laundry. 'Like to bark and snarl, do you? Don't fancy the taste of laundry, don't you?' A pair of water-heavy underpants soars through the early evening air and lands gleaming white on top of the dog's black head. The dog screeches in panic. It vaults prodigiously, yelping and scraping, and flounders over the fence top in its dazzling cap, and bolts off howling into the twilight.

'Miserable brute!' my mother shouts, arriving at the foot of the fence. She shakes a fist in the air, and bangs the fence with it. My father creeps out from behind the screen door. 'Has it left?' he whispers. He advances on to the lawn, looking carefully about. 'Has it gone?' he calls out. 'Yes, it's gone,' my mother cries, glaring back at him over her shoulder, fists on her hips. 'The big filthy coward doesn't care for the taste of laundry in the snout!' she shouts hotly, clubbing the fence again. 'Please, *please!*' my father protests, hurrying over to his helmet. 'The last thing we need is to harm that dog in any way. The old lady will sue us for every penny we possess!' he cries. 'Let her sue all she wants, that vile beast of hers owes me a freshly laundered pair of perfectly good unmentionables,' my mother cries back. She swings about and brandishes a beringed fist up at the second-story curtains next door. 'Have you taken leave of your senses!' my father hisses at her as he struggles with his helmet, which for some reason won't fit. 'I can't spend all my money on lawyer's fees,' he protests, wrenching the helmet off and battering its interior with his fist, 'what do I care about stupid unmentionables!'

'Great *Scot!*' says my mother. She draws back melodramatically. 'What is this hideous cadaver doing here?' 'That's extremely expensive carrion!' my father exclaims desperately. 'For god's sake, don't touch it!' he pleads, waving my mother away. With a sudden cry he flings his helmet at his feet. He wanders off clutching his bare head in his hands, shaking it from side to side. He stops wretchedly over the docile, recumbent lion. 'Look at this ruin!' he groans. 'What in gods's name am I going to do? I'll have to try to repair it myself. They'll charge me a fortune. A fortune!' 'I certainly hope you're not going to blame that all on me again,' my mother informs him, as she stoops to begin gathering the scattered laundry. She straightens for a moment to stare back in disgust with laden arms at the remains of the wildebeest.

While this entire scene has been taking place, I have wandered in circles about the dimming lawn – oblivious, helmetless, in a daze of personal anguish. My gun drags beside me in the grass like a broken leg. 'I forgot to load . . .' I moan, heedless even of the raw throb of my ears. 'I forgot to load my gun. . . . How can I be a hunter if I forgot to load my *gun*. . . .' 'Will you stop jibbering that nonsense!' my father calls at last over his shoulder. 'That's a training gun, you can't load it for god's sake, it doesn't take bullets! – Do you think I'd let a half-grown boy chase about a suburban neighborhood with a loaded weapon!' he demands. 'Now stop snivelling and come help me drag this wreckage over to the tent before it gets pitch black out here.'

We have a cold, cheerless meal that night, dispensing with a fire. My father retires immediately afterwards to his tent, where he labors with pliers and multi-feature safari knife and leather-working needle. He swears savagely every time his hand slips. I sway somberly in my hammock, doing my homework, my ears glistening with tufts of ointment. Eventually there is the sound of pinned mosquito netting being fumbled, and then being violently torn aside. My father emerges into the moonlight. Part of one hand is crudely bandaged with his handkerchief. He stands for a long while staring at the huge, bloody presence sitting low in the night sky. 'Have you done your homework?' he asks finally, still facing the moon. He turns about slowly, in thought. 'Let me see it,' he says. He reads, flapping away a cloud of gnats. A scowl appears on his face. 'No, no, this won't do, this won't do at all,' he says at last. 'For some reason,' he says, clearing his throat, 'for some reason you've chosen to emphasize certain aspects of certain events in a most unappealing manner. It just isn't appropriate, my boy, it can only give people a grossly unfortunate impression.'

He clears his throat again. 'Better let me correct it,' he says. 'Where's your pen? Your pen,' he repeats. I surrender it to him.

I watch him laboriously cross out most of what I've written, his bandaged hand an awkward paw for support. Grimly, he looks off to compose his thoughts. Then stopping once or twice to chew on his pen in search of *le mot juste*, he awkwardly inserts his revisions. 'There,' he announces at last. 'Now that's a much more reasonable and seemly account!' He grins at me. 'Better turn in, my boy,' he says. 'We've had a long day, you and I, haven't we? I think I've managed to fix the damage your stupid mother did. We should have fine sport tomorrow – just you wait and see how ferocious that lion can be when it's not impeded! You can't imagine how much I paid for it.' He looks at me. He leans close. The scent of cologne mingles with the odors of the wild. 'Perhaps I'll even let you try my gun for a bit,' he says softly. 'Would you like that? A hunter just like dad?' He winks. He pats my cheek. Then he steps over to the hurricane lamp and puts it out. He crosses back to his tent. The light goes off in there. After a while, I open the notebook and squint in the dimness at what he's written. What I can make out of his scribbling fills me with a familiar sense of gloom and outrage; and other emotions, more dark and inconsolable. I close the notebook and lie staring up into the night sky. The hyena laughs somewhere. A mournful whimpering answers from next door.

Footsteps sound beside me in the grass. My mother appears in the moonlight. 'Are you asleep?' she says softly. 'I came to say goodnight.' 'Goodnight, mom,' I murmur. She gives me a kiss. She remains beside me. From the tent, sounds of snoring rise towards the stars. 'Tell me something,' she says. 'Did you do your homework tonight?' I turn my head slowly. I look at her. Homework is my father's precinct. 'And did your erudite father peruse it as usual?' she goes on quietly. 'Did he say, as always, that many changes had to be made, for various reasons?' There's a pause. 'And did he make those changes himself, as he always does?' I stare at her. She smiles. She looks off at the moon. 'There isn't much lost on your old goony bird of a mom, you know,' she says. 'Well, you and I know what really happened, anyway,' she says, looking back at me. 'That he cannot change. We both know you showed you're a very brave fellow to do what you did out here this afternoon.' '*Mom*,' I murmur, twisting my head away in embarrassment and disapproval and distress. My mother smiles. 'Never mind,' she says softly. 'You go to sleep now, and tomorrow I just know there's grand hunting waiting for you. Tomorrow and many days after, even without bullets just yet, or genuine, born-in-the-wild lions. There'll be all the bullets and lions you'll want soon enough.' She runs her hand over my head. 'We'll have to get some more ointment for those poor, tormented ears of yours,' she says. 'And I must go now and attack a loaf for your sandwiches.' She turns, and goes back towards the house.

Storm

A storm comes on. I knock on the door of a house and ask for shelter. An old woman shows me into her kitchen. She hangs up my dripping coat and gives me a hot drink. The thunder rumbles all around; rain scatters on the windows like gravel. A girl wearing a bathrobe comes into the kitchen. She chooses an apple from a bowl of fruit. When she's left, the old woman says, 'Don't have any ideas about my daughter. She's mad.'

The rain falls without ceasing, turbulently, like a massive paroxysm of nature. The old crone sighs and says I can spend the night by the stove on the kitchen floor. I hear her slow steps on the stairs as she goes up to bed. I curl up against the warm wall in the blanket she's given me. I drowse, but I can't sleep. The gusts of wind rake the windows, as if trying to get in. Sometime during the night, the girl comes into the kitchen. She stands by the table. Trembling, she lets down her robe. The flash of faraway lightning falls softly across her bare shoulders. But after a while, when she sees I won't stir, she leaves.

Revolt

I hear about a slave revolt. I go down into the streets. It's night. Buildings are gutted, smoldering, some in rubble. Obviously there was a struggle of great violence. Under a sulfurous street lamp, a beautiful girl paces back and forth, apparently standing guard for the new regime. But all she has on are a red fez and a pair of satin harem bloomers. Her face is heavily made-up and her bare breasts are tipped with rouge. 'Now I understand,' I think uneasily. 'What they meant was *white* slavery. . . .' I move along with a show of nervous, obsequious modesty. I hear a clamor. I look up ahead. A furious crowd bursts suddenly into view. It's all half-naked women, tricked out in garter belts and lacy undies. With tassled whips they drive before them one of the masters of the old order. His fancy silk suit is savagely ripped and torn at, his pomaded hair, a spiky mess. The sight of his face makes me gasp. 'He looks – just like me!' I stammer. 'It's happened! They've discovered that in my heart of hearts I bear the tawdry sensibilities of a ponce!' I shrink back into the shadows of a ruined doorway and gnaw at my hand, watching horrified as my gruesome double comes stumbling past. His dyed, pencil-thin moustache is all aquiver, his eyes are fish-like with fright. For one brief instant as he passes abreast, his eyes find mine: a look of anguished recognition fixes me. Then the mob thunders down on his back, flailing and screaming. I press myself as far as I can into the doorway. The rout sweeps on past, and turns onto the next street. Breathlessly I hear the cries receding. I lower my arm, trembling, from my face. Somehow I haven't been recognized. 'I've got to get out of here,' I think. 'I've got to get back to the safety of my own room.'

I peer into the street. It's empty. But the pin-up of a guard is still at her post under the lamp. Cursing her sense of duty, I watch her, waiting for her gorgeous back to be turned. Feverishly, I dart out. My shabby raincoat catches on a nail. The pocket yawns enormously, and something topples out, and flops onto the sidewalk. It's a girlie magazine! I stare at it, riveted with horror. I reach towards it. I look about wildly. I break off and flee down the sidewalk.

I reach my room and frantically throw the bolt. I drop all the blinds. With a thumping heart I peek down at the street. It looks tranquil, as far as I can tell. But elsewhere, something dreadful is stirring, I begin to realize. I stare down at myself. 'Oh my god – not *now*,' I gasp. 'This is terrible!' I fumble with my pants, rearranging things. But I keep sticking out. 'Go down, go *down*,' I admonish myself desperately, fumbling. Sounds rise suddenly from out in the street. I look about in panic. I rush over to the sofa bed and tear off the blanket and start wrapping it around myself. There's a pounding on my door. I freeze. 'Open up,' a woman's voice shouts. 'Open up in the name of liberty!' 'Who is it again?' I inquire in a thin voice. 'I don't think I quite caught your – ' 'Open up!' the voice shouts back. 'Open up or we'll burn you out!' 'Alright, alright,' I mutter. I waddle over to the door and pull back the bolt.

The hallway is crowded with grim, voluptuous militia, half-naked in their red fezes. The smoky flames of wooden tapers throb among them. Swaddled in plaid, I look at them. 'Okay, it's over, you've got me,' I admit, and I hang my head, blushing. A great cheer goes up. Red-nailed hands seize me roughly. I don't resist as they start hauling me off downstairs. The stairwell rings with the hubbub of gloating cries, scornful oaths. Halfway down I decide suddenly that if I am going to face my end for being what I am, then I shall be just what I am. '*What I am!*' I think, flinging back my head. Hectically I search for the most gorgeous one of the lot in my vicinity. I spot her, over by the banister. With a defiant cry I heave myself bulging in my blanket onto her, plunging down through the crowd to press my kisses onto her silky, perfumed, struggling throat under a hail of shouts and blows – until the crescendo of clawing and battering suddenly overcomes me at last, and I dissolve into soft, triumphant darkness.

Music

I stop at an inn in the country. After dining, I sidle up to the proprietor, who is tending bar under a set of antlers. 'Here is some silver,' I tell him in a low voice. 'As you see, it is not of inconsiderable denomination. I would hope that, sometime later this evening, one of your lovely chambermaids might have reason to be sent up to my room to see me. . . .' The proprietor considers the coins on the dark, glistening bar. He looks up at me with an eye that is shrewd and comprehending. 'I certainly don't see why that couldn't be arranged,' he says to me.

A while later there is a knock on my door. I hastily stub out my cigarette. 'Come in,' I cry. The door opens. A very young, very pretty maid looks nervously into the room. 'I was told you wished to see me,' she says timidly. 'Yes, come in, come in!' I tell her warmly, smiling and gesturing for her to enter. She does, in uncertain fashion. 'And shut the door,' I add, smiling with avuncular good will. After hesitating, she does so. 'Excellent!' I declare. 'Thank you so much for coming.' I run my eyes over her hurriedly. 'Now I don't know if your employer explained to you,' I begin, 'but I happen to be a talent agent for a large musical concern. The whole year long I travel the countryside, searching the nooks and crannies for music and for – voices.' I falter for a moment, swallowing. 'Imagine how happy I was,' I go on, staring, 'when your employer confided to me that you sang like an angel!' 'He did?' says the maid, astonished. 'Oh yes, of course!' I tell her, my face aflame. 'Here. I would like you to sing some of this music – ' I take her by the elbow and turn her towards the sheet music set out on the music stand by the armchair. 'But I can't read music,' the girl stammers. 'Never mind,' I tell her heatedly, 'it doesn't matter, sing anything! Sing this: *la!*' She stares at me, frightened. 'Sing *la!*' I demand. '*La –* '

she begins falteringly. 'That's enough – ' I blurt out, shuddering. 'Out of my way – ' I mumble frantically, pushing her aside, knocking over the music stand as I hurry into the bathroom. 'What's wrong, is something wrong?' the girl cries frightened through the door. I press myself throbbing into the towels. 'It's alright, go,' I murmur. 'Are you alright?' she bleats idiotically. 'Will you leave me alone now!" I shout.

Later, I lie on the bed. There is a peremptory knock on the door. It opens without my bidding. There's a violent clatter against the wall above me. Things drop to the bedding and roll noisily along the floor: silver. 'You depraved *swine*,' the inn-keeper hisses, sputtering, almost incapable of speech. 'I took you for a man, not a – a – I demand you clear off the premises this minute!' he sputters. I look at him listlessly. I roll over towards the wall. 'Let me stay the night,' I mutter in a toneless voice. 'One hour!' he says. 'If you're not gone by then, I shall have you thrown out!' Several inarticulate curses follow. Then the noise of spitting. The door slams. I press my face into the pillow, eyes shut tight.

After a while I get up and slowly go about packing the music stand. Then I light a cigarette and turn out the lamp and sit in the darkness on the bed by the window. Down below in the back garden, the maid staff is gathered at a table around a lamp. They giggle and chatter animatedly – all about me, no doubt. As if to mock me, one of them – a plain, sturdy sort of girl – tilts back her braided head, and lifts a note like a swaying crystalline bell, up into the chill air of the night.

Grand Tour

My old man feels queasy when I show up, so my mother and I steer him to a bathroom. 'It's something I just ate,' he mutters. 'What did you have to eat?' I ask him. His skin has a ghoulish, greenish hue; drops of sweat stand out on his brow. 'What *didn't* he eat,' says my mother. I look back out the door at the restaurant. Waiters in greasy red are clearing off my parents' table. A pair of them struggle to shift a portion of a large dark animal off the table onto a trolley. Two hoofed legs drape over the trolley's sides. Ponderously the waiters start rolling their burden away. I see its blackened great head and mane. I turn to my father, thunderstruck. 'You ate part of a horse!' I ask. He gives me a greenish, sheepish look. A long, thick hair hangs out from his front teeth. A wave of violent nausea surges through me. I rush out through the tables, down into the street, and take cover behind a tree. Across the way passersby stop and watch. After a while, I clean myself with a handkerchief and come back stiffly to the restaurant steps. Dust and stench surround me. Even so I decide to wait where I am; I can't face the scene inside. 'This is just the third day,' I reflect, despairing. I visualize the landscape of our holiday unfolding in heat-shimmering distances, foul smells, cacophany; and the endless excruciations of my parents.

The two of them appear in the restaurant doorway. The sleazy maître d' escorts them. 'Where did you go?' says my father, in an irritated voice. 'Thank you, thank you,' he mutters to the maître d', dismissing him. He and my mother come down the steps as if these were coated with ice. I help them off the last one. The maître d' calls down farewell wishes in grotesquely distorted English. My mother whirls about and waves and shouts out a return of sentiments. 'My eye!' cries my father. He claps himself in agony. 'My eye!' 'Eh?' says my mother, turning back around. She regards my father in confusion. 'You nearly put out my eye with that stupid thing!' shouts my father. My mother looks shocked. She stares down at her complimentary fan from the restaurant. She looks up, abashed and confused.

The maître d' has now come down several steps and makes an unintelligible inquiry of concern. I gesture to him that everything is alright, an assurance he vaguely accepts after much nodding and hand-waving. I put my arms around my parents and herd them as fast as they'll go down the street. At the corner, I look back to give a final, reassuring wave. The maître d' is standing at the bottom of the steps, his hands on his hips, staring after us.

Around the corner lies a cafe. As we come abreast, my father suddenly stops. He continues dabbing the top of his cheek with his handkerchief while he plunges his other hand into his clothing. 'What's wrong?' says my mother. 'Nothing's *wrong*,' says my father, dramatically blinking and blinking above the handkerchief. 'I'm looking for my wallet, I must have something to eat, I'm starving.' 'But we've just – ' begins my mother. My father suddenly looks frenzied. 'I can't find it,' he cries. 'My wallet! My wallet's been stolen!' He heaves around. 'Police!' he shouts. 'Police! Police!'

Flood

Our house is flooded. The water rises over the lights in the ceiling. We swim about in the dining room, our napkins fluttering up around our heads from where they've been tucked into our collars. The food from the interrupted meal spins lazily about us. My father issues instructions and frantic slow-motion proclamations. But all that comes out of his mouth are great upheavals of bubbles. My mother drifts past me, stroking her hair over her ears to keep it neat. I paddle about, a little, diffident figure, peering at the dining room chairs as they tilt and slowly lift a leg and begin to drift upwards. The lamplight is dim and greenish under water, and the house around us a sad and unrecognizable place of disarray.

The next day there is greasy silt pressed into the corners and seams. The house is muggy, and a swampy odor hangs in the air. We have all the windows and doors open to aid in drying. At dinner the backs of the chairs are still clammy. They stick in queasy fashion to our shirts and our skin. My father eats in silence, looking grim and preoccupied. When he finishes he rises and carries his plate out to the kitchen. We hear him slowly mounting the spongy stairs. My mother looks at the table somberly. 'You see,' she explains, 'this flood is what happens eventually to all families, and your father knows this, and it makes him very sad that there is nothing he can do about it.'

Sand

News comes to us of my father. He's lying in the sands. 'You must go and recover him,' says my mother, 'and bring him back for a decent burial.' 'Yeah, yeah,' I tell her. 'Right now do you mind if I finish my breakfast?'

After breakfast I go upstairs to my room. Presently my mother comes to find me. 'Oh, this is appalling,' she says. 'What are you doing, just lying there?' 'I think I have the gout,' I tell her. 'My big toe is killing me.' I gesture along my leg on the bed towards my upright left foot. 'Nonsense,' she says, 'people your age don't have gout.' 'Why not?' I demand. 'Dad had it. I inherited it.' 'Stop this nonsense!' she cries. Her eyes suddenly fill with tears. 'Your poor father lies rotting under a foreign sun and his own flesh and blood won't lift a finger to find him.' I writhe frantically at this remark. 'Why should I?' I shout, swarming to a sitting position. 'There was only one reason he went chasing off into that godforsaken place. And what was it? I'll tell you what it was: it was because he heard they made terrific stewed fruit! So now *I* have to disrupt my entire life, *I* have to risk getting myself killed, because of *his* craving for stewed fruit? I say he can go to hell!' I lounge back, glowering. My mother stares at me with a trembling face. She rushes sobbing out the doorway. I lie, glaring after her; then I smash my fist into the blankets and curse and drag myself out to the head of the stairs.

'I'm sorry,' I shout down the staircase, into the stillness. 'I'm sorry, I'll go. I can barely read a map and you know how much I hate flying, but I'll go.' My mother appears in the kitchen doorway. She looks at me, grim-faced. 'Don't you ever raise your voice to me again like you did just now in your room,' she says. Her own voice is quiet, deadly. 'I said I'm sorry,' I tell her, chastened. I take a step down towards her. 'I said I'm going.'

'That's not good enough,' she says. 'Screaming at me like that.' 'Mom, I just wanted you to know how I felt,' I explain. 'And what about how *I* feel!' she shouts. She stamps her foot. 'I'm tired of hearing about your feelings, all I heard from your father was his "feelings"! What about me and my feelings? And what sort of a man are you anyway with your stupid gout and miserable fear of flying?' 'Don't tell me about being a man!' I cry heatedly. 'You're a damn fool, that's what you are!' she shouts back, and she wheels and goes through the doorway. I make a livid, obscene gesture after her. Then I wheel myself and stamp back to my room.

I eat my lunch alone. Afterwards I leave the house without speaking to her. I go downtown and after some confusion, locate the consulate I want. A grinning young Arab in a Hawaiian shirt shows me into a spacious office. A powerful air-conditioner drones. 'Isn't this heat something?' he drawls pleasantly. 'How about a diet soda?' He comes back from a small refrigerator with a can and a straw. 'Thanks,' I tell him. I wince. 'What's wrong?' he says. 'It's nothing,' I tell him. 'A touch of the gout, that's all.' He gives a nod of recognition, and smiles. 'I sympathize,' he says. 'Sometimes I have it so badly in this ear I have to lie all night with a huge ball of cotton wool soaked in paraffin stuffed in it.' I look at him. 'No, no – *gout*,' I tell him quickly. 'It's my big toe. Uric acid. Inflammation of the joint.' He looks back at me. 'Are you sure that's what is meant by "gout"?' he says. 'Oh yes,' I tell him, shifting in my seat, trying hard to remain amiable. 'But this condition you describe,' he continues, examining me askance, 'surely this is a condition of older people. Aren't you too young for it?' 'It is more common among older people,' I allow stiffly. 'But it certainly can occur if you're younger.' 'I see,' he says. He considers me in silence. I stare at the floor.

'Well, anyhow,' he says. He smiles. 'Here is the map you asked for.' He pushes it across the desk towards me. He folds his hands in front of him and inclines his head and looks amused. 'And what, if I may ask,' he says, 'could possibly interest you about our enormous, overheated, dismally sandy country?' 'Oh personal things,' I reply, shrugging. I feel his stare on me. 'And culinary things,' I add. I clear my throat. 'For instance, I have heard about your wonderful stewed fruit.' His stare becomes puzzled. 'Oh, *that*,' he says finally. He shrugs.

'It's not too bad, I suppose, if you like that sort of thing. . . .' Suddenly he looks off to the side and titters. 'We always have to warn our visitors, if you'll pardon me, to be very careful of it,' he giggles. He grabs his belly in both hands and grimaces violently. 'It cleans you out but *good!*' he cries, laughing uproariously. I stare at his gyrations, and then a sudden, terrible insight unfurls through my consciousness. 'Wait a minute,' I ask him, gripping my chair, 'you don't think someone could actually – I mean, under the circumstances, out there in the desert – you don't think it could ever be *fatal*?' '*Fatal?*' he says. 'Oh no no – well I suppose if someone were to just eat and eat and eat. But no one could be that foolish.' 'I'm afraid I know someone who could,' I mumble.

In a kind of daze I get to my feet. 'I must be going now,' I tell him. 'Thank you. For everything.' 'Not at all,' he says. He holds out his hand and bares his teeth. 'Eight fifty, please,' he says. I regard him blankly. 'Eight fifty,' I repeat. 'For what? For this map?' 'And the diet soda,' he says. 'The diet soda!' I reply. 'How much was that?' 'Two fifty for the soda,' he says. 'Six for the map.' 'But that's highway robbery!' I protest, coloring. He shrugs, grinning, holding up open hands. 'This air-conditioning,' he says. 'It's ridiculously expensive.'

I arrive home fuming. I slam the front door and stamp noisily into the hall, shouting for my mother. There's no answer. Shouting, I stalk into the kitchen. On the table is a note. 'I've gone to retrieve your father,' it says. 'Your supper is in the fridge. Take it out a while before putting it onto the stove. (It may need salt.)' I scream uncontrollably. As I come back out the front door, pain shoots suddenly through my foot so that I hop and stumble idiotically down the front steps. I hurry into the street, gnashing my teeth. I know exactly where she is. At the end of the block I lumber up the short bank of the defunct railroad tracks. I see her ahead, silhouetted against the setting sun, marching along towards the bus stop. A feeling of such utter pathos assaults me that for a moment I just stop. She is dressed for rescue, grotesquely: flopping sun hat, open parasol, my old Boy Scout pack and canteen on her back, her thin calves up to the knee in my hiking socks, which puff out in huge, clownish wads between the straps of her sandals. 'Mom!' I shout, hurrying again after her. She stops and slowly turns. She watches my approach. 'What on earth do you think you're doing?' I demand. She stares at me and starts to answer, but then her face just wobbles. I put my arms around her. 'Mom, mom . . .' I murmur, patting her shoulder as she weeps against me. 'The poor, poor man,' she sobs, 'all alone for the vultures to pick at.' 'Mom, it's alright,' I soothe her, a great lump swelling in my throat. 'I'm going, I told you, it'll be alright.' After a while, I turn her and lead her back slowly across the darkening tracks towards the house.

I put her to bed without bothering about supper. She takes one of my father's sleeping pills and is asleep before I have the door closed. I go up to my room and turn on the ballgame softly and sit with my foot up and the map and my world atlas in my lap. I look at them, musing somberly. Outside, the night is warm and still.

Towards midnight I wake up suddenly. I'm still in the chair. I rub my eyes. Then I stiffen. I turn off the radio and listen, darkly. A closet door slides open downstairs; clothing hangers rattle. I step over the atlas where it has fallen and go out into the dim hall, and after a pause, go softly down the stairs. The door is slightly ajar, the lamp is on in the bedroom. 'Mom,' I whisper desperately, and I push the door and peer in. I gasp. '*Dad!* . . .' I stammer.

My father looks at me from the closet — an eerily robust version of my father, one with dark-tanned skin, garishly blackened tufts of hair on his almost bald head, huge pitch-black sunglasses. 'Yes,' he says. 'Shhh — your mother!' He gestures with his head towards the bed, where my mother's long-nostrilled, barbiturated nose pokes above the covers. 'But my god,' I whisper, stepping into the room, 'we thought you were dead!' 'Of course,' he says. 'I sent the notification myself. And for all intents and purposes, continue to regard it as true.' I stare at him, unable to believe what I'm hearing. A bizarre, alien presence confronts me, come in slippers with long, curling toes. 'Dad, what's this all about?' I demand. 'Why are you taking all those clothes? What's going on?' 'I'm a new man, that's what's going on,' he says, adding another item to an armful of shirts. An open bag, sumptuously tooled, lies on the floor stuffed with his potbellied underwear. 'I feel like a million bucks,' he says. 'I feel like a kid again. Here – ' He shifts the load of shirts to wiggle something out of his breast pocket. He grins lustily, showing spendidly white teeth. 'Is that, or is that not, paradise?' he asks.

I look at the photograph of him in his new persona, sprawled under a tent awning amidst a heap of grinning houris, all wearing sunglasses and all as plump as he is. I think of a pile of roasted pumpkins. 'I just had to come back to get some things,' he grins, taking the photo back. 'I feel like an idiot in those bedsheets they run around in.' He lays the shirts into the bag and reaches into the closet for more. I watch him, stunned. 'But what about mom?' I ask finally. 'What about me?' 'You're perfectly old enough to take care of yourself,' he says. 'And as for your mother, she has her pension and her memories. And you,' he adds. 'But you don't seem to understand,' I tell him, distraught. 'Mom is suffering terribly! She thinks you're decomposing out in the middle of nowhere. She wants me to bring you back for a burial.' 'I'll send another message,' he says. 'I'll say I've been cremated. I'll say my ashes have been scattered over the sands.' I shake my head, my disbelief turning to pain and disgust. 'Dad, this is vile,' I tell him miserably. 'This is truly perverse.' He swings around towards me, glaring. 'Don't you sit in judgement of your father, my boy,' he says savagely. I flush and swallow. There's a menacing pause. 'There are certain things,' he goes on, 'about life, about which you are in no posi – ' He clutches suddenly at the closet door, grimacing. 'What's wrong?' I ask. 'My gout,' he mutters, clenching his teeth. 'Damn!' He shakes a stockinged foot. 'I have it too,' I blurt out. 'Nonsense,' he snorts, 'you're much too young for it. Anyway,' he says, easing the foot back gingerly into its ornate slipper, 'why are we arguing! I'm only here for a short while.' He grins. 'Come, I brought you something, I want you to have a taste of it.'

He stoops with a great deal of effort and at last brings out a little clay pot from the depths of the bag. He takes off the lid and holds the pot out to me, beaming. I peer into it, at the puddle of slimy purple and green and brown at the bottom. A terrible, pungent odor rises to my nose. 'What . . . *stewed fruit?*' I stammer. 'Not "stewed fruit",' he cries. 'Ambrosia! It's like nothing you've ever had before.' 'No, thanks, really,' I protest, turning my head away. 'I mean I'm not a great stewed fruit fan, and for god's sake, dad, under the circumstances – ' 'Oh but you must try some,' he insists, pushing the pot at me. 'No, but really,' I tell him, leaning away and holding up my hands. 'And for another thing I've heard it's really dangerous!' 'Nonsense, will you just take a little bit!' he cries, exasperated. I hesitate unhappily; then petulantly I swipe a finger into the pot and poke it into my mouth.

A taste of something pre-civilized shocks me – an intensely coarse sweetness that is part animal-fat and hair. I stand swallowing with all my might. 'Isn't it out of this world?' says my father, grinning expectantly. I open my mouth as if to answer, but the only noise that comes out is a gasp. I double over, clutching at my stomach with both hands. 'What's wrong?' my father asks. It feels as if someone were squeezing my intestines with a pair of pliers. Still doubled over, I whirl around and waddle frantically out the door, towards the bathroom.

I huddle on the pot, hanging on to the towel rack for support, sweat standing out on my forehead. Piercing shudders roll through me. I press my face into the towels, groaning. There's a knock on the door. 'I have to leave now,' says my father's voice. 'I'm saying goodbye.' 'No, dad, wait,' I call out, wincing. 'Just a minute.' 'No, no, I must be going, I have to make a connection,' he says through the door. 'Goodbye! Take care of your mother.' 'Dad, please, wait!' I cry, twisting painfully. 'Don't desert us like this!' But I can hear the slapping of his footsteps going down the hall; then the door closing.

I come out at last from the bathroom, white-faced and shaky-legged. The hall is empty. I go back into the bedroom. There's no sign of him there either; just some sand from his slippers by the half-empty closet. I look at the tracings of fine grain. Then I look at the bed, where my mother lies, snoring, her frail head showing out of the great rippled mass of bedclothes. After a long while, I turn off the lamp and go slowly back upstairs.

Barge

I buy a barge. I moor it in the Butterfly Quarter. Through my curtains I watch the girls making their way along the embankment to their rendezvous. They hold up the skirts of their sumptuous robes with delicate, powdered white hands. The big bows of their sashes are like butterflies when seen from behind. Plain-faced attendants glide along beside them, holding up the big, delicate parasols against the infringements of daylight and breeze.

In this setting I work all day at my trade, which is no trade at all. When dusk settles, the sound of a flute from one of the houses raises me from my couch and my pipe. I come out into the soft, dim air on deck. The lanterns are being lit on the balconies. A girl's voice joins the flute wherever it is. I lean with my elbows on the rail, listening. The barge rolls softly on the swell of the tide. I bring out some scraps of colored paper from the pocket of my gown, and I light them, one at a time. I lean on the rail, watching as they slowly drift, curling and glowing, towards the dark, shifting gloss of the water.

Armchair

I eat a heavy meal and doze in the armchair by the fire. Soon I am snoring. Two half-human monstrosities come creeping through the doorway into the room. One has a lizard's head; the other, a wild boar's tusked muzzle. The intruders crouch on either side of the armchair. Together they lift the chair and its snoozing occupant off the carpet. Powerful and adept, they carry me out the door without disturbing my repose.

Outside, they hurry their cargo through the spiky shadows of the wintry trees. An icy moon hangs over the dark street. Eventually there are some woods; then fields. The armchair wobbles out into them. The hair on my head stirs in the air as I am hefted swaying along the hard, dark furrows. The silence of night is all around me, save for the sound of huffing, the thud of bare, animalish feet.

The ground begins to rise. A ways along it, the monsters set down their burden. They pause, standing panting in the chill air. Saliva glistens on the boar's head's tusks. Cloudy hisses of breath rise about the flicking lizard tongue. Then the twosome stoop for the armchair once more.

Ahead, a copse of trees looms at the top of the crest. The monsters carry their snoring, slippered cargo up to it, and into its darkness. Forcefully the enormous, scaly and hairy arms clear a path through the low branches. A great tree rises in the middle of the copse, an ancient oak higher than the rest. Straining, grimacing lividly, the hideous pair lifts me in my chair up, up, slowly, through the great boughs. A squirrel leaps past overhead and stares at us, and darts away. At last we emerge, at the very top.

Moonlight floods down over the armchair. The stars glitter above, harsh and bright. On all sides fields spill away dizzily below, frost-grained, shadowed. The few, meek lights of distant houses glimmer on their outskirts. Deep in my treetop armchair I huddle in my sleep. I press my sleep-mild hands deeper into the warmth between my thighs. A night wind tickles my collar and I shiver slightly. The monsters grin down at me. They lift their horrendous heads and slowly, they exchange a wink. A lizard-like hand extends and settles onto my shoulder. Roughly, it shakes me awake.

The Mailman

I go to pay a friendly visit on a girl I've recently met. She answers
the door in a negligee. 'Gosh, I'm sorry,' I apologize, coloring
and backing in confusion down off the front step. 'I didn't mean
to interrupt any intimate – ' 'But you haven't,' she cries. She
throws open her arms. 'This is for you!' 'For me?' I reply. An
immense grin spreads out across my face. 'Well, how positively
and miraculously *delightful*,' I declare, and I bound up on the
step and advance across the threshold and shut the door behind
me. I stand over the girl, grinning down at her like an oversized
baboon. The girl grins right back. I stoop and wrap my arms
around her and give her a preliminary kiss of appreciation. 'Shall
we adjourn somewhere more comfortable?' I suggest intimately.
'No,' she whispers. 'Let's stay right here, where we are!' 'Here?'
I repeat. 'In the front hall?' I glance about one-eyed over her red
neo-beehive. 'But wouldn't that be a bit, well, you know –
kinky? I suggest. 'I *feel* kinky,' she whispers. Suddenly her
eyelids flutter. Her face lifts back in utter surrender. 'Kink me!
Kink me!' she moans desperately. My blood roars in my ears.
Furiously I maneuver her negligee most of the way off. We sink
down onto the throw rug. I start working away like a man
possessed. A loud knock on the front door makes us both gasp.
We lie frozen. The knock repeats. We stare at each other. 'Who
is it?' the girl cries over my shoulder. 'Mailman,' comes the reply.
'Leave it in the mailbox,' the girl calls back. 'It's right beside the
door.' There's silence. 'I need a signature,' says the voice.
There's another knock. 'Of all the *goddam* – ' I mutter. I signal
in vexed stealth to the girl and get up, fumbling with my pants
and shirt, and open the door a crack, blocking the way with my
body. A package and pen are shoved at me. I grab the package

and scribble on it hectically, tear off most of the receipt and thrust it and the pen back. But the mailman isn't paying attention. To my astonishment he cranes sideways, trying to peer in. 'Hey, excuse me!' I tell him, rattling the items in his face. This gets his attention. He grins. He takes his materials back and gives me a droll, appraising look up and down. I glare at him. He touches the bill of his hat and turns and starts to saunter off down the walk. But then he stops. He turns back half-about. He grins at me sidelong. 'Come here a second,' he says, beckoning. I stare out at him, flabbergasted. 'Come here,' he repeats. I peer off to my left, and off to my right. I peer back at him. 'Me?' I murmur, shaking my head, pointing a finger at my chest. 'Come *on*,' he says, with a fierce wave. He walks off a few more steps and stops. He beckons vehemently. 'Come on!' I shift about non-plussed in the doorway. 'Listen, I'll be back in just a minute – ' I mumble over my shoulder.

I step out, pulling the door to behind me, and go nipping down the walk in stockinged feet, the package still under my arm. 'Now what in hell is the problem here!' I demand, following the mailman around under the garage eaves onto the driveway. He stands there staring off, sucking shrewdly on a tooth. His uniform strikes me suddenly as absurdly adorned with braids, and suspiciously ill-fitting. 'So who are you?' he asks slyly, eyeing me askance. 'Who am I?' I repeat, taken aback. 'Are you the milkman?' he probes. 'Plumber? Door-to-door salesman? Are you the *garbageman?*' he suggests, leaning up close. 'Am I the *garbageman!*' I repeat, thunderstruck. I draw myself erect, taking in the jaunty, oversized silhouette of his hat. 'If it's any of your business, which it *isn't*,' I snarl, 'I happen to be a friend of the lady of this house. Who happens to be unable to come to the door at this particular moment,' I add, with a cough. 'Now if you don't *mind* – ' 'A friend . . .' he says, screwing up an eyebrow and considering the phrase. 'A *friend* . . .' he pro-nounces slowly. He sniggers, and lifts a corner of his lip. 'That's a new one on me, she must be trying out a new line,' he muses. He looks back at me and closes one eye and sniggers. 'You know, I don't believe I like your tone, *Mr Mailman*,' I tell him, shifting the package meaningfully. 'Are you in the act of insin-uating something highly ungentlemanly about a lady's reputation?' 'Oh, come off it,' he scoffs. 'I certainly shall not "come off it",' I inform him, tugging at my half-buckled belt, my color rising. 'I have the distinct impression I've been pressed out here for the sole purpose of impugning a lady's good name with some antique brand of smut involving the proverbial tradesman, and god knows what else. And I don't like it one bit!' I add. 'You know, you're too damn much,' he sneers. He shifts his bag about irritably; the faint, stencilled logo of a major drugstore comes into view. 'Do you really think I'm the mailman?' he demands. 'Do I *look* like a mailman? This whole stupid get-up is *her* idea, you pompous sap – just like everything else is!' I regard him speechlessly. 'What do you mean, "It's her idea, just like everything else is?"' I demand feebly, when I'm able to find my voice. My question sounds old and lumpish in my ears, like a stale tidbit from a burlesque routine. 'I mean: she's a pretty kooky type, if you know what I mean,' he says, grinning with nasty intimacy. He gives me a nudge in the ribs. I gasp. 'She didn't tell you what's in the package?' he leers, jabbing it with his finger. His face from very close looks jaundiced, ravaged by unspeakable corruptions. I stare down from it to the package with a sense of obscure revulsion, mingled with dawning dread. 'If that's what I *think* it is,' he goes on, his lip curling goatishly, 'neither you nor your *friend*, the *lady*, should plan on doing much *sitting down* tomorrow.' His eyes take on a salacious gleam. 'Maybe not much of a lot of *other* things . . .' he adds. 'Maybe not for the whole rest of the week!' He sniggers vilely, and rubs a bony finger along his nose, and drops a wink. Then he clouts me on the arm. I start back. He cries out an obscene valediction, and with that he rights his big bag and flops off into the street.

I stand in the driveway, in my stockinged feet, staring after him. I lower my head and stare at the package. Slowly I turn around, swallowing, and stare at the walk back around the garage. Suddenly I jump, gasping – a truck roars into the driveway behind me. It lurches to a halt. The door flies open. I gape horrified at the big, hand-painted lettering above the windshield. '"Pest Control",' I stammer. The driver climbs out and slams the door shut. It's a dwarf, in jet black overalls and a helmet and goggles. He hefts a gleaming cannister on his shoulder and sports what looks like a trumpet in his hand. He pulls up short when he sees me. He stares back at me, looking me up and down. Then he smirks, and starts jauntily towards the house.

At the Cabin

I meet a girl at a party. 'I have a cabin near here,' I tell her. 'Shall we go?' 'Alright,' she says. We sit in the darkness by the cabin window, passing a bottle back and forth. Sounds of the party reach us through the warm night. The liquor is acrid and very potent. Soon we are chewing away at each other mouth-to-mouth. Our teeth clatter against each other's, and we fall molten and grappling onto the counterpane on the bunk.

In the morning I come to with a thunderous head. I edge gingerly about the cabin, a bag of ice tied to my crown with a scarf. The girl sleeps, slack-mouthed, tumble-haired, pink in the cheek. Her neck and bare shoulder are marked with the telltales of our night, as if she had been lashed with a flower. I maneuver a chair up quietly to the bunk, and sit, coffee in hand, looking at her. She mumbles something, and groans in her sleep, and shifts about under the counterpane. She mumbles again. She's dreaming, I realize, in alarm. 'Wait a minute,' I murmur. I get nervously to my feet and start in queasy haste for the door. I come out squinting into the sunshine. 'I've got to get clear of here!' I think, wincing under my icepack as I make my way along through the still damp grass. 'In this state, I'm highly suggestible to anything at all!' I pause for just a moment to look back stiffly over my shoulder, and then I feel a strange pang. I grab out for a tree branch and hang on, gasping in bewilderment, as a rippling force makes me flinch, and then slowly start to loosely flap about, like a hinged puppet, odd mumbled phrases issuing from my lips. All at once I stiffen, quivering, my eyes rolling into my head. I gasp. And then it's over, and I slump against the tree, panting quietly. 'Well, really, that wasn't so bad now,' I think, a sleepy smile spreading across my face.

The girl wakes up in time for lunch. We lie together in the grass in our icepacks and scarves, picking lazily at a bowl of fruit. 'So tell me,' I ask her. 'Do you always have such pleasant dreams, like that one you had this morning?'

Ice

'Are you still so cold?' asks the girl in her startlingly low voice. 'Would you like another blanket?' 'I'll be alright,' I trill. 'I'll just keep drinking this.' I blow across the tea and shiver and pull the blanket tighter around me. 'These beach huts just aren't equipped for this kind of weather,' says the girl, looking out the window. She wears a blanket herself. Her breath shows. 'I wouldn't have thought it possible,' I tell her. 'Not in this part of the world.' 'It's very peculiar,' says the girl, reflecting fretfully. 'They're out there water-skiing, and here we are, like Eskimos.' She runs a fingernail along the windowpane, making a furrow in the hoarfrost. Outside, an ice-shrouded palm rattles against the corrugated roof. For fifteen feet in all directions, every frond, branch, trunk, and flower of voluptuous vegetation is sheathed with a coating of ice, as if sprayed with crystal. The sunlight splinters and sparkles and flashes wildly. In the distance, the tropical scenery goes on in all routine splendor. A small, bright-red powerboat drags a tiny sunburnt figure and its white trail across the blue waves, in front of the endless white beach and the green, breeze-stirred overgrowth. The blue sky, casual and imperturbable, overlooks the scene.

'Perhaps it's something we did,' I wonder jokingly, looking at the girl over my tea. She turns and grins bashfully. She shrugs. 'We just exchanged voices for a while,' she says. 'What could be the harm in that?' She looks at me from her blanket. I look at her. Our lame attempt at laughter puffs heavily in the air between us. 'No harm I can think of,' I tell her, shivering.

Dante

I go out for a drive. A pretty girl in shorts passes by on a bicycle. I crane my neck to ogle her into the distance, and unattended the car zooms off the road, careens frenziedly along a ditch and smashes into a tree.

I come to holding my head. There are bits of windshield glass in my hair. My first thought is horror over the car, which was borrowed from a friend. 'He'll kill me,' I think. I look around for the wreckage but I can't see it anywhere. I blink, trying to clear away the greyness which seems to have fallen over my eyes. Then I realize the grey is in fact a feature of the place where I am: a grim, rock-strewn ground I've never seen before, like a wasteland on an old TV show. The air is humid and foul-smelling. I notice now grey dogs slinking about everywhere. 'Oh my god,' I think. I get up. Dogs make me nervous. A couple of dingy weimaraners stop to look up at me with mournful eyes. 'Easy, easy,' I warn them and I step hurriedly over noxious piles of their organic litter. They slink off, whining. I hurry on a few steps and then I spy the figure of a dumpy woman in a shawl and kerchief sitting on a rock. Enormously relieved, I head towards her. 'Excuse me, hello there!' I hail her. She turns around. I get a terrific shock. 'Dad!' I gasp.

It's my father, dead these past three years. We stare at each other's grey face; we embrace. He looks miserable. 'My poor boy, how did you get here?' he asks. I tell him about the accident. 'Were you drunk?' he says. 'Why should I be drunk!' I demand, resenting the insinuation. 'I just wasn't – I don't know, I just wasn't paying attention, that's all.' He listens to this sourly. 'Was it a new car?' he continues. 'No,' I tell him. 'Not at all – it was a very old car! It happened to belong to a friend. Unfortunately.' This further admission of glaring irresponsiblity makes me hang my head. Then I get peeved at being made to feel so bad, when what's happened to me is bad enough. 'Anyway,' I say to him crossly, 'what about you, why are you dressed up in that strange outfit?' He looks like a madman with an Aunt Jemima fixation. 'Do you think it's my idea?' he says irritably. 'It's what they gave me when I arrived.' He wipes his sweating face with his shawl. 'It's been just terrible,' he complains. 'They have absolutely no idea what they're doing. I have to stay here with these wretched stinking animals in a place unfit for habitation, in a climate that is absolutely destroying me!' 'Where are we exactly?' I ask, looking out at the place under discussion. 'We're in a part of what the Judeo-Christian tradition refers to as Purgatory,' he says. 'Dante, the great Italian poet of the late Middle Ages, divided the afterworld into three areas: Hell – ' 'Dad I know all about that Dante stuff,' I gasp, 'you don't have to lecture me!' He looks at me distastefully. 'Oh,' he says. 'I've only been here every day for three years, but you know all about it.' 'For all three years!' I reply. 'With all these dogs? But my god, why?' 'What do you mean, why?' he says. 'Do you think I know? They keep telling me they've misplaced my papers or there aren't any vacancies or they're understaffed – anything, everything! They don't mind. They don't care.' 'That's terrible,' I tell him, genuinely feeling for him. I look again over the gloomy scene. 'Oof, the smell is awful.' 'Yes,' he says, 'you notice.'

Hello!' a voice calls. I swing around. I get another shock. Its the girl on the bicycle. She's on foot now, in full color, astounding in her red shorts and pink skirt. 'How's everybody feeling?' she asks brightly, coming up. 'How's your head?' she says to me. 'It's okay,' I tell her, dumbfounded. 'Say, didn't I – ' 'Yes, you did,' she grins. 'It's not my normal line of duty but we're a bit short-handed because of vacations so I'm filling in.' She laughs. 'I must say it's been quite an intriguing two weeks, being a quote angel of death unquote. But anyway,' she says. She gestures with the clipboard she has with her. 'Your papers have cleared already, so if you don't mind, please come with me.'

My father, who has been scowling at us impatiently, looks thunderstruck. 'Look here,' he protests, stepping in, 'this is an outrage. Every week I speak to someone else and nothing happens for three solid years! I can't continue to stay here like this in these humiliating clothes, in this reeking scrabblepatch. No one knows where my papers are! I demand relocation to a more satisfactory place! Where's he going? He's my son. I demand to go with him!' 'I'm very sorry but there's nothing I can do right now,' says the girl, calmly steering aside the storm of protest. 'I shall certainly mention your concern when I get back to the office.' 'But that's what they tell me every time!' my father cries. 'Please!' he implores, piteously fingering the fringes of his shawl. The girl smiles at him with the imperturbability of a nurse with a nervous patient. 'I'm afraid we really must be going,' she says, looking over at me. My father turns to me. 'See what you can do with them, perhaps you can do something,' he pleads. 'I'll try, dad,' I promise him. He looks utterly woebegone and helpless. I clutch him in my arms, then I wrench myself away and follow the girl through the rocks and the refuse. 'Please, don't forget me!' he cries after us. He waves from the crowd of curs milling around his skirts, a grotesque and pathetic figure, like something out of a seedy costume opera.

I walk along in emotional silence beside the girl. 'You know it really is dreadful that he has to be treated like that,' I say to her after a while. 'Can't somebody do something?' She smiles at my question without looking at me. She warns me to watch out for exposed roots underfoot. 'Your father,' she says finally, 'as I'm sure you know only too well, was and is a very difficult man.' 'That's true,' I admit, unable to disagree with this judgement. 'But, geez, the poor guy is undergoing torture back there.' She gives me a quick, hard look. 'That back there,' she says rather tartly, 'is not what torture is, *believe* me.' 'Oh,' I tell her. 'I see. . . .'

We go along in silence again. We are in the beginning of a woods now. The air is cooler and fresher, suggesting even the possibility of fragrance. The awful grey pallor is far behind; with every step the color returns to things, like a color TV set warming up. We mount a low rise, go around a bend and all of a sudden, at one stroke, we are in a brilliant, tropic-like forest thronging with fruits and flowers, noisy with the songs of birds and the tinkling of leaves. I stand stopped in my tracks, flabbergasted. 'Do you like it?' says the girl. She is grinning happily. 'I can't believe it,' I murmur, tears of astonishment and joy springing to my eyes. Through the vivid foliage I can see azure waterfalls splashing softly nearby through their own mists. I reach a trembling hand into the leaves at the side of the path and pluck a bright globe of heavy fruit. I stare at it in my hands, then I plunge my teeth into its scented, tender flesh. It tastes musky, of melon and honey and citrus. 'My god!' I exclaim through a full, overflowing mouth, staring back into the branches. Coins of small, shiny denominations clink against each other in the breeze. I reach in and start tearing out handfuls of stems. The girl laughs and puts her arm around my waist and gently pulls me away. I shuffle forward, wide-eyed, a clutch of coins in one hand, the vivid fruit in the other, its juices running down my forearm, the tears of emotion streaming down my cheeks. The girl watches me, delighted and amused. 'Oh you're going to love it here,' she promises. She holds up the clipboard and its papers. 'You're a very lucky young man, I've gone through all of these,' she says, 'and it seems every single little thing has been forgiven.'

Shelter

During the week there's a very bad storm. After a few days I work up enough courage to go over to my mother's house. My heart almost stops. A huge tree has crashed down across the roof. The place is in ruins. 'Mom! Mom!' I shout, clambering frantically in the rubble. 'Hello?' a voice calls from out back. 'Mom? – ' I shout. I rush around past the battered flowerbeds. Another leafy behemoth has toppled across the backyard. Beside it stands my mother. 'Are you alright?' I cry, running up to her. 'Oh, a little flung about, but surviving,' she says gamely into my chest, as I hug her. 'And how are you, my darling?' 'But what's all this?' I ask, turning from her and staring. A primitive but highly decorated shelter has been rigged up under the massive branches. My mother's telltale, inexorable hand shows – in the awful colored-glass knickknacks strung among the leaves, in the crocheted cushions plumped about, the ribbon-cinched twigs, the frilly rocking chair beside the frilly, much-repaired tea cart. 'You can't possibly be *living* out here,' I protest, flabbergasted. 'I most certainly am,' says my mother. 'I'm not going to be penned up with a herd of perfect strangers in some high school gymnasium.' 'But mom – ' I protest, taking in the full horror of the inventory under the branches. 'This is all so – so eccentric – and – *shabby*.' 'Excuse me,' replies my mother haughtily, 'shabbiness and eccentricity are in the eye of the beholder! A very blind and stupid beholder,' she adds. I hear her morosely. 'You couldn't get the neighbors to help out?' I ask in a lame way. 'The neighbors have enough worries of their own,' she says. 'As do you.' 'Yes, I suppose,' I admit. 'But under the circum – Now wait just a minute,' I burst out. I march a few steps in the grass. 'What in hell are these doing here!' I demand, gesturing savagely at where, like ghouls resurrected from the remotest, most lugubrious pit of my childhood, my last pair of dolls sit against the case of my mother's sewing machine, grinning with shiny sentimentality. 'They're lovely,' says my mother. 'They're keeping me company. They give me someone to talk to in the gloomy hours.' 'They give you someone to talk to!' I repeat, pronouncing the words with appalled amazement. I put my hands to my head. 'Mom, this is monstrous,' I tell her. I bend and snatch the dolls up. 'Put those down this minute,' my mother demands. 'Mom, if anyone should see these out here – ' I protest. 'They're mine, I shall do what I want with them,' she replies. 'Mom, these are my old, hideous dolls!' I plead. 'They *were* yours, they're mine now,' she says. 'I've lovingly fixed them good as new, and don't you dare harm a hair on their pretty heads. Put them back.' 'Jesus, Jesus . . .' I mutter. I drop the dolls into the grass. 'That's not how you found them,' my mother says. I roll my eyes. I give the dolls a rearranging shove with my foot. '*Not* like that,' she says. I throw my hands down in exasperation, and slouch off towards the house. 'I don't know why you're entitled to such dramatic moods,' my mother declares, stooping and propping the dolls back in their place. 'I'm the one who should be sitting howling in despair.' I don't answer. I stand contemplating the torn roof beams and crushed walls, which had once been home, before the storm. 'What an unmitigated disaster . . .' I mutter. 'What's that?' says my mother. 'I said: what a disaster,' I repeat somberly. 'Yes, of course, but we learn to keep going,' my mother says. 'I happen to be a hopeless optimist. I believe *everything* has a bright side, if you learn how to look for it. I've even found beauty in that mass of horror there,' she declares, gesturing at the house. 'And if you ask me nicely, I just might extend you the privilege of showing you some of the very beautiful drawings I've recently made.' I turn from considering the ruins, and stare at her. 'I don't have to show you,' she says. 'Alright,' I protest. 'Alright, I'll see them. But since when have you started making *drawings?*' 'Never mind,' she says. 'I certainly wouldn't want you to do me any favors.' 'Mom, I would like to see the drawings,' I tell her, slowly and fiercely. I watch her stoop back into the brocaded depths under the branches. With a pang of despair I note the carpet slippers she wears, festooned with pompoms by her own hand.

She comes out with some sheets of paper. 'Nothing but compliments please,' she instructs me. Helplessly I look at the drawings. Each one provokes an ache of poignancy and utterly unique horror. 'They're masterpieces,' I tell her, flatly, quietly, handing them back. She shrugs. 'For my humble part I think they're rather beautiful,' she says. 'I love them,' I murmur, wandering off down the tree trunk. I step over the dolls and lean with my shoulder against a branch, my arms folded. I sigh, in long stages, staring off at the eerie, rippled agitations left over above the horizon. 'So young and sad,' says my mother from behind me. I give a listless, melancholy snort of amusement. 'Tell me,' I ask her, not turning around. 'Honestly. Do you understand what goes on with the sky at all?' 'In all of my sixty-seven years,' she says quietly, 'never. Never once . . .' The two of us stand gazing out at the unfathomable, remorseless, yellowish grey heavens. 'Did I tell you,' I ask, 'that last evening, over my way, the wind or something had pushed the clouds into the shape of an elaborate dirty joke?' '*What?*' says my mother. She turns and stares at me. 'You like to pull your poor old mother's leg, you nasty, nasty boy . . .' she says after a while.

Plein Air

for Peter Lewis

It's late afternoon in the woods. The rain that's threatened all day has held off. I see ahead the crooked chimney of a hut amid a grove of birches. Outside, a couple of rude tables and chairs are set about. I knock on the ill-fitted timbers of the door, where a spray of orange berries hangs from a nail. An old crone answers. 'Yes?' she says. 'Something to drink,' I tell her. 'Something to eat.' She slouches off. I cast an eye around the place. The floor is just dirt, but swept clean. The bumpy, whitewashed walls display blue tiles here and there, and there are some colored glass things full of colored light on the mantle. A straw broom stands guard beside the grate, its twills clipped and trim.

I take the bottle and chipped tumbler I am handed out to one of the tables. I sit and smoke and look at the birches. It is the hour of contemplation. A hazy shaft of yellowish light slips through the grey, heavy sky and spreads among the trees, making the white bark brilliant, almost liquid-seeming. Two figures come into view. Woodchoppers, no doubt: one carries a lumbering tool over his shoulder. They're young. They tip their cloth caps to me as they come up and trudge across to the other table. The old lady appears with a bottle. They mutter perfunctory greetings to her, and pour out the first glassfuls. They refill, wiping their mouths on their sleeves.

Then the one nearest me reaches into his jacket. He brings out a leather-covered journal. It's a much-worn volume, slim and quite handsomely made. Intrigued, I watch as delicately he turns the pages one at a time in his big, grimy hands. Crude, careful images of wildflowers crowd the dog-eared leaves: birds such as the titmouse and the partridge; a fox with her cub; the piled trophies of the harvest garden. The fellow reaches blank paper, and carefully he places the journal before him. He feels about in a pocket and brings a stub of grease pencil out into the muggy air. Daintily he unpicks from it a spiral of encircling paper.

The old lady comes out the door with a heavy, steaming plate and a spoon. While I eat, I watch this woodland Giotto drawing the birches. He bends over the page. His mate sits with his chair tipped back against the log wall of the hut. His cap is over his eyes. He chews on a long stem of grass and murmurs lazy snatches of an old aimless song, and smoke drifts overhead from the chimney, out into the slowly fading light.

Traveller

I go along a dirt road. By a rude fence I see two dark-haired men, in white shirts, standing and weeping. I am hungry. I sit by the side of the road in the coarse, opulent grass and undo the bundle of the red-checked kerchief. While I eat, I watch the grieving pair, who stand very erect and silent as the tears drip down their cheeks. Their hands don't stir from their sides. They are brothers, I decide. 'It's a shame they don't have a guitar or other stringed instrument,' I think, 'to elevate their sorrow into art. But alas, this is a poor country.'

Treasure

The train slows down for a curve, and I jump. I lurch along wildly for a number of yards, but then I catch my balance and scramble down into the cover of the big ferns. I stare about. No one seems to have seen me. The last car of the train trundles into the curve; a roll of smoke trails back and a whistle screeches; then silence.

I take off my rucksack and get out the map. It shows the low ridge of the twin hills behind me. To the north and west, over there in the early daylight, lies the site. I put the map away and unsheathe my machete and start off. The undergrowth is thick, over-lush and monstrously humid. Flowers protrude, garish and gigantic, like ruptured cans of paint. I use the machete as best I can, but the going is slow. Every now and then I halt dead still and listen, to make sure I'm alone.

After some four hours, I reach the telltale slab of rock. I squat above it, peering down through the foliage and checking what I see against the map. It's definitely the site. It looks very promising. 'Memories can drift into very dense formations in this sort of topography,' I reflect once again. 'There could be rare value here.' I start down, gripping the vines and feeling my way. At the bottom I fit together the spade and begin immediately on the first likely mound. The sunlight falls misty around me through the greenery. My spade clanks against bits of rock schist and then makes the slicing thump of digging into rich, packed earth. Sweat drips from the end of my nose. After several feet, I see something. I get down on my knees and reach in, breaking away earth with my bare hands. An evergreen branch comes into view, hung with baubles; a wrapped and beribboned package; a hunk of plum pudding. I mutter a curse. 'Just another Christmas Eve,' I snort. 'They're a glut on the market.' I fling a lump of dirt into the leaves and sit back on my heels. I run a glistening forearm over my glistening brow. Then I blow out a breath and seize the spade again, cover over what I've done and go on to the next probable place. Almost immediately I turn up a lode: a full-scale summer evening, dotted with fireflies, poignant with a mother's voice drifting down over the fields to late-playing children. But the ensemble is simply too vast and rickety to be broken down for transport. 'There's no way on earth I could ever lug this out of here on my back,' I reflect grimly. Without wasting energy on the luxury of more curses, I start throwing dirt back on the scene.

All of a sudden I hear noises above me. I stare up at the rock. Frantically I throw on a couple more shovelfuls, snatch up my rucksack and lunge as noiselessly as I can manage into the cover of the undergrowth. I lie there breathlessly, waiting. After a few moments of commotion, a face peers down through the foliage from the top of the slab. It wears a bulky military hat, the hat of a sentry on patrol for poachers. It scans the area dully, stupidly, before pausing for a moment to stare right in my direction. I lie in the leaves, immobile, my heart pounding. Slowly the heavy eyes move on again; at last, the face withdraws. The noises move off, on down the circuit of patrol. I remain where I am, my jaw clenched, waiting for the silence to grow well-established. When this is so, I clamber back out and resume my digging, with furtive intensity, working right at the base of the rock, at the drift point. Finally, I'm in luck. My spade cuts away the dirt from a young man and then a young woman, sitting hunched together in separate gloom, surrounded by letters, flowers, torn but recognizable photographs – all the paraphernalia of a love affair and its end. This is a real find. 'And by god, don't you know they look enough alike to pass for brother and sister,' I congratulate myself, carefully freeing the girl's shoe from its boot of soil. 'I'll bet I can push them as incest. Aristocratic families will pay a fortune for this sort of item.' I ponder happily the details of various possibilities as I dismantle the find and pack it up piece by piece into my rucksack. It barely fits. I heft the load and grunt under its weight. The real labor still lies ahead of me. I look over the site for the last time, for any signs of my presence. There're none. I check my pistol and then eye the terrain overhead. Then I take hold of a vine and ponderously I start the climb up, wary and huffing, back through the jungle to the railroad.

Towards Asia

A girl walks out of the water. She is plump and dark, with eyes the color of olives.

She comes up beside me on the rocks. About us the dusk is humid and the sun sinks into its own reflection on the grey waves as if into a pool of melting wax. The girl recites the story of her little brother. . . . So frail, so sad and helpless he lies on his pallet all day, a sickly orphan, dependent utterly on his only sister for what food and care and brief shelter he has in this world. . . . The girl glances at me slyly as she drones her plaint. The sun sinks away and a humid moon hangs in the sky. I lie back on the rocks, feeling the coins in my pocket as I listen to the slow, soft drone of the girl's voice, cadging and unhurrying, as I smell the musky scent of her dark, damp hair, of her body under its damp, threadbare dress. A small figure moves near us in the dimness. A face shows over the girl's shoulder — a frail, somber face of a young boy. He kneels there, looking down at me with solemn curiosity while the girl refines her plaint yet once more, probing for an additional nuance, trying now the savor of a particular, intricate phrase, reshaping unhurrying a certain figure to suggest a new coloration, a subtle readjustment in the artifice of her plea. . . . A breeze off the straits stirs over us. The water laps softly at the rocks, at the girl's languorous connivings. Lights glow on the distant shore under the evening sky.

Engineering

My mother is on the roof. 'What are you doing up there?' I call to her heatedly. 'You'll kill yourself. Come down!' 'I'm perfectly fine,' she calls back, teetering over the eaves. 'I'm just reading one of your late father's engineering books, on flying and so forth. I want to see how it works in the flesh, it's the only way I grasp things.' She extends a wavering arm, in the manner of a wing. 'Are you out of your mind?' I shout at her. 'You can watch all that stuff on TV if you have to. Come down here!'

In the living room I consult the program listings and turn on the set. 'Anyway, what could you hope to understand about high-level *aerodynamics?*' I ask, reaching for the dusty volume by my mother's side. 'Why not?' she demands. 'I have two eyes and a brain, don't I?' I look up at her, flabbergasted. 'Mom, are you nuts, this isn't engineering, this is one of dad's weird sex books, in French!' 'What!' she says. 'Oh for Christ's sake,' I tell her, and I toss the book irritably onto the coffee table. She shrugs. 'I'm sure I don't know what you're talking about,' she says. 'That's exclusively engineering. Anyhow, go fix the TV reception, I can't see a thing.' I get to my feet and stand behind the big box, sourly maneuvering the rabbit ears. 'Stop!' my mother cries. 'Mom, you don't have to shout like that,' I mutter. 'That's it, that's perfect!' she shouts. She leans forward, avidly, ignoring me as I look at her. I shake my head. I walk around a couple of steps and consider what's on the screen. A naked man strapped into feathery wings lumbers idiotically after a girl in frilly undies who rushes squealing back and forth in front of a blackboard on which she hectically scribbles mathematical equations. My mother stares at the action. Then she throws up her hands in disgust. 'Ach, I need to watch *this?*' she protests. 'I already know all about it!'

Window

My mother and I are watching TV. It's late at night. I hear a scratching noise from the rear of the house. I turn my head. 'What's that?' I ask. My mother turns also. Then she turns back to the TV. 'It's probably your late father,' she says. I look around at her, shocked. 'He's always trying to get in,' she says. The colored light from the TV screen washes over her face.

I get up in silence and walk back through the house. I stand at the pantry window and look out. The back lawn is in moonlight. A flickering white tubby form slinks about at the fence. All at once it comes hurrying towards the house. I shrink back, aghast. It's my father's ghost. He comes up into the flowerbed under the window and starts rattling and scratching at the pane on tiptoe. I stare from four feet away at his grisly, desperate face, at his naked shoulders framed in the glass. A cry bursts out of me. 'Dad!' I call. His eyes widen in his head. His grappling becomes frantic. He flaps at me to come open the window up. But locks barnacle the frame. The window is locked against him. I gesture helplessly. I hurry around into the kitchen. The back door is girded with padlocks and large bolts. I come back into the pantry and stare in helplessness out at him, holding up useless hands, shaking my head, feeling stricken. Suddenly the pathos is just too much for me. I break away and go back into the other part of the house. I stand in the living room doorway. My mother sits in her chair, staring grimly at the TV screen. The screen suggests a window into a fiery but mundane world. 'Why are you doing this?' I ask finally. 'Mom? Why won't you let him in?' My mother scowls, staring straight ahead. 'I'm sick and tired of him, that's why,' she mutters. 'He's dead, isn't he? He's dead!' she bursts out. 'Let him leave things be – life is for the living!' she protests.

Tweed

My mother comes to me with a jacket. 'This was your father's,' she says. 'What do you think?' I shrug. 'I don't know,' I tell her. I try it on. The shoulders are too wide and bulky for me. My forearms protude past the bottoms of the sleeves like peg legs. The tweed is scratchy and smells un-nice. 'It's not for me,' I tell my mother, taking it off and handing it back to her.

That night I wake up suddenly. My father's ghost stands shimmering beside my bed. 'What's the matter, you don't like my coat?' it says. 'Dad,' I say. I sit up against the pillows and rub my eyes wearily. 'It's a fine coat, it just doesn't fit me.' 'It's a *fabulous* coat,' says my father. 'You couldn't find a coat made that well anywhere in the world any more. You should be thankful you have even a *chance* to own a coat like that.' 'Please,' I explain, 'I love the coat. I was honored to be considered a legatee for it. But I wonder if you've noticed, I happen to be tall and on the thin side while you're short and – and broad.' 'I was as slim as a reed when I was your age,' my father says, drawing himself to full, wavering height. 'Slimmer than you are, if you want to know the truth. Of course I always had very broad shoulders.' 'You looked great, dad,' I agree. 'I've seen the photographs. But do you understand what I'm telling you? The sleeves barely reach past my elbows. It looks ridiculous on me.' 'You could have it altered,' he says. 'I suppose so,' I admit forlornly. 'What do you think tailors are for,' he says. 'Why, any tailor today would give his eyeteeth to work with cloth like that – I'm sure they haven't seen its like in years! Have you felt that tweed, have you run your fingers over it?' 'Yes I have,' I tell him. 'And my neck. It's a great tweed, a true tweed. Like heather, and bramble.' 'I don't know what you mean by "bramble",' he says, 'it's as soft as cashmere against the skin. But "heather" is very accurate, very *juste*. A tweed that caliber, it's like wearing the earth of the highlands around your shoulders. The Scottish highlands, where tweed comes from.' 'I know perfectly well where tweed comes from!' I tell him. 'In point of fact it's from a part of Scotland which is a bunch of offshore islands, for your information, not highlands.' 'You don't know what you're talking about,' says my father. 'Tweed is from Scotland – the highlands.' 'Look, why are we arguing about this,' I tell him. 'The point is, I like my clothes to fit. I have several nice jackets that meet this specification already, so thank you very much all the same.' 'What, that ridiculous black thing you wear, with the funny collar?' he says. 'Please,' I tell him. 'It's very late, I'm tired, I have to get to sleep, I'm very sorry about the coat. Can we say goodnight?' 'Yes, goodnight, goodnight,' says my father. 'If I were alive, you wouldn't even come near that coat, you would be lucky just to be allowed to *look* at it.' 'Gee, thanks so much,' I tell him, plumping my pillow. 'Do you know what it's like being dead and having your precious memories flung back in your face?' he says. 'For pity's sake the coat just doesn't fit!' I protest. 'What do you want from me?' 'Don't you raise your voice to me,' he says. 'Don't you think just because I'm gone you can forget your place with me.' 'But what *do* you want?' I ask him. 'Why are you making such a terrible fuss about this?' 'I just want to pass on to you what was mine,' he says. 'You're my son, I want you to have the things that were mine. . . .'

I don't know what to say to this. The room falls silent. My father's ghost trembles pathetically in the dimness. 'Alright,' I mumble finally. 'Alright . . . If it means that much to you. Alright. I'll wear it . . . even though – *No*,' I blurt out desperately, 'I won't, I *won't* wear that itchy, stumpy, evil-smelling thing! I'll accept it and cherish it as a gift from you, but I won't wear it, because it simply doesn't fit, and that's all there is to it. Dad,' I say. I push off the covers and get out of bed. 'Dad, don't be like that. Where are you going, come back.' I go over to the window. 'Dad,' I call out, over the dark bushes.

'What's all the shouting?'

My mother stands in the doorway in her nightgown. She blinks at me sleepily. 'Oh, he got all upset about that stupid tweed coat,' I tell her. She looks at me. She looks away and shakes her head, wearily. 'Even in the grave,' she says, 'he's a lunatic.' Before she closes the door she says, 'Go to bed, go to sleep. I'll give it to the neighbors in the morning.'

In a Bottle

I have a bottle in which I keep my father. Fate has decreed that he die and return as a ghostly miniature in a glass container. Fate has decreed further that he do so dressed up as a cavalier, a role in which he liked to fancy himself in life just past. It is not however a lean, lithe, glimmering figure of a cavalier my father cuts. His is portly and solid and squat. But he is properly equipped with a great, opulently feathered hat on his head; a soft spray of ruffles under his double chin; lacy, lampshade cuffs at the ends of puffed sleeves; an embroidered sash diagonally over his girth, from which wobbles the deep, bowled guard of his rapier; suede boots that struggle, rumpled, up to his mid-thigh. Spurs clank faintly when he walks.

The bottle itself is furnished simply, to my father's needs. It holds a bed, a carpet, a couple of chairs, and a table at which my father spends most days fittingly at work on his memoirs. He looks sober and substantial and squire-like as he scratches away with his quill, his inkpot open on one side of the pages, his great hat carefully set down on the other.

Once a week, on Sunday, he makes a practice of reading aloud his progress, in a tiny, orotund voice. These are not pleasant times for me. Sometimes I can't restrain myself from breaking into his declamations to let him know what I think: that his language is ostentatious, his tone cornball and melodramatic, his selection of facts preposterously self-serving. Naturally I don't use these exact words, but even so my father is violently insulted. He draws himself erect in his finery to dismiss my opinion out of hand. I am callow, I am uninformed; I know, for all intents and purposes, nothing about anything. Haughtily my father flaunts his seniority, the numerous achievements of his lifetime. 'You should listen,' he concludes,' and perhaps learn something for a change.' 'Perhaps, perhaps,' I mutter, shifting in my seat, as his piping drone resumes.

Then there are days when memoirs are not the issue. A black mood descends on my father. He slumps in his chair in sumptuous, velvety gloom. His splendid hat lies upside-down on its feather on the floor. The deckled pages of his manuscript are scattered over the carpet, useless. My father drinks from a flagon and rails against his death and his imprisonment as a homunculus in a knickknack. His hair is tangled, his little eyes are red, drunk, obsessed. He pleads with me suddenly to pull the cork from the bottle, to release him from captivity. But I don't think this a good idea, as I try to explain. Besides, I don't see how he could ever hope of fitting through the neck of the bottle. He curses me for this. He seizes his rapier from his other chair and thrusts bellowing at the confines of the bottle. Again and again the glinting needle of his sword buckles against the glass walls. With a howl he heaves the rapier from him and tramples his hat on the way to the bed, where he sprawls in agony, his teeth sunk gnawing into his wrist, the tears coursing down his cheeks.

When my father's exhibitions reach this piteous stage, I take the bottle down from its wooden cradle on the mantle. I hurry with it into the bathroom. I fill the tub with water and I set the bottle into it. The gentle undulations of the surface exert a calming influence on my father's anguish. His writhing begins to subside; his sobbing diminishes. I stir the water quietly with my fingers. At last my father's hands slacken and fall away; his breathing changes. His room bobs placidly. I listen for it to fill with vinous snores. My father's suede is scuffed, his velvet bruised, his lace torn in places; but at last, he sleeps. Gingerly I lift the bottle out of the tub and dry it with a towel. Tenderness and irony mingle in me equally at these moments. I carry my little, sodden, miserable father back into the living room. Without jostling, I lift him and gently as I can I set him back snoring onto the wooden struts of his cradle.

Waves

I have to go home to visit my mother, who lives on the other side of the country, but I'm terrified of flying. So I hire a boat. We set off under a fair sky. Outside the harbor there's a headland. We clear it, then pull in to shore. 'What's up?' I ask, coming up behind the skipper who's tugging on a rope. 'This is as far as I go,' he says. 'Are you kidding?' I tell him. We've been out about three-quarters of an hour. 'This is a recreational vehicle,' he says. 'This is as far as she goes.' 'But I hired you to take me to the other side of the continent!' I point out. 'Isn't that tough,' he says. I stare at his huge muscled back, speechless. 'But how am I going to get there?' I protest finally. 'Do I look like a travel bureau?' he says. He tosses my bag onto the peeling wharf and with an outsized hand indicates the gangway plank.

From shore I watch his wake narrowing into the distance. I can't believe it. I pick up my bag and turn around and trudge disconsolately up into the village on the hillside above. At the first cafe, I go in and order a cup of coffee and sit with it, staring glumly out to sea. 'How will she ever understand?' I think, about my mother. She's been looking forward to my visit for months, and I've spent all the cash I had on the boat rental. I get choked up thinking about it, and have to get out my handkerchief and blow my nose.

At this point I realize that my waitress is laughing at me. I turn my head and regard her over my handkerchief. She's young and sly and cute, now that I take her in, with exotically curly hair. 'You're funny,' she says, and she gives me a little look and walks away. I turn in my seat and watch her stroll back to the kitchen area. A grand blush begins to heat my entire body. When she reaches the service alcove, she spins around and grins straight at me, as if she knew I'd be watching. I blush more fiercely and turn away and stuff my handkerchief in my pocket. I pick up my coffee. I peer back over my shoulder. She's whispering with another waitress, the same age and sly style she is. She sees me looking and she stops talking and smiles. I smile back, sheepishly. I watch her bend forward. She takes the hem of her skirt in both hands. Suddenly she jerks the skirt up above her waist. The cup spills out of my hands. I hear them howling with laughter behind me as I spread paper napkins over the grimy puddle. My face is burning.

She appears at the side of the table with a tray and a dish towel. 'I'll get that,' she says. She's still chuckling. I watch her mop it all up. Then she drops into the chair opposite and considers me brazenly, clearly extremely amused. 'You're making fun of me,' I tell her. 'You're so funny and sad,' she says. She leans forward with her elbows on the table and her cheeks in her hands. 'So what's the matter?' she says. Her eyes have a twinkle in them. I stand up and find the last of my change and throw it down on the table. 'None of your business,' I inform her.

Twenty minutes later she knows everything. She sits mulling me and my story over. 'I'll help you get back to visit dear old mom,' she announces finally, and she breaks into a grin. 'Yeah? How?' I demand scornfully, getting riled again at her manner. 'And is there perhaps something wrong with a son wanting to visit his mother?' 'I have friends going out that way who can give you a lift,' she says, ignoring my second question. Then she reaches across the table and presses a finger to my lips and shakes her head – all this meaning I should now hold my peace. 'I'm off at six,' she says, soft and sly.

Her place is a couple of blocks from the cafe. It's small and pretty, like she is. My head goes spinning. At ten o'clock she puts a hand out to the old, barnacle-encrusted alarm clock on the window sill by the bed, and gives it a shake, and says it's time for me to go. She repeats the directions to where I'll be leaving from. Then she kisses me sweetly on the nose. She stands in the doorway in her sea-green bathrobe and waves to me, grinning, as I stumble off light-headed and wet-nosed down the cobblestones.

The night has clouds, and the moon bobs in and out, making things picturesque but highly perplexing. At last, after several backtrackings, I recognize a landmark from her directions, and I scramble down through the trees, smelling and hearing the immediate sea. A jetty appears ahead of me. My heart sinks: no boat is in evidence. I hurry up to the edge. Not a thing in sight anywhere. I drop my suitcase and let out a groan.

'Hello up there!' a voice cries. 'Ahoy!' I look around, unable to locate a source, finally I make out a woman treading water at the bottom of the jetty stairs. 'Are you all set?' she says. I regard her in bewilderment. 'Where's the boat?' I ask. She lets out a good-natured laugh. 'We don't need any boat,' she says. 'We'll get there fine just by ourselves, in about a week or so.' I stare at her. I look off in horrified confusion at the vacant waves. Suddenly the face of a nasty little imp starts yukking it up back up the cobblestones. 'It's all some kind of practical joke!' I realize, my heart dying inside of me. Once again I'm the butt of a gag – the whole trip has turned into one vast, sadistic nightmare! 'I just want to go home to visit my mother!' I moan pathetically. 'What's wrong?' says the woman. 'There're two of us, we're going to change off so we don't get tired.' A second woman pops up beside her, as if on cue. 'Let's go!' she says, blowing water out of her mouth. 'Or we're gonna miss the tide.' 'Oh do shut up!' I snarl. I glare down at the pair of them miserably. 'What are we going to do, *swim there?*' I demand, flapping my hands mockingly. 'Well what else?' says the second woman, as if any alternative would be the strangest thing in the whole world. 'All aboard!' cries the first woman. She has turned in the water, and gestures to her back. It's a broad, shimmering back. I look at it, stupefied. 'This can't be true . . .' I mumble, as my mind begins to fill with the extraordinary glimmerings of long-ago, imaginary scenes. 'Hey, all aboard means gimme your bag and let's go!' says the second woman. I can't think what to do. Finally I just shrug and troop down, realizing all things are apparently far beyond my understanding. The seond woman takes my bag and balances it on her head with one hand and with the other pulls me, splashing awkwardly, on to the first woman's back. 'Everything okay?' calls the first woman. 'Then hold tight!' I look down and gasp and hang on fearfully, as the powerful fish tail furls and unfurls, and I surge homeward out into the waves.

The Stranger

A car pulls up in the driveway. A man gets out and starts unloading shabby luggage onto the cement. I walk out to him. 'I've come to stay with your widowed mother, to take care of the darling,' he tells me. 'What are you, some kind of nurse?' I ask, eyeing him unamiably. 'No. A friend,' he says. I go back into the house, rubbing my cheek. My mother is up in her sewing room. I stand in the doorway. 'There's a guy out here who says he's a friend of yours and has come to take care of you,' I tell her. She puts her sewing down on her lap, and turns and stares at me over her glasses. '*What?*' she says slowly. 'A guy,' I repeat. 'Did he give a name?' she asks. 'What does he look like?' I shrug. 'He's in his fifties, thin, grey crewcut, eyeglasses, dressed sort of cheap Western. Brown from the sun. He looks like maybe a ranch hand.' My mother stares at me. She shakes her head. 'How extraordinary,' she says. 'Where is he?'

We go downstairs and out to the driveway. The stranger is standing by the pile of his baggage, smoking a cigarette. He throws it aside when he sees us and straightens erect, smiling hard and wiping long, thin, brown hands on his dungarees. My mother stops a good ways from him. 'How do you do,' she says uncertainly. The stranger bows to her and grins in extravagance. 'So,' he declares. 'I've come!' There's an awkward silence. My mother draws back, to full height. 'My good man,' she declares. 'I'm afraid there's been some unfortunate misunderstanding. I'm sure I haven't the remotest idea in the world who you are.' The stranger tries to grin roguishly at this, despite the transparent nervousness in his manner. His Adam's apple bobs up and down. 'Dear lady,' he exclaims, forcibly debonair, 'don't deny me, come from so far away, bearing so many splendid gifts.' He gestures dramatically at the luggage. My mother and I regard the shabby collection. We look at each other. 'Perhaps with these treasures and pretty things,' he continues desperately, 'I can win a place in your home, in your heart – at your side, sweet lady,' he says, fixing a melting look on my mother. He squats suddenly and begins unstrapping one of the suitcases. My mother stares at him startled and confused. She turns to me. 'Go inside,' I tell her. 'Now don't you listen to him,' says the stranger, shifting on his heel, grinning. 'Mom, go inside,' I repeat. The stranger rises to his feet. I step in front of him and grab a handful of his collar. 'Get your squalid junk off our driveway, hoss, and clear out of here this minute,' I snarl. His eyes look back at me wide with fright behind his glasses. I can feel his body trembling. I hear our front door close. I shove him away and stand over him, fists clenched, while he loads his battered luggage into his car. He doesn't say anything. With my fists on my hips I watch him back out into the street, and slowly drive away, staring out the window at me. He goes out of sight. After a while, I let my hands down and turn and go back inside.

We eat dinner that night in preoccupied silence. Strange thoughts won't leave my head. 'You know,' my mother says finally, looking abashed, 'I can't help wondering what it was he had in those awful suitcases. . . .' I put my fork down slowly and stare at her. She shifts in her seat. She laughs. 'I mean, what *sort* of presents? . . .' she says.

Drinks

My mother and I drive out to a famous resort for a drink. Inside, she gets lost. After wandering in search of her for a while, I shrug and go back to the bar and order myself another round. By late afternoon I feel a pleasing numbness. My mother appears at last through the oaken doors. She looks put out. 'I was gone all this time,' she says, 'and you didn't alert the authorities? You didn't care what happened to your mother, you just sat here throwing down one drink after another?' 'Glad to see you! Have one!' I tell her pleasantly. I push the peanut bowl towards her and signal the bartender. I stifle a belch. 'Oh, I knew you'd be alright, and so you are,' I tell her. 'Nonsense,' she says haughtily. She wriggles onto the stool and glares at the drink in front of her. 'So where were you?' I ask, in a more serious tone, trying to placate her. 'How do I know?' she cries, tossing a hand irritably. 'This stupid hotel has so many nooks and crannies! I went into some sort of closet by mistake, and I would still be there this very minute if a maid hadn't finally let me out. The people who work here must all be deaf, I was shouting my lungs out!'

I put my glass down to keep from spilling it. Then I hang my head and grip the bar, shaking with laughter. 'What's so funny?' demands my mother. She picks up her glass and grins. She flaps her hand at me in a gesture of dismissal. I sit beside her, hanging on to the bar and quaking. 'Locked screaming . . . inside a closet . . . for two hours . . .' I sputter. Some beer trickles the wrong way out my nose. I wipe at it. At last I have enough control of myself to sit up, wet-eyed and gasping. 'Everything okay here?' says the bartender, coming over. 'Certainly not,' says my mother. 'I was a prisoner all afternoon in one of your evil-smelling closets.' 'I beg your pardon?' says the bartender. I put my arm around my mother, grinning fondly, as she recounts her adventures in great detail.

Later, when we we're ready to leave, our check is taken back. 'Drinks on the house,' says the bartender. 'Sorry for what happened.' 'It's not your fault,' my mother reassures him, 'and you're a very nice man.' 'Thank you,' says the bartender.

You should get lost more often,' I tell her, weaving beside her through the reception lounge. 'Next time maybe they'll give us dinner.' I stumble over the edge of a carpet and rush ahead on hurried, sinking steps to catch my balance. My mother comes up beside me, roaring with laughter. 'Tell me,' she says, taking my arm, beaming and appalled, 'how many bottles did you have?' 'Oh, just twenty or thirty,' I tell her. 'I know my limit.' We come out merrily into the evening. I salute a group of doormen smartly. Ahead of us, over the parking lot, the famous mountains loom against the dimming sky – slighty forbidding, like drowsing monsters. 'Oh look!' my mother cries. She tugs us to a halt. She reaches a hand out in front of her in the gesture of a herald. 'There on top,' she cries. 'Oh look!' 'I can't,' I inform her. I pull free and wobble a step and slump luxuriously across the waxed hood of an expensive car. 'I believe you're drunk,' my mother says. 'I have a sot for a son. Oh what a magnificent sight you're missing, come look!' I grunt vaguely in reply, smiling into the crooked pillow of my arm. Beyond me the last light of the day blazes eerily on the pale bulks of the far range. My mother stands gazing at this apparition, her face uplifted, a heroine from a great drama of nature, while I nestle amiably fuzzy against the warm metal curves of the car.

Soap Bubble

A great soap bubble wobbles down onto our lawn. It sits on the grass, trembling and glassy. My late father steps out of it. He is naked, potbellied and stout like a big, curly-chested baby. He comes striding towards the house on pale bare feet.

Later, after we've visited, we go out onto the lawn with drinks in hand. Under the shade of the oak tree we admire the glistening, trembling membrane of the bubble. Overhead, leaves rustle in the breeze. Small white clouds push along high above in the sunshine, and the bubble trembles, incandescent where it sits, as if stirred by a kinship of the airborne. Finally my father hands me his glass. He goes behind the oak, and I hear the splash of his urine. He comes back out. He claps me sentimentally on the back. We embrace. The cheeks of his buttocks jostle as he steps awkwardly into the clinging, filmy wall of the bubble. His grey hair lifts a moment in the breeze, then will no longer. With his exposed, trailing hand he gives a last, hurried wave, and then the hand too becomes a glassy shadow like the rest of him, and the bubble wobbles slowly from side to side, then lifts and goes wafting heavily sideways out through the shade trees and off into the blue, endless heavens.

Meteor

Instead of sleep I look out my window. The night is full of meteor showers. I watch them flit through the starry sky towards the horizon. Late in the night I lie on the couch, wishing a meteor might land in my room. . . . The window swells with pale blue light. A softly shimmering blaze settles onto the carpet. It steadies, and it resolves into a girl wearing pale blue pajamas. I make room for her on the couch. She tells me about her life in the sky – how brief it is, how dark the distances between the stars. But how exquisite the sights, slipping into the atmosphere blazing softly. . . . 'And now it's over,' she sighs. She yawns. 'And here I am with you.' She smiles at me sleepily, and reaches for my hand. She takes it in hers. . . . I smile wistfully, lying with my chin in my hand, gazing out my window at the night sky, and the dreaming stars.

On a Train

I open the door of a train compartment. There's a girl inside. She glances up from her magazine. 'Are any of these other seats taken?' I ask her. She shakes her head. I close the door and sit down. I look at her while she reads. I turn my head and gaze out the window. 'How can I demonstrate in a captivating way my love for her at first sight?' I wonder. Suddenly a gigantic rosebush appears in the window, and slowly pushes its way in, filling up the entire compartment. 'For Christ's sake,' the girl cries, from somewhere in the leaves. 'Help, I'm choking under all these blossoms!' 'Don't worry, don't worry!' I shout. I hack and batter and punch at the tangled branches and greenery and pink petals. At last I force the rosebush out. I slam the window on it. 'I'm sorry,' I protest breathlessly. 'Are you alright?' I help the girl sit up. 'I meant to give you an unusual present of flowers, not suffocate you,' I explain. 'That's very sweet of you,' she says, panting. She brushes leaves off her lap and rearranges her blouse. 'But you know, sometimes a single flower can be just as effective.' 'You're absolutely right,' I agree. 'Wait one minute.' I go out into the corridor, rubbing my scratched arm. I stalk up and down, peering. I let myself back into the compartment sheepishly. 'I feel like a fool,' I confess. 'I had a crazy idea there might be a flower somewhere.' The girl looks at me in fond amusement. 'I think you're sweet,' she says.

We sit together with my arm around her. She gazes out the window, smiling and lost in thought. A tear starts down her cheek. 'What's wrong?' I whisper. She shakes her head. 'Nothing,' she says. 'I can see ahead in the future, that's all.' 'Then why are you sad?' I ask. 'Because first we'll be very happy,' she says, 'then we'll be sad. That's the way it will be for us.' 'No,' I protest. 'That's not true at all. I've fallen in love with you! I'll be with you always!' She only smiles, hearing what I say. 'Go look outside the door,' she says, wiping a cheek. 'The door to the next car. That's where the flower is.' I return to the compartment with a dark red rose on its green stem. 'You were right,' I tell her, in a subdued voice, somewhat shaken. 'About the flower.' I give it to her. I sit back down beside her and put my arm back close around her, and in sudden despair I kiss again and again her protesting mouth, her damp cheeks, as the train sways through a curve, and straightens, swaying the other way, and rushes on. Outside through the window, an early summer storm erupts, whirling rose petals over the green landscape.

The Vision

My mother isn't in her room. I go outside to the dark driveway. She's curled up in some blankets in the back of my pickup truck. 'Why on earth are you out here?' I demand. 'I was having a vision,' she says. She stares up fixedly at the crescent moon, the scattered silences of the stars. 'What was it this time?' I ask, trying to keep patience in my voice. The metal rim of the pickup bed is cold under my hands. 'Dogs,' she says, her gaze drawing inward. 'Many, many dogs . . .' 'Any particular breed?' I inquire. And I regret this wisecrack as it leaves my mouth. But she is oblivious to it. 'I don't know breeds,' she says. 'They were very large and thin. Their bones showed through.' 'Were they friendly to you?' I ask, after a pause. 'You know me and dogs!' she says. She laughs, so I have a glimpse of unadulterated fright. I feel a stab of panic. 'But now it's over,' I ask her. 'This vision.' 'I hope so,' she says wanly. She swallows. 'Please, drive me somewhere.' 'Now?' I ask. There's silence. 'Please,' she says. 'But you'll get pneumonia,' I tell her. 'Not if you go slowly,' she says.

I make my way around to the cab of the truck. The plastic seat is cold and stiff. I start the engine and let it idle. I look over my shoulder through the rear window. I can see the top of her head, the wisps of grey hair – white hair – lifting in a stir of wind. I have to turn away. I hunch over, squeezing my hands between my legs. My eyes feel prickly and swollen from interrupted sleep, from emotion that threatens to be almost unbearable. I stare numbly at the dashboard. After a while, I bring my hands up and put the truck in gear, and start slowly down the driveway.

Cement

I am at the beach with my mother. I bury her up to her neck in sand. 'Alright, now please let me out,' she says finally. 'It's hard to breathe.' 'Only if you pay me a tremendous amount of cash,' I inform her, teasing. I start to dig her out; but I can't. The sand is like stone. It's turned to cement. 'Please, stop joking, get me out,' my mother pants. 'I can't breathe.' 'I'm not joking, something's wrong,' I protest. I scratch at the cement desperately. I pound on it with my fists. The surf surges around us, splashing my mother in the face. 'Help me, help me,' she bleats wildly. 'I'm trying, I can't do anything!' I cry. 'I'll have to get help!' I rush down the beach, waving and shouting, frantic. Some men are drinking beer by a pickup truck. They run back with me with shovels and pickaxes.

I wander about holding my head in my hands. They smash up the cement, their pickaxes swinging high and low, violently. 'Careful, oh please be careful,' I plead, walking back and forth, helpless. One of them crouches by my mother, cupping her chin out of the water. Her eyes are haggard with terror. 'Can't breathe . . . can't breathe . . .' she keeps bleating, through clenched teeth. 'You'll be okay, you'll be okay,' I promise her desperately.

Finally they have her out. The seawater gushes and foams into the rubble. Other, different men appear; they bear my mother over the dunes, carrying her high in a litter. An oxygen line runs into her nose from a cylinder. A catheter bag sways from a litter handle, its hose running up under her pale thighs.

I follow behind in a distraught daze, plodding through deep sand carrying our sandy beach towels, my mother's much-ornamented beach bag. 'How did it happen, how did it happen?' I moan, over and over again. A small plane flies low over the beach, dragging a long, fluttering sign. I give out a sobbing cry, imagining the sign bearing her frail name, the helpless dates and particulars of her obituary.

247

Blood and Flowers

I have a drink on a hotel terrace. The bay is at my elbow. Bougainvillea overflow their railings. The sun is on its way down, but still strong. My mother appears, dressed sleek and informal, sunglasses up in her hair. She orders a drink from the white-jacketed waiter. I light her cigarette, then my own. We blow the smoke into the breeze. 'Where are you shooting next?' I ask. She shrugs. 'Somewhere hot and tropical,' she says, looking off at the bay. 'Somewhere with tigers and giant snakes, and flowers like severed heads.' She taps restlessly on the table with her cigarette holder. 'You know, I thought your last film was sensationally marvelous,' I tell her. She turns back and smiles at me, dazzling, dark carmine. 'You say the sweetest things, my darling,' she says, reaching up to take her drink from the waiter's tray. A photographer seizes this moment to spring up beside her and start snapping with his big black camera. My mother hisses at him. 'Will you have the bare manners to leave us some privacy!' I shout, but he's already scurrying off with his booty. 'Scum!' spits my mother. '*Salaud!* Come on, let's go for a drive.' She throws down her drink and snatches up her purse.

Outside the hotel, there's a red sports car, brand new, a blood-colored beauty. 'Where did you get this from?' I exclaim admiringly, getting into the passenger seat beside her. 'Don't ask silly questions,' she grins behind her sunglasses, knotting a leopard-skin-pattern scarf under her chin. She starts the engine. It thrums powerfully. We jolt backwards, swerve forward, and go roaring out through the hotel gates, spraying a shower of gravel. We take the coast road. The sea flashes off to our right. Pine trees skim past. 'Jesus, this is some car!' I shout, over the din and the wind. 'What?' my mother cries. 'The car!' I shout. 'Yes, isn't it a marvel!' she shouts, the wind tearing at her scarf.

'I've only taken it up to a hundred kilometers, that's nowhere near its limit! Who knows how fast it will go! – Faster, faster!' she laughs, and we surge forward. I glance with concern at the speedometer. It's well over one-twenty. The road hurtles at us like a furiously untangling line of rope. 'Easy, easy,' I call out, hanging on. We throb through a bend. The road veers inland. Mimosa blur past on the hillsides. I look at my mother. The famous profile is grinning, intent, almost wild with life. The road bends sharply ahead in the distance. 'Careful of this little bridge up here! I shout. 'What's that?' she shouts. 'The bridge! Care-ful – ' I shout. I flinch back, staring horrified. 'The bridge – watch out – turn – turn the – !'

Brakes screeching wildly, we spin sideways and crash through the wooden railings and plunge out into the air. Screaming, I am torn loose, and flung twisting and tumbling in slow-motion headfirst into the shock of the stream, and blackness. I come to with my face pressed into the weeds. My head is thudding. Stunned, I push myself up and look about. The car rests upside-down, brilliant red on the sloping flowery bank. Its tires continue to spin in the silence. My mother protrudes from it near the bottom. 'Mom, mom – ' I blurt out, clambering through the water towards her. She lies with the back of her head and a shoulder in the stream. A dark hideous stickiness shows on one side of the scarf's leopard skin. I crouch over her in the water, gaping, beside myself. She smiles up at me. 'I'll get you out!' I tell her frantically. I set my weight against the bright red metal and strain, but nothing happens. 'Don't . . .' my mother mur-murs. 'It's no use . . .' I look about helplessly, at the pink masses of oleander, the wild white roses crowding the dark under-carriage of the car, the slowly spinning tires. I fall to my knees. 'I'm afraid . . . my back . . . is broken . . .' says my mother. She laughs slowly, falteringly. 'You'll be alright, we'll get you to a hospital, you'll be fine,' I tell her desperately. 'Is my make-up . . . still on? . . .' she asks. 'Yes,' I tell her. 'Good . . .' she says. 'Give me . . . a cigarette . . . please . . .' I fumble in my wet jacket and bring out the pack. 'They're soaked through,' I tell her. 'Never mind . . . Put one . . . in my mouth . . .' she says. 'At the side . . . please . . .' I place the sodden cigarette in the corner of her dark red lips. Wild roses frame the action with their creamy blossoms. 'Thanks . . .' she says, the cigarette bobbing. 'Now wipe . . . my brow . . . please . . .' With a trembling hand I wipe away the thread of blood trickling along the edge of the leopard-skin pattern. 'Mom . . .' I blurt softly, turning away. 'I was . . . great . . .' she says. 'Wasn't I? . . .' 'Mom, you were the greatest!' I assure her, in tears. 'The greatest!' A smile flickers, half-smile, half-wince, on her lips. 'Yes . . .' she murmurs. 'You tell them . . . how well . . . I went . . .' 'I will,' I whisper. The smile flickers again, one last, painful time. 'Such a . . . pity . . .' she murmurs past her cigarette. 'Wrecking . . . my lovely . . . wild car.'

Winding Sheet

'What time is it?' asks my mother, turning just her eyes. 'Mom, you keep asking,' I tell her. 'I don't know. It can't be more than an hour since we got here. Please – try to relax.' 'I'm trying,' she says. 'I'm trying.' But her brow is deeply furrowed, and her eyebrows pull down exaggeratedly, like a caricature of despair. She keeps shifting about on the pallet, crossing and recrossing her gnarled feet. 'Oh when are they bringing me my sheet,' she moans. 'Mom, they said soon,' I plead with her. 'They didn't give an exact minute. It won't be long – please.' I get up and go over to the door. 'I can't see anyone,' I tell her, turning back into the room. 'They're very busy. . . .' 'Do I still look alright?' she puffs. 'You look fine,' I assure her. 'I told you, very Plantagenet.' I come over to the pallet and stand beside it, making a show of mildness and quiet. I smile down at her. 'How do you feel?' I ask quietly. 'Do you have any signs of rigor mortis?' She winces. 'Don't use that awful word!' she puffs. 'I'm sorry – ' I apologize. I try to go on evenly. 'Are you feeling any immobility, in your extremities – can you move your hands and fingers – mom?' 'Yes, I think so,' she says. She manipulates her fingers dutifully. Her hands lie close to her sides, looking absurdly thick-fleshed and huge at the ends of her gaunt wrists. 'You're lucky,' I tell her. 'I would think most people in your position wouldn't be able to do that.' She doesn't reply. She stares up at the ceiling, puffing. She twists about. 'Oh I wish this hadn't happened, I'm so frightened,' she moans. 'Mom, it'll be alright,' I protest. I make myself pat her hand, which is startlingly cold. Her face looks like a frail, stricken animal's. 'Really, believe me,' I plead. 'There's nothing to fear. They're coming in a minute.' Her black, shining eyes move sideways and fix on me, clinging. 'I'm so sorry you have to go through this . . .' she murmurs thickly. I shake my head. I can't speak for a moment. 'Nonsense,' I whisper. Her eyes linger on me. They brim with panic and drift away. 'Please, why don't they bring me my sheet!' she moans. 'Where are they!' 'Mom, I'll go and get someone!' I tell her. 'Just try to relax!' I implore. 'I can't,' she puffs.

I come out into the hall. It's empty. I hurry along it. I turn a corner, into another corridor. It's empty too. I go down it. A sense of frenzy starts to mount in me. 'Hello!' I call out. 'Hello!' Finally I stop, and turn back. My heart is beating wildly. I turn the corner and see the figure of the chaplain standing in my mother's doorway. I rush towards it.

'It's alright,' the chaplain says, smiling peaceably. 'It's alright. It's over.' I step past him and stare into the room. The mortician looks back over his shoulder as he finishes wrapping my mother's feet. 'I'm sorry we were so long,' he says quietly. My mother lies wrapped in a dazzling bundle of cloth. All that shows is her face, which is inert, exhausted beyond all endurance, her eyes half-lidded, her jaw slack. She looks like a tallow mask, the features pinched, almost as if about to drip.

A great soft sob erupts from me, and I hang my head. The chaplain's hand presses my shoulder. 'Yes, yes, it's alright,' he says softly. His arm comes around me, making me feel its pressure. 'I'm sorry,' I sob, shaking my head. 'It's just – she suffered so much – she was so frightened – ' His arm holds me against him. He smiles at me. 'Be consoled,' he murmurs, smiling. 'If you could only have seen how joyful she was – the look of joy on her face when she saw us come in with her beautiful sheet, and spread it wide open, so white and radiant for her.'

Grass

I go to the graveyard after dinner. My mother's ghost stoops beside my parents' headstone, pulling a weed. 'Hello, dear,' she says. 'Just tidying up a bit. I don't know why they bother to pay the people here, they don't do a thing. How are you, my darling?' I give her a kiss, pressing my lips to her flickering cheek. 'Looks very nice,' I tell her, indicating the paired graves. 'It's a handsome site, and a handsome marker,' she says. She considers the gravestone. 'It's what a gravestone should look like: simple lettering, very elegant and plain. You chose well,' she says. 'You did right for your poor departed mom and dad.' 'Thanks,' I tell her. I look about. 'Where is he? I brought him some pickles, at least to sniff.' 'Oh how sweet of you,' she says. 'He's turned in already. But you can leave that right over there, he'll be sure to pounce on it when he wakes.' I put the jar down in the grass. 'Yes, that worm is still giving him hell in his ear, poor thing,' she says. 'You don't think we could get a doctor to come and look at it?' 'Mom, doctors don't really like to make house calls to cemeteries,' I point out. 'I suppose you're right,' she says. 'I'm afraid there's nothing for him to do but put up with it,' I tell her. I shrug. 'I'm sorry. It just goes with the general condition.' 'Is that so?' she sighs. 'My, what a knowledgeable young man you are. Well, just wait, one day you'll be buried six feet under with the worms gnawing away at you, and we'll see what wise things you have to say then.' 'I won't say a thing, because I'll have myself cremated and stored away in a silver urn,' I tell her. 'My, what a clever lad you are too,' she says. I give a smile at all this bantering. 'So tell me, how are you, mom?' I ask gently. 'Are you getting used to this?' 'Oh, you know me, I'm fine,' she says. 'Fine. Very peaceful. The worms don't seem to like me at all, which offends me greatly. Oh, it's a bit startling now and then,' she says, looking down at a flickering hand, 'to be able to see right through one's mouldering body. But we have to take things as they come, and make the best of them.' I nod, contemplating her bare, crooked feet, which never did have the hammer-toe operation they needed. I can make out the darkness of the grass through them. 'I'm sorry,' I say quietly. 'Nothing to be sorry about,' she replies. 'All part of the grand scheme.' We fall silent. I look off at the graveyard, and then up into the night. The night sky is shot through with the benevolent plentitude of stars. 'When I get low,' my mother says beside me, 'I just lift up my eyes.' She indicates the expanse of the heavens. 'I gaze up there for a long, long time every night,' she says. 'The stars are my friends. Each one of them has a soul, you know. I've given them names.' 'I believe they already have names,' I murmur. 'Not my names,' she replies. 'That one over there, shining for all its worth, that's you. That big gleaming greenish thing near it, that's your father. . . .' 'And which one are you?' I ask. 'Oh, I haven't quite made up my mind,' she says. 'I'm up there all right. But it's a very special one, my particular star. Very special indeed, you can bet your boots on it.' Together we scan the constellations. My mother exhibits a hand, wavering and pale. 'I'm a star already, just look at me,' she says.

The Horsefly

I have my eyes painted – blue, the color of the sky. I remember the sky of my childhood. I have the glazer paint in the tops of the trees that framed that long-ago, faraway blue. The treetops would sway, I remember, and I would hear the noise of the wind in the branches, a noise that for some reason nagged and irritated me, that agitated me with its restlessness. The wind would blow in my face all afternoon, and I would realize, with fretful insight, that wind was in a literal sense 'moving air', come from great distances and rushing through our trees on its way to somewhere else. . . .

Other recollections return to me, and each time I call the glazer back. I feel the light flick of his delicate brushes, and the steady prop of his hand under my chin. Now I see the house where we lived, the dark cool veranda in the back. I smell the damp, painted cement of the walls and the floors. Then I wander out into the backyard and creep among the bushes and kneel on the hot ground and feel about in the leaves for blackberries. The glazer paints my dirty hand, full of the dark, sweet, densely celled berries. . . .

Then a truck waddles heavily in through the back gate. It stops under the oak tree in a low, tired cloud of dust. The color of its matronly, swelling hood is a much-faded red, rusted and pitted, coated with the dust of the roads and the fields. The driver comes around to the back, wiping his neck with a handkerchief. He sets up his cumbersome scale and brings out his paper bags. His vegetables lie in piles in tilted wooden crates. There are green beans, long and irregularly twisted, and potatoes and onions, and peppers, red, green and yellow; and fruits such as oranges and peaches and pock-marked apples, and half-maroon, half-gold mangoes. The same film of dust coats all these, but their richness persists, and here the glazer truly outdoes himself, capturing the subtle balance of forces in my memory of the dull sheen of the dust and the persistent vividness of the cargo in its wooden boxes. . . .

Having accomplished this feat, the glazer amuses himself by repainting the driver in his own likeness. . . . The driver-now-glazer reaches in between two crates and brings out a small, rumpled bag and carefully spreads its mouth and offers it to me. It's licorice. He takes a black stub for himself and asks me my name. I tell him, and then I have an inspiration, and I ask the glazer to paint in some brushes and a palette and French easel beside the truck. The once-upon-a-time driver rolls up the rumpled bag and stashes it away and wipes his hands carefully on his loose, heavy trousers. In his new role he picks up his materials and follows me around to the veranda at the side of the house. The glazer paints the blue-flowered jacaranda tree there, to give his likeness shade while he works. I show him where, on my birthday, I carved into the bark the awkward letters of my name. . . .

Then I leave him and go around on to the screened veranda to join my cousins, who are visiting. My mother is telling us a story in the heat of the afternoon. On the easel the sketched clouds pile up slowly from the horizon; the glare of the sun is thick on the hedges, the shadows lie deep and reddish inside the veranda. My cousins and I sit cross-legged in sandals on the floor, our mouths open in attentiveness. The damp sweat glimmers slightly on our foreheads and cheeks. My mother sits with us, her skirt spread out among us, its long folds rendered in long, softening hollows of shadow. She tells us a story about a river that flows faraway to the north, and when we cross that river, the kingdom we find beyond. . . . She tells us, I remember, about another river further distant, and the country we come into there. . . .

The glazer's double smiles, listening as he works on the other side of the veranda screen. He takes a step back quietly, to consider his progress. The glazer tilts back my chin and peers in over his own shoulder for a look. He smiles too. Deftly, with his subtlest brush, he mixes green and blue and adds a drowsy horsefly to the veranda scene, a scrap of glitter that has come wandering out of the heat, into the story and the shade. . . .